The Money Bird

This Large Print Book carries the Seal of Approval of N.A.V.H.

The Money Bird

Sheila Webster Boneham

THORNDIKE PRESS
A part of Gale, Cengage Learning

GALE
CENGAGE Learning®

Detroit • New York • San Francisco • New Haven, Conn • Waterville, Maine • London

GALE
CENGAGE Learning

An Animals in Focus Mystery.
Thorndike Press, a part of Gale, Cengage Learning.

Thorndike Press® Large Print Mystery.
The text of this Large Print edition is unabridged.
Other aspects of the book may vary from the original edition.
Set in 16 pt. Plantin.

LIBRARY OF CONGRESS CATALOGING-IN-PUBLICATION DATA

Boneham, Sheila Webster, 1952–
The money bird / by Sheila Webster Boneham. — Large print edition.
pages ; cm. — (Thorndike Press large print mystery) (An animals in focus mystery)
ISBN 978-1-4104-6517-7 (hardcover) — ISBN 1-4104-6517-9 (hardcover) 1. Rare birds—Fiction. 2. Large type books. I. Title.
PS3602.O657155M66 2013b
813'.6—dc23 2013038086

Published in 2014 by arrangement with Midnight Ink, an imprint of Llewellyn Publications, Woodbury, MN 55125-2989 USA

Printed in the United States of America
1 2 3 4 5 6 7 18 17 16 15 14

For the retrievers who have
brightened my life and my home:
Labrador Retrievers Raja, Annie, and Lily,
and Golden Retriever Sunny

AUTHOR'S NOTE

This is a work of fiction, so I have taken the liberty of creating a fictional bird, the Carmine Parrot, to represent the many species that suffer individually and as whole populations from wildlife trafficking and habitat destruction. The examples of smuggling mentioned in *The Money Bird* — tiny birds packed into curlers, primate infants carried under clothing, birds and other animals stuffed into boxes under floorboards and seats — are all too real and horrifying. So too is the worldwide slaughter of animals for their parts, which are used for everything from fur coats to traditional medicines to hair clips, jewelry, and decorative items. To learn more, I suggest you start with http://worldwildlife.org/threats/illegal-wildlife-trade, or contact the World Wildlife Fund, 1250 24th Street NW, Washington, DC 20037, (202) 293-4800.

money bird: the last bird the dog retrieves in a retriever field trial; without this bird, the dog and handler win no money.

One

The man with the gun stood half hidden in chest-high brush to the west of Twisted Lake. Drake crouched a hundred yards to the east, gaze fixed, muscles twitching. The only thing obstructing my view of either was the cloud of no-see-ums whirling around my head. Daylight was dying, and the eastern bank of the lake was already lost in shadows, so I knew I wouldn't see clearly for much longer. The breeze had all but died in the last half hour and the bright scent of day bowed to darker notes of mud and rot.

The man, Collin Lahmeyer, tucked the 12-gauge under his right arm and picked up an orange canvas-covered training bumper with the other. He let it drop from his fist and bounce at the end of a half yard of thin nylon cord, then swung his arm and let fly toward a small island fifty yards offshore. Drake quivered as he watched. He shifted one foot forward an inch but held his ground when his partner, Tom, murmured, "Wait."

The cylindrical bumper stalled high in the air, vivid as blood against a bank of charcoal clouds. Drake tracked the object, his focus so tight that he didn't so much as twitch when the shotgun's long barrels rose and the gunman shouldered the weapon. A single blast cracked the August dusk and made my eyes blink and my shoulders tighten. I've been photographing field dogs in training and competition for years and I knew the shells were blanks, but every blast still somehow caught my reflexes by surprise.

The training bumper plummeted into a tangle of goldenrod, thistle, and bindweed. Tom whispered one magic word — "Fetch!" — and Drake was gone from his side. The big dog leapt from the bank at a full-out run and was swimming before he hit water. His shoulders muscled through the light chop and his thick tail worked like a rudder to keep his heading true. He swam to the island, charged from the lake in a glittering spray, and disappeared into dense brush. Fading blossoms of ironweed jostled one another, mapping his progress. He quartered for five or six seconds, moving back and forth through the brush, searching. The wild swaying of the plants stopped, signaling that he'd found the bumper, then resumed as Drake turned back toward the lake.

The gunner, Collin Lahmeyer, had a better view of the dog than did Tom, his owner and handler. I had the best view of all. I'm Janet MacPhail, professional photographer and lifelong cynophile. I'd been shooting the Northern Indiana Hunting Retriever Club's practice session since late afternoon, hoping to capture some of those beautiful dogs in photos I could sell to publishers and, often, to the dogs' proud owners. I peered through my viewfinder, up to my muck-smeared elbows in ragweed and burdock. I didn't expect to get a decent shot against the dark water and smoldering horizon, but the zoom let me follow what my naked eye would never pick up.

Collin gave a thumbs-up, indicating that Drake had his "bird," the foam-filled canvas bumper, and called, "There's your money bird!" In a field trial, the money bird is the last bird the winning dog retrieves, the one that brings home the cash prize. There was no cash here, and the bird was made of batting and canvas, but Tom Saunders looked like he might pop his buttons, if there'd been any on his faded U of Michigan sweatshirt. Tom and I had started seeing each other back in May, but we'd had only a couple of weeks before he and Drake headed off for a summer of fieldwork in New Mexico. Tom is an ethnobotanist. He teaches in the anthropology department at the local campus, but he likes to run off to exotic places to do research between terms. We'd developed quite an electronic relationship over the summer, and although I declined all invitations to head west for a visit, I had to admit that I was both thrilled and terrified to have him back in town. As I stood watching the man work with his dog in the sultry dusk, the Janet demon in my head whispered *time to jump his bones.* Good Janet pointed out that poor proper Collin Lahmeyer might never recover from the spectacle, and besides, the ground was soggy and the mosquitoes ravenous. Romance could wait.

I knew that Drake needed only one more qualifying run to complete his MH, his Master Hunter title, and the way this training session was going, he looked ready to me. Not that I know much about training retrievers that I haven't gleaned from listening to friends involved in the sport. I have an Australian Shepherd myself, and we pursue other sports. I knew, though, that

Drake had been entered in a Hunt Test the end of May and should have finished his Master Hunter title there, but he pulled a shoulder muscle two days before the event. Several people advised Tom to give the dog painkillers and run him anyway, and, gutsy Labrador Retriever that he was, Drake would have worked through the pain if his beloved Tom asked him to. Tom refused — another feather in the cap he wore in my viewfinder. Now, after two months of R and R in the high desert, the dog appeared to be back on top of his game.

I glanced at Tom. He was talking to a man I didn't know while watching for Drake to reappear from the brush. I looked through my viewfinder again. Drake burst from the brush and was almost back to the water when he veered away from the lake, back toward the west side of the island. The cover there was lower and more sparse than where the bumper went down, but I still couldn't see what he was after. He was quite a sight, though, his wet coat sparkling in the low-angled light.

"That's not like him," said Tom, blowing one long, shrill blast on his whistle. Drake looked over his shoulder, his glossy black coat set off by the orange bumper in his mouth and the black-eyed Susans scattered behind him. I clicked off several more shots. *Click click click.* Drake held for a pair of heartbeats, then went back to what he was doing. Whatever it was, it was strictly against orders. Tom blasted the whistle again. I glanced at him, and noticed the stranger walking back toward the road, where we had all parked.

The dog turned around and made for the water. I could no longer see the orange bumper, but he had something in his mouth. The water around him fanned into a gilded wake as he swam. *Click click.* As he came closer, a strip of orange canvas showed in his grip, but most of the bumper was obscured by something else. I tightened my focus and zoomed in on his face, but I couldn't tell what it was. Fabric?

Drake exploded onto the bank, set his burden on the grass, and shook a thousand water diamonds into flight. I clicked off a few more shots. Drake picked up the bumper and his other find, climbed the low bank, and sat six inches in front of Tom, sweeping the grass with his tail and offering up the bumper and what appeared to be a canvas bag. I swung the camera their way.

Tom reached to take Drake's gifts, his face aglow with love and pride. But the look was fleeting. The muscles around his eyes and jaw tightened, waking a butterfly of fear in my own chest as I wondered what had put that look on Tom's face. I zoomed in tight on Drake's head and sucked in a breath as I saw what Tom had seen.

An erratic crimson trickle wound through the silvered hair of Drake's lower jaw and fell, drop by drop, onto the darkening ground.

Two

Tom set the bumper and the bag on a boulder, wiped the blood off Drake's face with the hem of his sweatshirt, and checked Drake's mouth, inside and out.

"He seems to be fine. Maybe just jabbed himself on something. I don't see any more blood," said Tom, standing up and wiping his hand on his jeans.

Drake stepped toward the canvas bag, nose working, and Tom told him to settle. The dog lay down sphinx-style in the grass, nostrils twitching, neck stretched toward the sodden object on the big rock.

The bag was about ten by fifteen inches with a half-open zipper along one long side. It showed signs of having once been white or beige, but the bottom third was stained dark and a trail of chartreuse duck weed angled across the fabric. A shoulder strap dangled from one corner. The other end had torn free and was fringed with stray threads.

Water drained from its corners, arced along the curve of the boulder, and dripped onto the clay below.

Tom lifted the bag and turned it over and back. There was nothing distinctive about it. No writing, no logo. Tom pulled the zipper open, gave the bag a couple of shakes to throw off the bulk of the water, and peered inside. "Oh my God! Yuck!" He tried to pull the bag away, but I grabbed his hand and peered in. Tom burst out laughing and elbowed me. "Gotcha!"

"Funny." I elbowed him back as I pulled the bag closer and looked inside. "What's that?" Something lay along the bottom seam. In the fading light it looked a bit like a fish bone, whitish against the rust-tinted base of the bag and thicker at one end than the other, but I doubted there were any fish with bones that big in Twisted Lake.

Collin stepped toward Tom. "What is it?" he asked, fishing around in his pocket for something.

Tom glanced at Collin, then at me. "Looks like a feather."

"A feather?" Collin and I harmonized.

The soaked barbs were flattened against the quill and hard to make out against the stained fabric, but I could see that Tom was right. It was hard to say what color it was, but at eight or nine inches long, it came from a fairly big bird. "Weird." I gestured toward the dark stain on the bag's lower portion. "What do you think that stain is?"

"There's something else," Tom said. "Looks like money."

"Money?" Collin and I were starting to sound like parrots.

"Yeah. Well, a piece of money. Looks like a corner torn from a bill. There are two zeroes, so I think that makes it part of a C-note." Tom started to reach into the bag, but I caught his arm.

"Maybe we should call someone."

Both men looked at me. One blurted, "Why?" and the other, "Who?"

I wasn't sure myself, but the last time I picked up an abandoned bag and removed its contents, it turned out to be evidence in a murder case and I spent some very uncomfortable moments explaining my actions to the police. I looked into Tom's eyes and said, "Think about it. That little island isn't exactly on a walking path. You wouldn't get there by accident. And besides, this is private property, so why was anyone with a bag of feathers and money here in the first place?"

Tom peered into the bag again. "It's not exactly a 'bag of feathers and money.' "

He must have felt the sticky warm air temperature rise yet higher, because he looked at me and backpedaled. "You're right, though, it is an odd place for anyone to be who doesn't belong. But you could probably wade to the island from where Collin threw the bumper."

"You need a boat. Or you could swim," said Collin. "There's a drop off there. My father-in-law used to keep a diving raft out there. Safest place for kids to go in head first."

We stood in silence and stared at the bag for a bit, until Drake yawned loudly and snapped us out of it.

"I'll call Jo and see what she thinks we should do." Detective Jo Stevens was the lead investigator when three members of our local dog-training community were murdered six months earlier. After a nerve-wracking start involving that other found bag, Jo and I had become friends. She'd know what to do.

Collin pulled a plastic bag from the stock of poop bags in his pocket and held the open end toward Tom. "This'll keep your car clean."

Tom folded the canvas a couple of times and slid it into the bag Collin held open. The water dripping from the fabric settled into the bottom crease of the plastic and I watched as it took on a distinctly pink cast. "That's odd."

Collin leaned in for a closer look.

All three of us watched the puddle forming under the canvas turn ever pinker, and I stared into Tom's bluebird-blue eyes and said, "It's blood."

"Maybe from Drake's mouth?" asked Collin, looking at the dog.

"It took a lot of blood to make a stain like that," I gestured toward the bag, "and to survive the swim. If it is blood, maybe what we saw on Drake came from the bag."

Both men insisted that it couldn't be blood and I was about to argue when something, more feeling than sound, made me look across the water. Drake, his sharp gaze also directed toward the island, moved up against my knee and let out a soft, un-Drake-like grumble. I scanned the vegetation beyond the faraway shoreline through my viewfinder, zooming and sharpening shrub by shrub. "There's someone out there."

Collin and Tom followed my gaze. Nothing for half a minute, and then a dozen hollering crows exploded from the island's single tree, a ghost-pale old sycamore. I turned to Tom and heard myself say, "Murder."

Three

Tom froze, no doubt hoping he had heard wrong.

"What did you say?" Collin asked.

I snapped the cap onto my lens and tried to fend off the shadow beginning to spread through my mind. "Crows. A murder of crows." *Be a good name for a group of humans,* I thought, as I smacked a humongous mosquito and peeled her corpse off the sticky veneer of bug juice and sweat on my arm.

We walked toward the road without speaking, all three of us swatting at my deceased tormentor's gluttonous relatives. Drake trotted close to Tom's left knee, tail waving and tongue dripping. I envied the men's long legs as I clambered down and through the drainage ditch that parallels the road and then fought my way through face-high weeds on the upward slope to the road.

Tom looped the bumper's nylon line

through the wires of Drake's crate and tied it loosely, letting the canvas-and-batting cylinder hang to dry. He tossed the plastic bag into a corner of the van bed. "Up ya go," he told Drake, and the dog hopped into his crate and turned, tail thumping in anticipation. Tom emptied a sandwich bag of premium grain-free kibble into a stainless steel bowl and set it in the crate. He twisted the top from a beat-up water bottle, emptied half into the water bowl in Drake's crate, and leaned back against the van's bumper while Drake, in typical Labrador style, inhaled his dinner. "Drink?" Tom waggled the bottle at me, and swigged it empty when I declined.

We had parked on Tappen Road, a narrow gravel lane off Cedar Canyons Road north of Fort Wayne. Heron Acres, two hundred acres of lake, woodland, and uncultivated open ground, belonged to Collin Lahmeyer's in-laws, who let Collin and his retriever group use the place for training. This was the group's first time back since early June. Collin's family takes up residence in the cottage at the far end of the lake for most of the summer, and between various grandkids and granddogs racing around the lake and grounds, it gets a bit congested for training. I'd been out a couple of times in

June to photograph birds, but was always early enough to be long gone before summer fun started. It was a beautiful place, but across the road a crop of McMansions was springing up with alarming speed, and Tom feared it was just a matter of time before Heron Acres felt the weight of bulldozer treads.

To the west was another expanse of semi-wild ground owned by the Treasures on Earth Spiritual Renewal Center, brainchild of one Regis Moneypenny. Tom and I had speculated on whether it was the man's real name and decided it wasn't. Whoever he was, he had attracted a well-heeled congregation, or clientele, or whatever they called themselves. The collection of Lincolns, Beemers, Lexuses, Caddies, Mercedes, and one bright red Jag I had seen in the center's landscaped lot attested to that.

One of the vehicles had apparently strayed onto Tappen Road by mistake. There was nothing but corn on one side and Guernsey cows on the other between where we stood and the dead end a half mile farther on, so no reason for anyone to drive down there unless they were lost. The curvaceous metal body crept toward us like a giant black beetle, the tinted windows watching like so many eyes. I expected one of them to open and reveal a human being in need of directions, but the sedan kept moving, barely, until it passed us. Then it slowly accelerated, making scuttling sounds in the gravel, headlights igniting as the car turned east onto Cedar Canyons Road.

We looked at each other and shrugged in unison. "Creepy," I said.

Tom removed the empty bowl from Drake's crate and shut the door. "Our turn. Can I buy you some supper?" And darned if the man didn't wink at me just as I turned away.

I suppressed the little tingle in my belly, walked to my van, and fished my cell phone from under a bag of desiccated liver in my tote bag. The number was ringing by the time I got back to Tom. He raised his eyebrows, and I answered his unspoken question. "Jo Stevens."

When I finished the call, I shoved my cell phone into my pocket and said, "I need to get home. Jay's been locked up since mid-afternoon."

"So how 'bout I grab something on the way and meet you there?"

It was after eight and I hadn't been planning to eat more than some fruit when I got home. Fruit surrounded by Edy's ice cream. As usual, hunger and hormones won the day, or evening, and Tom and I set out separately for the same destination.

FOUR

Jay met me at the door. As I watched his bum wriggle and the light dance through his eyes, I remembered some know-it-all telling me at my last photo club meeting that bob-tailed dogs can't express their emotions as well as their tailed brethren. I recommended she spend a few minutes with an Australian Shepherd and then get back to me. As if he'd read my mind, which I wouldn't doubt for a nanosecond, Jay stood smack in front of me and bared his incisors in a goofy grin, his hips still doing the hula.

I shoved some magazines aside and set my camera case on the kitchen table. Then I straddled my dog, wrapped my arms around his neck, and smooched the silky top of his head. It's not a maneuver I'd recommend except for dogs and people who absolutely trust one another, but we qualify. After a few seconds we disengaged and crossed the room. "Out we go," I said, flipping the deadbolt and pulling the back door open. The sensor picked up Jay's movement and lights came on in the backyard. I'd had several new ones installed, all triggered by motion detectors and backed up with batteries, after I was attacked by a gun-toting intruder last spring. Granted, it was hardly a case of random violence, and was unlikely ever to happen again, but the lights still made me feel safer. The lights, and the new touch-pad locks that let me do away with the key under the geranium pot. And my vow to always, always listen to my dog and cat if they ever acted weird again.

Jay stayed outside to patrol the yard and update his territorial notices. Back in the house, I looked around and was just gearing up for a tidying frenzy when my orange tabby, Leo, waltzed in and yawned at me, his long striped tail held high like a shepherd's crook. He hopped onto the chair nearest me. I bent toward him and we bonked noses, feline for "Hi, where ya been?" and then I scooped him up, kissed him, and hugged his vibrating body, smooshing my face into his tawny fur.

I could stay like that, glued to one of my animals, for the rest of my life, but a pesky whisper in my brain kept hissing about the state of the house, so I put Leo back on the chair and began triage. Tom kept his place so tidy that I'd become a tad more conscious of my disinterest in housekeeping, at least when I knew he was coming over. First, to the bedroom with the pile of clean undies I had set on the kitchen table earlier to make room in the dryer for Jay's bedding. I grabbed my running shoes from beside my own bed and my lime-green gardening clogs from in front of the open closet and was about to toss them in when my old book bag caught my eye. It hung from a plastic hanger, and its size and deep red hue sent my mind racing back to Twisted Lake. Who leaves a canvas bag containing a feather and torn money on someone else's private island? More troubling, what could possibly stain the canvas that rusty red? Blood. I was sure of it, no matter what Tom and Collin thought. A lot of blood, I thought, to saturate the fabric enough to survive the swim back to the mainland in Drake's grip, even if the canvas was waterproofed.

A car door slammed outside and brought me back to the task at hand. I tossed the shoes into the closet and slid the door shut. Then I snagged the half-empty diet root beer can from the nightstand, whirled down the hall to the bathroom, tore the used towels off the shower and towel rods, raced back to the bedroom, and dropped them into the hamper. I also dropped in the root beer can, dousing the towels with the remaining fluid and making me mutter something I was trying to expunge from my vocabulary. I retrieved the can and crumpled it in revenge, slammed the hamper lid, and hustled back to the linen closet across the hall from the bathroom door. As I hung a pair of nearly matching towels on the towel bars, I heard the front door open, followed by Tom's, "Honey, we're home."

The scent of fried chicken and the bang-bang-bang of Drake's tail against the wall lured me into the kitchen just as the back door flew open and Jay exploded into the room. The two dogs acknowledged each other with a quick sniff, but were more interested in the containers Tom set on the table. They positioned themselves shoulder to shoulder, noses twitching in the aroma that poured from the red-and-white bucket on the table.

Tom wrapped me in his arms and kissed me, one of those delicious kisses that could have gone on and on and morphed into something more serious, but a terrifying image of our two dogs choking on chicken bones while we were distracted broke the spell. Besides, the antihistamine I took before I went to the lake was long gone and the one I took when I got home hadn't kicked in yet, so I pried my lips off Tom's and gasped, "Can't breathe."

At the same instant, he said, "Chicken bones," confirming that I am in serious trouble with this guy because we're definitely on very similar wave lengths.

Drake was nearly dry, but still too damp for carpet or couch, so I pulled a baby gate out of the laundry room and barricaded all of us into the kitchen. Piles of reading matter on every horizontal surface aside, I do have my limits, and damp dogs do have to stay off the carpets and upholstery. I turned to get some plates from the cupboard and tripped over the dogs, who were jockeying for the best view of what lay beneath the lid Tom was peeling off the bucket.

"Okay, that's it. Everybody out!" I pulled the door open and directed the two reluctant canines out to the backyard. Leo followed them. Tom tucked the bucket of chicken into the curve of his arm and grabbed the bag of sides. With his free hand he pulled two bottles of Killian's Red from the fridge and scurried after the dogs, calling back over his shoulder, "Soup's on!"

All I had to do was shut the door and follow.

Five

Tom and I sank into my Adirondack chairs with plates on our laps and the buckets of food on a side table between us. I'd bought the rusty old table at a garage sale a couple weeks earlier for a pittance and made it sing with tangerine spray paint. The bug lights by the back door cast an odd yellow glow over the yard and the three eucalyptus candles made it smell vaguely like vapor rub, but the neighborhood mosquitoes apparently found the atmosphere even more disturbing than I did and we weren't eaten while we ate.

"Leo, my man." Tom set his plate on the table, gathered the cat like a baby into the cradle of his arms, and gently massaged Leo's chin and chest. The cat squinted at Tom, his amber eyes aglow in the candlelight. He *mrrowled* and accepted the snuggle for a third of a minute, then wriggled free, sauntered to where Tom had told the dogs to lie down, bonked noses with Jay and tolerated a sloppy swipe of the dog's tongue. Then he turned his attention to Drake. Leo sniffed the Lab's damp head and legs daintily, giving the impression that he didn't want to inhale too deeply. Drake kept his silvering chin pressed to the ground and his dark eyes on Leo, forehead furrowed as if he were waiting for bad news.

"Not a big fan of *eau de* lake water?" Tom appeared to be addressing the cat.

Leo gave Tom the "foolish human" look, then turned back to Drake, crouching to sniff the dog's lips.

"Wonder if he smells the blood," I said through a mouth full of chicken.

"What blood?" Tom clearly was not as obsessed with the bloody bag as I was. He watched the cat settle belly-down into the grass, tuck his paws under his chest, and wrap his tail along his left side with the white tip twitching next to his elbow. "Ever feel like he thinks people are too stupid to live?" Tom's new to cats. In fact, he had told me a few weeks earlier that Leo's the first cat he's ever really gotten to know, and Tom had fallen hard for my little orange tabby.

"Nah." I tossed a chicken thigh bone onto the paper towel I'd spread for refuse. "He just doesn't suffer foolish questions easily."

"Ah."

"Speaking of questions, what do you really think about that bag?" As I spoke, Jay and Drake swivelled their heads and aimed their ears toward the yard next door. My neighbor Goldie had just stepped through her back door wearing a caftan that glowed neon lime under her yellow porch lights.

Tom followed my gaze and smiled. You have to smile when you see Goldie. Parts of her never left the sixties, when, true to Scott McKenzie's song, she had gone to San Francisco, worn flowers in her hair, and changed her name from Rachel Golden to Sunshine Golden and, ultimately and legally, Golden Sunshine. She came back here a decade ago when her parents died within two weeks of each other, leaving her the house and a tidy pile of money. She had filled the yard with flowers and had been my friend through bad times and good.

Jay looked at me, back at Goldie, back at me, twitching to go but obeying my command to stay. I told him he was a good boy, and free from the "stay" command, and he raced for the fence, Drake right behind. Leo jumped out of the way, glared at the dogs, and shook a paw as if flinging away his disgust at their lack of manners. Feline dignity restored, he trotted after them. The commotion caught Goldie's eye and she waved. That was our signal to join the gathering at the fence.

Six

"She doesn't look good, does she?" I asked as I put the remains of the cole slaw in the fridge. I had been speculating on Goldie's health all summer, to myself and to Tom. It was all I could do. I'd tried everything from conversational fishing to direct questions, and Goldie always insisted that I was being silly and then changed the subject.

Tom dropped the chicken bones into a garbage bag, pulled it from the trash can, spun it, tied the knot, and looked at me, the closed bag dangling from his hand and a weary look on his face. "She's not well."

"That's what I think. She's lost too much weight and her color is off." I tossed Jay's eyeless, one-eared squeaky bunny and a newish floppy-legged fleecy sheep into the living room to clear the kitchen of dogs and started a pot of tea. "I've asked and asked and she says she's fine. Maybe she thinks she is fine. I just . . ."

A hand on my arm stopped me mid-wish and I turned. "No, Janet, I mean, she's not well." Tom's brown eyes, usually so warm and open they make me hungry, had gone a little murky, and a sliver of fear pricked at my mind. "I ran into her at the co-op a few days ago." He hoisted the bag in his hand and turned toward the back door. "Let me take this out. Then we'll talk."

I think my jaw dropped open, and I know my knees started to give. I sank into a chair at the table. The bunny and sheep appeared in my lap. The dogs watched me, mouths open in panting grins and eyes sparking with anticipation. I tossed the toys, but my heart wasn't in it. Dogs know, they just know, and the next thing *I* knew I had a black chin on one thigh, a white paw on the other, and four worried eyes telling me that I was never alone. I ran a hand along each lovely skull, the black hair on Drake's crisp and cool, the copper and silvery merle of Jay's slippery as silk. I folded at the waist and laid my face between theirs and felt my eyes fill, not just for Goldie, whatever was wrong, but for all the sorrows that chip away at our souls.

Tom let the door bang shut, breaking the spell. The dogs ran to him and I mashed the heels of my hands into my eyes to make my tear ducts behave.

"Settle, guys." Tom spoke softly and pointed toward a spot along the kitchen wall. In cooler weather I keep a big dog bed there, but in summer Jay prefers the cool vinyl, so the bed was stashed in the laundry room. The dogs looked at Tom and back at me, probably in hopes that I would countermand the directive. I shrugged at them and they went and lay down.

The kettle began to whistle, so I got up and grabbed it. I poured a bit of boiling water into my ancient bone china pot, swished it and dumped it, drizzled in some loose jasmine green tea, and filled the pot to steep. I focused on taking deep, cleansing breaths to calm myself, and teared up again as I realized that Goldie had taught me to do that. *Shake it off, MacPhail.* I set the pot and two mugs on the table, sat down, and braced myself. Tom was about to tell me whatever bad thing he had learned about Goldie when the doorbell rang.

Seven

"Wowser!" I said. "Who *are* you, and what have you done with my friend Jo?"

The woman on my front porch wore a V-neck peach-colored silk blouse and a skirt three shades darker that draped softly around her slim form. Gold chandelier earrings sparkled beneath her wavy short brown hair, and a delicate gold chain hung just below the notch of her collar bones. Quite a contrast from her usual khaki chinos, white shirt, and navy blazer. "You have makeup on!"

I was used to seeing Jo Stevens in her tough-cop guise and was surprised to see her cheeks go a soft rose. "Oh, come on. I dress like a girl occasionally."

"I'll say!" Tom stood framed by the kitchen doorway, each hand in a dog's collar. All three males had pretty much the same adoring look on their faces, although Tom's tongue didn't actually hang out. I realized with a start that my right hand was trying to fix my own messy hair, and I made it stop. Tom sent Drake and Jay to their spot in the corner, then bowed and gestured Jo into the kitchen, and I felt even frumpier as I watched her glide to a chair. But as she passed him, Tom turned and winked at me and bowed again. "Milady." As I moved by him he pinched my butt, and I swatted at his hand with deep and unreasonable pleasure.

Jo declined my offer of tea. She asked Tom how his summer research in New Mexico went, then got down to business. "So what's up?" The notebook and pen she usually stowed in her breast pocket emerged from a drawstring pouch lavishly embroidered and beaded in shades of sea and sky.

Tom excused himself to retrieve the canvas bag from his car while I gave my five-second rendition of Drake's mysterious find and then asked, "Hot date?"

Jo grinned at me.

"Come on, girlfriend, give it up!" But Tom's return put the kibosh on the juicy details. He handed Jo the plastic bag containing the canvas tote. She lifted it toward the ceiling light. "Huh." The water pooled along the plastic seam still had the pink cast I had noticed at the lake. Definitely not a reflection of the setting sun.

Jo glanced at Tom, then looked at me. "So?"

"So, I think that's blood on the bag, and there's a torn bit of a hundred dollar bill inside. At least that's what we think it is."

Tom added, "And a feather."

"Maybe a game bag?" She glanced at her watch. Not the big round face of the black-banded Fossil she usually wore, but a dainty little gold number that shared her wrist with a delicate gold bracelet. "I mean, if someone was out there hunting, they'd need a game bag to carry their victims home, right?"

Tom and I looked at each other. I hadn't thought of that.

"That whole area is posted no hunting, so it's unlikely," said Tom. "And anyway, it was a long red feather, not from any local game birds I can think of." He looked at the bag in Jo's hands. "And that's not a typical game bag."

I smiled at him, encouraged that he finally seemed to be on my side, and added, "Besides, why would a blood-soaked bag with part of a hundred dollar bill in it be lying out on a little private island like that?"

Jay and Drake both lifted their heads and looked at me, attuned as always to shifting emotions in their human companions. For my part, I was attuned to Jo's apparent lack of concern. Or maybe it was annoyance. She *was* off duty, after all.

Jo sighed. "You have a permanent marker handy?"

I produced one and she made some marks on the plastic bag.

"Okay, I'll look into it. It is a little weird, but there's no evidence of a crime." She stood and smoothed her skirt. "Tell you what. One of you meet me there tomorrow and I'll take a look at the island. Right now, I'm off duty. Gotta go."

The dogs started to follow but Tom signaled them to lie down and stay, and they did. We walked Jo to the door and made arrangements for the next day, then watched her get into the passenger side of a nifty little sports car. Couldn't tell you what kind, other than low and sleek and an indefinite color under the glow of the streetlight. I couldn't see the driver, either.

"Hunh." I didn't exactly want to be Jo's age again, but still, another sprig of loss grew in my heart.

Tom wrapped his hand around mine and gave it a little squeeze, making me wonder, not for the first time, which came first, the astute people-watching skills or the anthropological training.

"She looks great." I was startled by the whiny little edge in my voice.

"She does," he agreed, and the sprig in my heart morphed into a sequoia of jealousy that I knew was stupid, and yet, there it was, until he said, "Then again, a bit young and skinny. And there's not nearly enough dog hair on her duds." He pulled me back from the door, pushed it shut, wrapped his arms around me, and kissed me silly. When all rational thoughts were cleared from my head, he slid his cheek along mine and said, "Maybe we should make ourselves comfortable."

"Mmmmm." We turned away from the door and stepped over the dogs, who had crawled closer for a better view. Drake slapped his tail against the cool vinyl and Jay waved a lazy white paw our way, then they both sighed and went back to dozing. Tom draped his arm over my shoulder and steered us to the living room couch, where we were beginning to get serious when a knock on the back door launched the dogs off the floor and turned our heads toward the kitchen. The door swung open and a plate of cookies barged through, followed by Goldie, her long braids like liquid silver against the fuschia caftan and her smile like the sunshine for which she had named herself. A pang of guilt hit me for having let my hormones keep me from asking Tom what he knew about her health, and now that would have to wait again.

"You have to come eat these," she called from the kitchen, seemingly oblivious to the passion play underway in the living room. "I don't know why I baked so many. If I eat them all myself I'll be a blimp."

Tom pulled himself off me and then pulled me off the couch. We both refastened and tucked in clothing as we followed our noses to the kitchen. Jay and Drake were already standing by the counter, muzzles aimed toward the plate of cookies that Goldie was uncovering. They were having an olfactory orgy this evening.

"I just heard from my source at the county building. That preacher, that Regal Moneypincher . . ."

Tom choked on his cookie and I said, "Regis Moneypenny."

"That's the one. He's buying up land all around Cedar Canyons Road and plans to put up some kind of commune or something." Goldie used the back of her wrist to wipe a stray curl from her forehead. "Not my kind of commune, you know. We worked and shared and had barely a pot to, well, cook in. No sir, he's planning some kind of walled, gated, gotta-have-a-lotta-money place."

"Sounds like most of the new developments around here," said Tom, grabbing another cookie. "These are great. What *are* they?"

"What do you mean, . . ." I began.

"Lavender and white chocolate."

". . . your 'source' at the county . . . ," I stopped as Goldie's words sank in. "Lavender and white chocolate?" I reached for one. "Really?"

"He's going to ruin that beautiful land up there."

Tom nodded and said something like "Rmftt" through a mouthful of cookie.

"What kind of source, Goldie?"

"Secret."

I flashed on an image of Goldie meeting a guy in a trench coat in the shadowy concrete parking canyon of the City-County Building. "Who?"

Goldie looked over the top of her glasses at me. "What kind of secret would it be if I told you who?"

"She could," Tom said, elbowing me and winking at Goldie, "but then she'd have to kill you."

Goldie pulled a chair out from the table and sat down with a huge sigh. "It's no laughing matter. Those little lakes and the fallow fields up there are on the migratory flyways for birds and butterflies both, and besides, how could anyone want to bulldoze and pave that lovely part of the county?"

"We were just out there," said Tom. "Didn't see any new development going in."

"No, he's just applied for the permits. My *secret* source," she stressed the word and looked at me, "said there were all kinds of things on the building list. Not just houses. Weird things."

"It is a spiritual center of some sort. Maybe they need another church?" I envisioned the palatial building they had now and thought it seemed doubtful, if obvious.

"Ladies," Tom said, "I'm going to call it a night. I have to work on a paper in the morning, and Janet, you're out early, too, right?" He pulled a plastic bag out of a box on the counter and shoved several cookies into it. "So I shall gallantly protect you from these calories, and ride off with my faithful dog." He gave me a quick kiss, whispered "I think she's here for a while," and left.

I tried to listen closely to Goldie, but couldn't keep my thoughts from wandering. If Moneypenny was planning to develop the area around his spiritual center, there would be more people than Goldie eager to stop him. Especially if he was planning to build "weird things," whatever that meant.

"What do you mean by 'weird things,' Goldie?" I asked.

"An aviary, for one. Big one."

That didn't seem too weird to me, although I wasn't sure how it fit into a Spiritual Renewal Center. If there was something odd about his proposed buildings, though, could there be a connection between his plans and the bloody bag Drake had found? I didn't care what anyone said, I was sure the stain on the bag was blood, and the thought of what that might mean made my stomach turn. I set my half-eaten cookie on a napkin and put the kettle back on. I could tell that Tom was right, Goldie did seem to be good for at least another hour. Still, it wasn't even ten. I realized that I was disappointed that Tom had left, and a little angry at both Tom and Goldie. What were they hiding from me? And what in the world was going on at Twisted Lake and Treasures on Earth? I was suddenly determined to find out, with or without their help.

Eight

The next morning I was out the door early despite the fog in my brain from lack of sleep. Goldie had stayed until nearly midnight. I tried several times to steer the conversation to her health, but she was on a roll about land-raping developers and crazy cult leaders, and she dismissed my concerns about her with a cheery, "Bah! I'm *fine,* Janet!" By the time she left and I'd showered, taken Jay out one last time, and locked up, it was nearly one a.m. Even then I tossed and turned for at least another hour, pondering the meaning of Drake's bag and its contents, Goldie's evasiveness, and the likelihood that I would oversleep.

I didn't. I woke up about two minutes before my alarm was set to go off and dragged myself out of bed. A prominent women's magazine had commissioned a photo essay on a day in the life of a woman veterinarian, and I was scheduled to spend every day that week traipsing around my vet's clinic with my camera. It's a two-vet office. Jay and Leo usually see Paul Douglas, but I would be shadowing his partner and, as it happens, his wife, Kerry Joiner. Dr. Kerry Joiner had officially linked up with Dr. Paul Douglas, in business and in life, a couple of years earlier. I knew her mostly from dog-training classes and dog shows. She was perfect for the magazine article — five years out of Purdue vet school, petite and perky as the Pomeranian she owned, strong enough to hoist a hundred pounds of dog onto an exam table, and lots of fun to be around.

The clinic was in turmoil when I arrived. The lobby, at any rate. One of the two veterinary technicians had called the week before from Key West and announced that she wasn't coming back. The other called in sick half an hour before I arrived, and the second receptionist wasn't due until nine o'clock. Peg, the office manager, was scurrying between the clamor of Monday-morning phones and the chaos of Monday-morning clients. This particular Monday morning was deafening, and as I walked by the front desk I heard Peg mutter something about sedatives.

I spotted my across-the-street neighbors,

Mr. Hostetler and Paco, the Chihuahua, at the far end of the waiting room. Mr. Hostetler's five-year-old grandson, Tyler, was leaning into his grandpa and gently stroking Paco. I waved as I asked Peg, "What can I do?"

Peg turned grateful eyes my way and slapped a file folder into my hand. "Any chance you could escort the Willards to exam room one?"

I had the oddest vision of rats, and realized the name made me think of that old movie about a kid named Willard who sicced his trained rodent on his enemies. Turned out in this case we were faced not with a rat but a brat. I missed out on having children, not by design, but I have learned a few things from my years as a dog and cat owner. One thing I know for sure is that young animals have to be trained. All kinds of young animals, including the human ones. Lacking direction, some young animals do everything in their power to discourage their mothers — and anyone else within earshot — from ever reproducing again. The Willard child was one of those.

The Willard puppy was named Hummer. Big name, whopping big puppy. His file showed that Hummer weighed sixteen pounds at his last visit, when he was seven weeks old. Now, a month later, he had more than doubled in weight and had a surplus of puppy energy. Not that I'd expect less of a Golden Retriever crossed with Something Really Big. The shape of his head made me suspect Newfoundland in his lineage, and I considered suggesting water dog training to channel his enthusiasm. Then I really looked at Mrs. Willard and decided that mud and wet dogs were probably not her thing.

When Hummer heard me call his name, he spun toward the sound and leaped at me, yanking Mrs. Willard out of her seat. If he'd had better traction on the vinyl floor, his owner might have found herself skidding face-first behind him. Luckily for her, the pup's cartoon scramble over the slick surface gave her a chance to get her strappy Ferragamos under her, and she clattered toward me, her arm pulled taut along with the leash that was, apparently, purely decorative. The rest of the clients in the waiting room hugged their pets or pet carriers close.

"Hummer, stop that!" pleaded Mrs. Willard. Hummer planted his humongous feet against my waist and pasted a fist-sized glob of sticky drool to the smock I'd borrowed from the missing techs.

I was wondering how we might set up a photo of a slobbered-up vet for my photo essay when a high-pitched scalpel of a voice began to chant, "Hummer, stop that! Hummer, stop that! Hummer, stop that!" The owner of the voice jumped up and down on chubby pink-clad legs a couple of times, then grabbed the leash halfway between her mother and Hummer and pulled with all her four-year-old might.

Hummer spun away from me, circled the screeching kid, and wrapped his leash twice around her ribs before you could shout, "Down! Stay!"

"Tiffany dear, please be quiet." Mrs. Willard was remarkably calm.

Tiffany dear was remarkably loud, and she raised the volume when Hummer gave her face a good slurp. "Aaaaaaa! Bad dog! Bad dog!"

Pandemonium broke out in the back room as a chorus of barking and howling mingled with Tiffany's racket. A couple of dogs in the waiting room joined in. Paco started a staccato series of barks but was quickly stifled by Mr. Hostetler's hand around his muzzle, a motion mirrored by Tyler, who had clapped his hand over his own mouth and widened his eyes. A dainty little Border Collie whined and strained against her leash, hot to organize the unruly mob. Hummer bounced up and down against the howling kid, woof-woofing and mouthing bits of clothing. Mrs. Willard reached for Hummer's collar, then snatched her hand back with a gasp and looked at it.

"Did he bite you?" I asked. I didn't think the big galoot would do it on purpose, but those needles they call baby teeth can cause some damage if you get in the way.

"I broke a nail! Awww, I just had them done!" She held her hand in front of her eyes, a pout wrinkling the otherwise perfect skin around her mouth. I never have any nails to break, so the apparent depth of the tragedy was lost on me.

I wanted to chime in with the screamers. Instead, I tossed the file folder onto the counter and said, "Let me help." I got the back of Hummer's collar in my left hand and put my right hand on Tiffany's chubby little shoulder. "Quiet!" Child and dog both froze and stared at me. I unhooked the leash from Hummer's collar and unwound it from Tiffany, then put it back on the dog. Tiffany burst into tears and resumed screaming, but at least the puppy was under a semblance of control. I told Mrs. Willard to bring the folder and follow me. As I led the unruly horde down the hall, applause broke out in the waiting room. My debut as a veterinary assistant was off to a rip-roaring start.

Nine

As any experienced dog breeder will tell you, not all females are endowed with a full set of mothering instincts. Judging by Tiffany dear's too-well-fed form and too-expensive-for-kids couture, I could see that Mrs. Willard was at the head of the line marked "Instincts for Feeding and Clothing the Young." Judging by Tiffany's exquisite brattiness, I assumed that Mrs. Willard had skipped the line marked "Managing Unruly Offspring." Perhaps she relied on other people to do it for her.

I have no burning desire to manage anyone's children, but Tiffany dear forced my hand. She leaned one dimpled hand of her own on the seat of the bench in the exam room and swung one pink-stockinged foot back and forth, peering at me from the corner of her eye. Each forward swing of her leg brought the toe of her shoe a little closer to Hummer's head. The puppy was lying down and panting happily, and I wanted him to stay that way until Dr. Joiner arrived. A shoe to the ear wouldn't help.

"Careful you don't kick your puppy." I forced myself to smile.

Tiffany dear stuck her tongue out at me. Her mom giggled and squirmed in her seat. She reached out to stroke her daughter's curly brown hair, but the kid dodged her hand, so Mrs. Willard scratched Hummer's head instead. A glint below her throat caught my eye, and I looked at the pendant hanging from a delicate chain. It looked like a cross with half a heart hanging from one side, and although I thought I had seen something like it before, I couldn't think where.

My attempts to remember were cut short when Tiffany pointed at me and whined, "I don't like that." *That?* I thought. But the kid went on, "It looks like Polly and I *hate* Polly." She stuck her lower lip out so far I thought she might trip over it.

"Well, that one is green, dear," said Mrs. Willard, "and Polly is blue, so it doesn't really look like Polly, does it?"

"I hate Polly!" Tiffany's voice escalated in pitch and volume with every word. "I hate all the birds!"

I turned to see what in the world they

were talking about. On the wall behind me was a painting of a green parrot of some sort. I turned back to Tiffany, smiled at her, and said, "I think that's a very pretty bird. Why don't you like it?"

Without a word, Tiffany popped off the seat and danced a pirouette. As she turned toward the wall behind her, the poster of "Cats of the World" caught her eye. She scrambled onto the bench and ripped a ragged triangle from the bottom third of the poster.

Mrs. Willard turned her head toward her daughter, and said, "Tiffany dear, please don't do that. Be good and we'll stop for ice cream on the way home."

Just what this kid needs, I thought. *Calories and sugar to reinforce her bad behavior.*

Tiffany's hand started to reach once more for the wounded poster, but Mrs. Willard didn't move. I suppose she was in nail-preservation mode. With reflexes honed by years of handling unwilling and untrained animals, I took hold of the little dear just above her elbow and, with marvelous restraint, pulled her gently around and sat her down on the bench. "Please sit down, Tiffany." I tried to keep the snarl out of my voice. "That bench is pretty slippery. You might fall off and hurt yourself." She glared at me, glanced at her mother, and started to cry. The kid deserved an academy award. I kept the smile pasted to my face and left the room.

Dr. Joiner was squatting in front of a large cage watching a newborn tan-and-white Bulldog nestle against his mother's warm belly. Agnes, the mama dog, didn't seem to mind that her puppy's shoulder was firmly planted against her stitched-up incision. She had taken to her new son immediately, not always the case with caesarian deliveries, and she looked immensely pleased with her offspring.

"Who or what was carrying on out there?"

"The Willard kid."

Dr. Joiner stood, her face scrunching up with obvious dread. "Oh, no. Don't tell me they're here for me?" I nodded. She slumped against the door frame and whined, "Why can't she see Paul instead?" She was still muttering as she stalked down the hall toward the room. I thought of retrieving my camera but decided to wait for more appealing subjects than the Willards for my photo shoot.

"They are really weird," said Dr. Kerry.

"Who?"

"Willards." She stopped, took my arm, and leaned in so I could hear her lowered voice. "Money out the yin yang, and apparently nothing to do with it except buy expensive stuff." She released my arm. "Sorry. I shouldn't be gossiping about clients."

"Mum's the word."

"I love their pup. He's such a big sweet galoot. She told me they paid $1,800 for him."

"But he's a mixed breed."

"Right. But they were sold a bill of goods along with him. Golden by Newfie cross labeled 'Goldenlander.' Can you believe it? Even came with papers from some fly-by-night registry. No health clearances on the parents, of course."

I understood her frustration, having spoken to many pet owners, and said, "People think if you cross different breeds you automatically get healthier dogs."

Dr. Joiner shook her head and muttered, "So gullible."

We rolled our eyes at one another and walked the last few yards to the exam room door.

Hummer had restarted his engine and was bouncing around as wildly as he could manage in the three feet between the bench and the examination table. Dr. Joiner bent to pet him and Mrs. Willard told him over and over again to sit. He didn't mind any better than her kid, but he hadn't destroyed anything. Everyone in the room focused on the puppy. Everyone except Tiffany. She was somewhere behind me, and I was just turning to see what the little dear was up to when the metallic protest of a drawer being yanked open filled the room.

"Tiffany dear, don't do that." True to form, her mother again made no move to restrain the child, and her voice was too tentative to have any effect. I thought back to my own mom, who in better days had brooked no nonsense from me or my brother, Bill, especially in public — clearly a different breed of mother from Mrs. Willard.

The oblivious child was on tippy toes, reaching a hand above her head and into the drawer. I half hoped she'd accidentally jab herself with a syringe full of anaesthetic, although the possibility was remote since I knew from my tour of the clinic that they don't keep syringes or drugs in the exam rooms. So, for the second time in five minutes, I gripped Tiffany's chunky arm and pulled her away from trouble. Or so I thought.

TEN

Trouble seems to be my new middle name. Not that I cause it. I just find it lately. I mean, how many photographers find blood-stained bags in idyllic settings or uncontrolled children in veterinary clinics? I was wondering whether I should switch my photographic specialty from living things to, oh, say, architecture when Dr. Joiner's voice brought me back to the moment.

"Is it broken?"

Tiffany dear had yanked the drawer far enough out of its slot that it stuck when I tried to push it in. "I think just off track." I released Tiffany's arm and tried to give her the glare my mom used to use to scare the bejeepers out of me and Bill. Either I wasn't as terrifying as Mom or Tiffany was gutsier than I was as a kid, because she glared right back at me. I was reluctant to turn my back on her — an instinct that turned out to be sound — but someone had to, so I squatted to examine the bottom of the injured storage unit. I pushed up on the handle and jiggled the drawer to the right, felt it fall back into the track, and tested it. "All better."

Tiffany stood against the wall, kicking the new paint with her heel. The hostile glare had been replaced by a chilling gaze that bespoke more plotting than an Agatha Christie collection. I thought the leash should be on Tiffany rather than Hummer, but knew that it would be every inch as ineffectual as it was with the pup as long as Mrs. Willard held its other end. In any case, the child's mother hadn't said a word as her daughter terrorized the exam room, and in the aftermath she looked calm as a sleeping dog. I wanted some of whatever she was taking.

"Well, then, let's have a look at this puppy." Dr. Joiner talked a little too fast and smiled a little too cheerfully.

I unsnapped Hummer's leash and handed it to his owner. As I hoisted him onto the exam table, I checked the whereabouts of the demon child. She was still busy planting black scuff marks on the wall to my left.

Dr. Joiner pronounced Hummer's heart and lungs healthy, gave him his shots, and began to trim his nails. He wriggled and squirmed, alternating between licking Dr. Joiner's face and trying to eat the clippers, so I encircled him with my arms to immobilize him, or at least slow him down. Unfortunately, holding him still made me a sitting duck.

Come to think of it, I wish I had been sitting. As it happened, I was on my feet and leaning forward against the table to hold the puppy for his pedicure. Mrs. Willard sat on the bench, still filing her own broken nail and smiling like the Mona Lisa. And for a brief instant I had no idea where Tiffany dear had gotten to. Then, in the time it took to clip one puppy nail, little hands shot up under my smock, latched onto the top of my easy-waist pants — both pairs — and slid them down to my ankles.

"Owww!" A sharp pain shot from my butt to my brain. I didn't immediately recognize the sensation, but quickly realized it was caused by enamel penetrating flesh.

"Wha . . . ?" Dr. Joiner stepped back from the table, startled.

"She bit me!"

The vet glanced at Hummer's distinctly male abdomen and looked confused. I pushed the puppy toward her, determined to free my hands so I could swat my assailant.

Mrs. Willard stood at the end of the table, nail file in hand, staring at Hummer. "He bit you?" She turned enormous contact-turquoise eyes on me.

"Not your dog!" I growled, craning my neck over my shoulder and running a hand over my complaining behind. "Your kid!"

Tiffany dear was backed up to the wall again, grinning at me. For an instant, I could have sworn I saw long fangs dripping gore. I looked at my hand and showed the smear of red across my palm to Dr. Joiner. She scooped the bewildered looking Hummer into one arm and opened the door to the back room with the other. "We need some help here. Now!"

I realized with horror that the only one who could be in the back room was Dr. Douglas. And before I could react to the thought, there he was.

Dr. Joiner shoved Hummer into her husband's arms and pushed the two of them toward the door to the waiting room. "Janet's been bitten." She grabbed Tiffany's hand and hauled her away from the wall and toward her mother. "Paul, please keep the Willards out front for a few minutes." To Vampira's mother she said, "Make your daughter sit down and stay put."

Mrs. Willard gaped at the blood on my

hand and, for the first time, came to life. "Oh my God!" She pulled her daughter to her. "She could get sick!" At first I thought she was concerned for me. Bites of any kind are dangerous, and a friend who runs a preschool had once told me that human bites that break the skin often result in horrifying infections.

"I think I'm o . . . ," I started to say, but Mrs. Willard cut me off.

"Have you been tested?" It was becoming clear that Tiffany got her weapons-grade screech from her mother. "Oh my God, Tiffany!"

"Tested?" I asked.

Dr. Joiner put a hand on Mrs. Willard's shoulder and aimed her toward the door. "Your daughter just bit this woman and injured her. You could show a little concern for Janet."

Dr. Douglas seemed to be trying to catch up on the situation. "You got bitten?" He looked doubtfully at the puppy slurping happily at his chin. As he walked past the examining table, I bent over to pull my pants up under my almost-long-enough smock, confusing him even more.

"The dog didn't bite her," said Dr. Joiner, "but watch out for the kid." She gave her now-grinning partner a final nudge and pulled the door shut.

"Okay, let me see."

"It's fine."

"It's not fine. She broke the skin. Let me see."

"No, rea . . ."

She crossed her arms, cocked a hip, and waited, her green eyes daring me to object again. With a sigh, I pulled my pants back down to my knees and leaned forward against the steel tabletop.

"Wow. That's bigger than I expected."

"Hey!"

"The bite. It needs a stitch or two, and antibiotics."

"Can't you just clean it and stick a bandage on it?"

She stood up and reached for some Betadine and a cotton pad. "I'll clean it and tape a pad to it, and then you're going to the ER."

"No!"

"Don't argue, Janet. I can't treat you, and you know as well as I do that you don't screw around with bites." The muscles around my eyes and in my fanny flinched as Dr. Joiner dabbed at the wound. She taped a gauze pad bigger than some bikinis to me and signaled me to pull my pants up. "I should fire you, you know."

"Oh yeah?"

"Yeah. How dare you flash my husband?"

"Well, if you remember, I was shanghaied for this duty. You can't fire a slave."

"Listen, we'll pay for everything. Get HIV and hepatitis tests while you're there. Wouldn't be surprised if the Willards raise a fuss."

"But *she* bit *me*!"

"Just trying to be proactive."

"Wow," I said, looking at my blood-stained hand. "Just wow."

"I know." She sighed. "I'll have Peg drive you. Nancy will be in soon and she can get the phone."

"But . . ."

Dr. Joiner signaled "stop" with her hand. "The only butt I'm interested in at the moment is yours. Get it taken care of."

ELEVEN

Peg laughed all the way to Parkview Hospital. Or most of the way. She paused for a moment of outrage when I told her how Tiffany dear had ripped the poster and jammed the drawer, but my painful humiliation at the hands and jaws of Mrs. Willard's demon spawn sent her into whoops of laughter.

"I'm not laughing *at* you, you know," she gasped between giggling sprees. "But you have to admit it's pretty funny. Not that a kid who bites is funny, but . . ."

I gave her a dirty look but she was watching the road and missed it, so I complained out loud. "It hurts like hell. That kid is headed for big trouble if you ask me." My body listed toward the passenger window to spare my damaged cheek.

"Yeah, they better wash her mouth out with soap so she doesn't get sick." She wiped at her eye.

"Yuk yuk." I thought about Dr. Joiner's instructions. "Did Kerry tell you I need HIV and hepatitis tests?"

Peg nodded, then grinned. "No wonder Dr. Douglas had that funny grin on his face when he came out!"

"Great. I suppose this will be the topic of many a tasteless comment every time I come in for the next few months."

"Oh, more like years. You'll be . . ." The rest of the sentence disappeared in an incoherent squeal that turned into more giggles. Peg finally got a grip and repeated in a voice two octaves too high, "You're gonna be the butt of a lot of jokes."

I scowled out the window.

Peg recovered some control and, aside from her periodic giggle, we rode in silence until I said, more or less to myself, "Treasures on Earth."

"Huh?"

"Treasures on Earth Spiritual Renewal Center. Mrs. Willard's pendant. It's their logo."

"Never heard of it. But I think Mrs. Willard's husband is a minister of some sort." She seemed to be pondering something. "Wonder how a minister's wife affords those clothes."

Mrs. Willard didn't strike me as a seeker

after spiritual enlightenment, but her duds certainly fit with the cars I had seen in the parking lot at the Center. I started to ask Peg what else she knew about the Willards, but the throbbing in my backside distracted me. "Why do these things always happen when my doctor's office is closed?"

"Same reason these things always happen to people's pets when we're closed."

Same reason we find suspicious items in the middle of nowhere during dog training sessions, I thought.

Peg braked in front of the ER entrance.

I winced as I straightened out of the car. A security guard young enough to have a scattering of pimples across his cheeks hustled up to the car. "Do you need a wheelchair, ma'am?"

I wanted to slap him. When did I become a ma'am? "Thanks, but definitely not." The last thing I wanted to do was sit down again, which of course is what the clerk told me to do while I gave her my information. Peg hustled in from parking the car and explained that she would be paying on behalf of the clinic.

"What species of animal bit you?" The clerk's hands hovered over her keyboard. Her short green nails matched the beads at the ends of hundreds of tiny braids hanging from neat cornrows, and her name tag dubbed her LaFawn.

"Homo sapiens."

She started to type, apparently on autopilot, and then stared at me as the information sank in.

"A person bit you?"

"Yes."

She gaped at me. "Why?"

"Because I'm so sweet?" I shrugged, and sighed. "Because she's a little brat."

LaFawn snorted and her beads clacked as she shook her head in disgust. "What did her mama do?"

"Not much. She was injured earlier." LaFawn's eyebrows rose. "Broke a nail."

Another snort, then back to work. "Where were you bitten?"

"All Paws Veterinary Clinic."

She looked at me as if I had a brain injury. "Where on your body?"

"Oh." My hand went involuntarily to my left buttock. "My butt." I could tell she was trying hard to suppress the grin that played along the edges of her glossy red lips. "Go ahead and laugh at me. Everyone else has."

LaFawn leaned across her desk, a conspiratorial smile lighting her face. "I got bit in the butt once." Pregnant pause. "By a skeeter." LaFawn and Peg cracked up. I gave the clerk my best dirty look and she adjusted herself in her chair, cleared her throat, and wriggled her fingers in preparation. "Okay then! Are you taking any medications?" And so on.

LaFawn directed us to follow the blue line down the hall and around the corner to where we would find a waiting area. She tried to insist that I occupy a wheelchair for the journey, but I was more insistent that I wasn't interested in sitting down just yet, and off we went, one of us limping and the other still grinning her face off. A whirl of color flew into my peripheral vision as we passed another long corridor labeled Nuclear Medicine, and I turned to see a figure in white slacks and a loose-fitting tunic striped lemon, lime, and strawberry. What stopped me mid-stride was a vision of silver braids looped over the woman's crown, but the vision disappeared through a doorway before I could call her name.

Goldie.

My feet seemed to take root as I stood at the intersection of the hallways. A series of images slid through my mind and suddenly took on a meaning I had pushed away for months, although I had suspected that something was off. I flashed on Goldie buying mountains of vitamins and herbals at the co-op last spring. Saw palmetto. Green tea. Cat's claw. Goldie looking thin and pale. Tired, though she tried to hide it. What was it Tom wanted to tell me? He had left shortly after Goldie arrived the night before, saying he'd stop by late this afternoon after he showed Detective Jo where we'd found the bag at Heron Acres.

"Janet?" Peg had stopped and turned toward me, and all the jokes had abandoned her. "What's wrong? Are you faint?"

The warmth of her hands on my arms unfroze my feet, and I let her steer me into the waiting room, but I still refused to sit. I fished my cell phone out of my purse, but the battery was dead. "Give me your cell." She handed it over and I tried Tom's office, cell, and home numbers, and left "call me's" with Peg's number on all three. I figured I would update the message as soon as I was near a working phone of my own.

The image of Goldie walking into that room wouldn't get out of my head, and within minutes I had assured myself that nothing was wrong. She was probably there for a mammogram. She was fanatical about getting them, on time, once a year. And since spring she'd been slathering on high-test sun screen whenever she was out, so no wonder she looked pale compared to past summers. As for the supplements, she'd been into herbal therapies for forty years. I told myself she'd just been stocking up.

Peg leafed through every year-old magazine in the waiting room and gently relieved one of a recipe. I paced the floor and had put in several miles by the time someone could see me eighty minutes later. The nurse got me into a gown and situated face down on the exam table. I thought I'd be relieved to get the ordeal over with, but when the doctor walked into the room and I heard his name, I wished I had simply treated my injury with copious amounts of alcohol, taken internally.

Twelve

"You know how sometimes something you once wanted finally shows up at the worst possible moment?" I was sprawled on my stomach, a position I seemed to be assuming a lot lately. At least I was on my own bed and fully clothed this time. I was nose to nose with Jay, holding the phone with one hand and popping chocolate chips into my mouth with the other. In deference to my current weight-loss attempt I had stripped my cupboards of junk food, but twenty minutes of scrounging had turned up half a bag of these little darlings.

Goldie was still ranting about "some people's children" and I wasn't sure she'd heard me, but I plowed on.

"So there I was, in one of those stylish hospital gowns, belly down on an exam table with goose bumps all over my bare behind 'cause it was freezing in there, and in walks the doctor."

"I bet it wasn't a woman, huh?"

"Oh no."

"Probably not a kindly old fart either, huh?"

"In your dreams."

"Greek god?"

"Close."

"So, tell me."

"Neil Young."

"The singer?"

"High school heartthrob."

"Ohmygod! Neil the Hunk?" I had mentioned my girlhood lust for Neil to Goldie before. "He's a doctor?" She squealed the last two words.

"That, or he just plays one in the emergency room."

Goldie seemed to have caught Peg's laughing disease, so I fiddled with Jay's ear until the hooting on the other end of the line subsided.

"So, Goldie, what were you doing at Parkview?"

Silence.

"Goldie?"

"Oh, sorry, I'm making tea, trying to reach the oolong at the back of the cupboard."

Uh huh. "So, Parkview?"

"Just some routine blood work. Annual physical, all that jazz."

Something was very wrong here, and although the frightened mortal part of me didn't want to know what it was, the friend part of me did. "Goldie . . ."

She cut me off. "So tell me more. You've wanted Neil Young's paws on your bare tush since you were sixteen. What an opportunity!"

"Goldie . . ." I thought of pressing for more information. Then I decided maybe the phone wasn't the best medium for such a conversation and shifted back to my own story for the moment. "I haven't exactly been holding a torch for him all these years."

Jay inched forward, pointing his twitching nose toward the diminishing pile of chocolate chips and flicking his gaze back and forth between them and me.

"You can't have chocolate." I snarfed the last few chips to save him from possible poisoning. Theobromine, a chemical found in chocolate, is toxic for dogs. It's the one reason I might hesitate to become fully canine, given the chance.

"Why can't I have chocolate?" Goldie sounded confused.

"Talking to Jay."

"So then what happened? Neil the Hunk is hunkered over your butt. Did he kiss it and make it better?"

"He put in a couple of stitches, gave me a prescription for two weeks worth of horse-size antibiotics, and went on to normal emergencies."

"That's all? No old home week?"

"He didn't know who I was."

"Sure he did."

"He was polite, professional, and showed no hint of recognition."

"How do you know? You were face down."

"Funny."

"Okay, brass tacks. Did you see whether he was wearing a ring?"

"Nope."

"Well, there you go. You should have made your move."

"No, I mean I didn't notice. I didn't have a very good view of his hands." My brain zoomed in on an image of Tom's smiling face and a wave of guilt sloshed over me.

As if she had read my mind, Goldie said, "I don't think you should tell Dr. Tom about Dr. Neil."

Despite my own twinges of conscience, Goldie's comment hit me wrong. I mean, I like the guy a lot, but neither of us had made any firm commitment. "I'm not married to Tom." Goldie let that go, although I knew her well enough to think I'd be hearing more on the subject later.

"So you were naked with Neil the Hunk and you didn't do anything about it?"

"I wasn't naked. I was draped. All that showed was the bite."

"Bite, butt, close enough."

"You try feeling sexy with a numbed fanny and a hospital gown."

"That is a real bite in the ass," and I thought *I'm never going to hear the last of this.* Goldie's voice brightened as she thought of something else. "You have to go back to get the stitches out, right?"

"In your dreams. If I had to, I'd get Kerry, you know, Dr. Joiner, to do it, or just die with them in place. But they're the dissolving kind."

I didn't tell Goldie, but I was relieved that Neil hadn't recognized me. Despite the years, hearing his voice had made me yearn for something long gone, something we share only with those who knew us as children. And I had to admit that, from the little I could see when I snuck a backward glance, Neil wore the intervening years well. The body that had once been all elbows and Adam's apple had matured well, and a glance over my shoulder had shown me that he still had those famous bedroom eyes, although they now suggested silk sheets and champagne rather than a quick fumble on a vinyl backseat. He struck me as the kind of guy who might prefer to unwrap a package of his own choosing rather than have one served up fanny first.

And that image, naturally, led my canine-oriented mind to an image of Mark Soudoff's Miniature Schnauzer Heidi flinging her tail in Jay's face at obedience practice last week. She wasn't in heat. In fact, she's spayed. But that never stops her flirting, and Jay flirts back, although he was "tutored" long ago. Of course, if he gets too fresh, Heidi offers to pin his ears to his nubby little tail. At the moment, Jay was gazing at the empty chocolate chip bag as a promising substitute for sex. He cocked his head, still flicking his gaze from me to the bag and back.

Goldie asked, "What?"

"Oh, just wondering if Neil likes dogs." I winced as I forgot myself and rolled into a sitting position. Jay raised his head and listened for a moment, then leaped off the bed and raced out of the bedroom.

"Well, there's a big black dog getting out of a car in your driveway, and he's with a fella who does for sure like dogs. Looks like he comes bearing dinner. Again."

I wasn't sure if the flipflop in my chest was guilt or anticipation, but realized with a flush that I was glad the big black dog was here with his man, and not just because I wanted to hear about Tom's trip to the lake with Detective Jo Stevens. I said goodbye to Goldie, rolled off the bed, and limped to the front door.

Thirteen

As you might expect, I often do have my camera handy when I need it, but not this time. Drake stood on the front porch with my evening paper in his mouth, tail waving and eyes gleaming. Tom stood beside him balancing a container of salad on a pizza box, eyes gleaming, my mail in his mouth.

"Are you two related?" I asked, taking the slightly damp paper goods from them and ushering them toward the kitchen. I limped along behind and tossed the mail and paper onto the pile that had sprouted on the table. "Let's eat outside."

Tom was already elbowing the back door open and sending the dogs out. He winked at me and asked, "Buy you a beer?"

"By all means." He paused in the open door while I grabbed two Killians and a bottle of low-fat ranch from the refrigerator, then tucked the salad dressing between my arm and my ribs to fish a couple of forks and knives from the dishwasher. Good thing I'd run it last night. *Note to self: pay more attention to the house.* I glanced at the empty napkin holder on the table and ripped a length of paper towels off the roll beside the sink. *This is getting to be a habit,* I thought as I nodded at Tom to lead the way.

We settled into our usual spots at my tangerine table, dogs lying at a discreet distance where they could maintain eye contact without being told to go lie down. As soon as he had slugged back some beer and stopped moaning about how good the pizza tasted, Tom wiped his mouth and began to speak.

"Jo wasn't too impressed with our crime scene."

"Did you take her to the island?"

"Nope." He took a big bite.

"Why not?"

"Mmm." He swallowed and slugged down some more beer. "No boat."

"There is a boat. It's tied to a tree behind where Collin stood to toss the bumper."

"Nope."

My brain was working on the boat's disappearance as I asked, "Well, did you see anyone else out there?"

"Nope."

"It was there yesterday."

"Maybe. I wouldn't swear to that, though."

"I would. Hang on."

Two minutes later I held the viewer of my camera in front of Tom and showed him a photo of an aluminum bass boat bobbing in the late-afternoon sun. "I took that yesterday."

"Okay." He watched me ease myself back into my seat. "You're limping. And you don't want to sit. Somebody bitecha in the ass?"

"Who told you?" Tom was pretty good friends with our shared vet, Paul Douglas, but I was appalled at the idea that my vet had told anyone, even Tom, about my assault.

"No one told me anything. I was kidding. You really got bitten?"

"As a matter of fact . . ." I told him about my morning. Most of it. I didn't tell him that my high school heartthrob had worked on my lacerated behind.

By the time we'd finished our stories we had also finished the food and drink and the evening invasion of mosquitoes had begun, so we went inside. The dogs found a long rope toy and started a friendly growly game of tug, and Tom and I settled onto the couch. Tom wrapped his arm around me and pulled me close, clearly interested in another friendly game, but first I wanted to know more about what Jo had to say.

"Already told you, Janet. Not much. Really. There just wasn't much to see from where we were standing, and other than the bag and your creepy feeling . . ."

"It wasn't a 'creepy feeling.' " I squirmed away from him and smoothed my hair. "But I'm sure there was someone out there, someone watching us."

He pulled me against him again. "I just meant that you had the creepy feeling we get when we know someone's watching."

"And what about that car? Don't you think that was strange?"

"Car?"

"Tom! The black sedan that drove by us. That road is clearly marked 'Dead End.' There's a sign right at the corner, and another right before that old barn. Other than kids looking for a lovers' lane, or us, there's no reason for anyone to get down that far. And that was not a kid car."

"Hmm. Oh, speaking of people being out there, I forgot to tell you. I saw a friend of yours out there the other day. Friday, I think. I was out there with Drake. Yeah, Friday."

"A friend of mine?"

"Yeah. Said you told him to go out there to shoot birds."

"What?" My mind was clearly switched to mysterious events mode, because I took Tom's words in the firearms sense.

"Had a big lens. Said his name was Anderson. Said he was sorry you weren't there and he'd call you soon." He nuzzled my neck, pulled me close to him, and lowered his voice. "Didn't catch his first name."

"That is his first name. Anderson Billings." Anderson had taken several of my photography classes and I recalled telling him about Twisted Lake as a good spot for birds.

Tom put an end to further conversation. I gave resisting a passing thought, but there's something irresistible about a man who smells of wet dog and pizza. There's also something disconcerting about having a pair of furry muzzles thrust into the action just as you get horizontal.

"What say we reconvene down the hall, *sans* dogs?" Tom asked, pushing himself off me and standing up. "You are bad dogs!" he laughed, scratching a head with each hand. Jay and Drake wagged and panted agreeably. Then he took my hand and pulled me to my feet.

A couple hours later I woke up and

glanced at the clock on my night table. Half past nine. Leo was purring on the rocking chair in the corner, but we were alone. Then I heard the kitchen door close, and heard Tom softly telling the dogs to be quiet. A baby gate clicked into place in the kitchen doorway. And he was back, his skin cool against mine. "Oooh, you're nice and warm," he crooned, wrapping me up in his arms. Leo mewed a protest and curled into a ball.

"You always go out in the backyard nekkid?"

"Wasn't. I had a towel. And I didn't go out, just let the boys out and locked up."

I was starting to doze off again when Tom spoke. "Been thinking."

"Mmmm. Not unusual in a college professor."

He squeezed me but didn't say anything. I got the feeling he had something important on his mind, but I was too warm and muzzy to do anything but wait. I droned, fighting off sleep, "Okay, professor, you've been thinking."

He rocked me back and forth a couple of times, and settled his cheek against my hair. "Uh huh." He pulled me a little closer. "Been thinking Drake and I have lived alone too long. I think it's time to expand the family."

I lay perfectly still, instantly awake. All I could think was *no no no, don't ruin a good thing.* I didn't have a lot of experience, but what I did have suggested that I wasn't very good at long-term commitments. Or more to the point, I wasn't very good at picking men who were good at long-term commitments. Besides, I'd gotten along fine without a long-term commitment ever since my marriage went belly up a quarter century ago. We lay without speaking, my thoughts bouncing around my brain like Mexican jumping beans, for what seemed like hours, although according to the clock I was staring at, not even a minute clicked by.

"You awake?"

I considered not answering, but instead asked, "Can we talk about this tomorrow?" *Or maybe never?*

Tom didn't say anything for a few seconds, then kissed my cheek, rolled out of bed, and began to dress.

I rolled over and watched him in the dim glow from the lights outdoors. "Tom?" An icy wave of nausea washed over me as I thought about past failed relationships and wondered whether I was the one who always ruined everything.

"Got to get to school early tomorrow. Papers to grade." He sat on the bed and kissed me again. His face was in shadow, so I couldn't read his expression, but I felt as if he were sitting on my chest rather than beside me. "Besides, you're sleepy and I'm wide awake, so I may as well go do something useful and let you sleep." He ran a feather-light finger down my cheek. "I'll call you tomorrow."

I heard the baby gate pop open, and Tom's soft "Drake, here." Then Jay was on the bed beside me, shoving his head into my hand and flipping himself over for a belly rub. When I heard Tom's car start, I wrapped my arms around my dog, buried my face in his ruff, and tried to go to sleep. I didn't have much luck.

Fourteen

I hadn't planned to take a day off from the veterinary photo shoot, and if I had, I wouldn't have chosen to spend it nursing a sore backside and trying not to sit too hard, but there I was. By morning the drugs had all worn off, leaving me sore and less than euphoric. My left buttock was swollen and felt like the demon Tiffany was poking it with a hot little pitchfork.

I tried to explain to Jay that I really wasn't up to our morning constitutional, but he danced around my feet and grinned at the leash hanging by the door until he convinced me to pull on a pair of loose-fitting yoga pants and a baggy Eeyore tee. I ran a comb through my hair and checked for smeared mascara under my eyes. Why spend time on my appearance when I'd be sweaty and windblown in twenty minutes? Jay's front paws tapped a routine around me that would put Gene Kelly to shame and, as I pulled the laces on my Asics tight, his muzzle darted in under my face and slurped my chin.

Mr. Hostetler was sitting on his front steps across the street. Paco, his Chihuahua, stood at the end of his leash, and Mr. Hostetler's grandson, Tyler, knelt next to Paco with a brush in his hand. Paco yipped once and his companions waved. Jay and I walked over to say hello.

"Mrs. Janet," asked Tyler, his little forehead wrinkled up, "are you okay?"

"Sure, Tyler. Why?" I had forgotten for the moment that Tyler was at the veterinary office the day before.

"The veterinarian said that little girl bit you."

Mr. Hostetler reached out to pet Jay, who was exchanging a mutual sniff with Paco, and said, "I hope it wasn't a bad bite."

I smiled at Tyler and said, "You heard right, Tyler. She bit me, but I'm okay."

He cocked his head and asked, "But why?"

I wanted to say because she's a little monster, but Tyler was asking a serious question and I wasn't at all sure I had a serious answer for him. I was afraid I would let him down when I said, "I don't really know, Tyler."

He shrugged and said, "Okay." He turned

to pet Jay, and said, "I'm combing Paco."

A few minutes of small talk later, Jay and I took our leave.

We usually walk the eastern end of the River Greenway where it skirts the slow brown Maumee from Maysville Road east toward New Haven, but once I was buckled into my van I decided to head downtown. I parked on Vermont and we walked through Lakeside Park, starting among the tea and shrub roses that mingle north of the massive white pergola. Spent and unpruned blossoms drooped among buds and flowers in calming pastels, welcoming yellows, playful oranges, passionate reds. We crossed under the stout vine-covered columns of the pergola and scurried down the western steps of twin staircases to a brick-and-concrete walk. Jay expressed mild interest in a little spaniel mix who was cooling off in one of the two round pools aligned with the long rectangular reflecting pool, and the riot of yellows, oranges, reds and whites bubbling out of concrete pots along our path made my heart smile.

The cring-cring-cring of a bicycle bell burst through the hum of traffic and twitter of birds, and a lavender bike with fluorescent pink tails streaming from its handlebars caught up and wobbled past. Brown pigtails set high on the sides of the rider's head swung and bobbed, and the bike swayed from one training wheel to the other with every pump of a pedal. The rider wore pink leggings and for a moment I feared it was Tiffany, but quickly recovered my senses. A man and woman followed on matched mountain bikes.

We dodged west between Lake Avenue and the small body of water that gives Lakeside Park its name. We waited at the curb for a pack of helmeted velo-jocks in lycra body suits to whoosh past us, spines arched, legs spinning, and then crossed the street and headed southwest on Delta past two smaller ponds. All three bodies of water were home to what looked like hundreds of Canada geese and mallards. A single swan hunkered on the shaded grass south of the middle pond. A trio of crows burst from a beech on the far edge of the pond and suddenly I was back at Twisted Lake. At least I wanted to be. I knew I probably wouldn't get there for a few days, but decided to swing by my brother Bill's place later to borrow his kayak just in case. I'd call Detective Jo in the morning and if the cops hadn't checked the island by then, I'd go take a look myself.

Jay stopped to update one of his sites, hiking his leg so high he nearly fell over, and then we turned right and jogged along the sidewalk between Edgewater Avenue and the Maumee River for half a mile to where the street fishhooks north. My *gluteus maximus* worked through the soreness, leaving me free to savor the rich scent of late summer gardens along the way. That, and the hazy light of the morning, lifted my mood ever higher. We crossed over where Columbia Avenue bridges the Maumee, formed where the St. Mary's and St. Joseph's rivers merge maybe a hundred and thirty yards north of the bridge. From there we picked up Clay, ducked under the Norfolk-Southern overpass, crossed to the north side of Main because the sidewalk is better, and headed east past the art museum. Forty minutes after we set out, we reached Freimann Park, where a handsome young couple veered toward us, hand in hand. They wore matching navy tees and neatly trimmed beards. Jason and Jason. Honest. I know them from photo shoots for the kennel club. We made the usual small talk while their Great Dane, Oscar Wilde, got reacquainted with Jay.

I decided to splurge on breakfast at Park Place, and hoped that Jasper Jesperson was working. He was assistant manager, and another regular client for annual photos of his four stunning Himalayan cats. He had no qualms about letting Jay into the sidewalk seating area or about stretching the truth a tad in my dog's defense. A few weeks earlier a customer had objected, and Jasper had told him that Jay was a service dog. When the skeptical complainer asked why an obviously healthy person would need a service dog, Jasper had stage whispered with a straight face that if I, "poor dear," started to slip into one of my "states," Jay would knock me down and sit on me until it passed. He added that "stress seems to set her off." When he heard his name, Jay had confirmed the fantasy with a woof, then curled up with his chin on my instep.

Jasper wasn't there, it turned out, but Alison, the hostess, knew the story and seated us near the railing, where Jay could lie at my feet but be technically outside the restaurant perimeter. As I eased my sore behind into a chair, Alison cooed at Jay and told him how silly the rule was considering the daily offenses of sparrows and pigeons. She had a point, I agreed, indicating a sizeable splat on the far side of the tablecloth.

"Ewww!" She wrinkled her nose and scurried off to find the bus person.

I looked around for abandoned reading

material, but the only thing in sight was a philatelic magazine, of all things, so I settled back and gazed across Main Street. The raised beds in Freimann Park were a floral riot of flaming cannas, sunny marigolds, red-orange tithonia, shocking-pink zinnias, frothy-white alyssum and petunias, true-blue salvia, and iridescent purple-leafed Persian shield. The colors of August. At this distance it seemed that some of the flowers, orange and yellow and indefinite dark, took flight from time to time. Butterflies.

Despite the occasional twinge when I forgot myself and shifted too far to the left, I began to settle into a delicious calm. Jay sprawled on his side at my feet, eyes squinty with pleasure and mouth open to accommodate his soft panting. I pushed my concerns about blood-soaked bags as far back in my thoughts as I could and chitchatted with the bus boy as he replaced my tablecloth. Then male voices made me look at three men being seated two tables away. The one with his back to me caught my eye. I thought later how ironic it was that I should recognize him from that angle, but at the time I just wondered how I might escape without coming face to face with Dr. Neil Young.

FIFTEEN

I did not escape. One of Neil's companions smiled at Jay and the other two turned to look, and the next thing I knew Dr. Neil Young was standing in front of me with a grin on his face. Not just *a* grin, but *the* grin, the one that made me and my friends in high school all giggly and stupid. It was still slightly lop-sided, which gave his face just the touch of imperfection it needed.

"Janet MacPhail." He held out his hand.

I took it. "Neil Young."

He laid his left hand over mine and I glanced down. No ring. I looked back at his face and smiled, and we stood that way for a second or two longer than seemed comfortable. I extracted my hand and said, "It's been a long time." He didn't react, so I held out some hope that he hadn't known whose posterior he was embroidering the day before.

"How have you been, Janet?"

Acutely conscious of looking frumpy, especially as I took in the sheen of his gray suit jacket and the ice-blue tie that exactly matched his eyes. He wore a lapel pin that seemed to be a cross of some sort, but it was too small to see from where I stood and I wasn't about to lean in closer.

Right on cue, but with no trace of sarcasm that I could detect, Neil said, "You look terrific." He glanced at Jay, who had stopped panting and seemed to be sizing up the good doctor. "Nice looking dog."

"Thanks." I noted that he made no move to pet him.

He looked at me again. "Really, you do. It's great to see you." He glanced at his friends, then fished a card from his pocket and laid it in front of me. "Look, I'm sorry, but I really need to get back to them. Business. But, well, I'd love to see you when I have more time."

I'm embarrassed to say it, but the teeny bopper inside me felt a little giddy at the thought of Neil the Hunk wanting to talk to me. Grown-up Janet whispered *Really? You're giving me your number, not asking for mine?* I also felt a tad guilty. Then again, Tom Saunders didn't have dibs on my time, or me for that matter. My brain was trying to parse the questions dancing through it when I realized Neil was still there, still talking to me, and was pointing a pen at me. "If you write your number down, I'll call you. I mean, if that's okay?"

"Oh." I took the pen. "Sure, why not?"

He slipped the card into his shirt pocket and nodded at me. "Soon."

I paid my bill, picked up Jay's leash, and skedaddled as quickly as possible. As Jay and I retraced our route to the car, I wondered how it's possible not to lay eyes on someone for thirty-some years and then run into him twice in two days. I also wondered aloud, "What the hell am I doing?" Jay bounced up to my chin level a couple of times and wriggled his rear end, which I assume meant, "Having fun, Janet! We're having fun!"

Right. "Okay, calm down. He probably won't call anyway. He never did in high school."

Half an hour later we pulled into my driveway. There was something swinging from the front doorknob, so I put the car in the garage, refreshed Jay's water, and opened the front door to a big summery bouquet. I snatched the delivery tag from the door, carried it and the flowers inside, and cleared a space on the kitchen table. The greeting card that was taped to the vase showed a Golden Retriever wearing glasses and a stethoscope, and inside it said, "Heel!" The vets and staff at the clinic had all signed it, and someone had written in a tidy hand, "All kidding aside, heal quickly — no ifs, ands, or butts." *Ho, boy.*

I took a quick shower. As I dried my hair and mentally checked my schedule for a time to take care of my roots, another part of my mind went to a vision of Neil's hair. Still that lovely dark blonde. No gray. Interesting. Come to think of it, his skin was still tight and smooth. Dye job? Facelift? Or maybe just young genes. Which made me giggle, because of course he had Young genes.

As if to reinforce the giggle in my head, a muted tinny rendition of "Walking on Sunshine" wafted around the bathroom, and I fished my cell out of my pants pocket, which happened to be in the hamper.

It was Neil. He told me he'd been thrilled and delighted to see me. *Thrilled and delighted?* He also wanted to know if he could buy me dinner.

"Maybe another time? I need to go see my mom."

"Does she still live in your old house? I could pick you up there."

I hesitated, then told him she was at

Shadetree Retirement Home. I wasn't sure why, but I didn't want to tell him that Mom had Alzheimer's. "But I have some work to do first. I probably won't get to the nursing home until late afternoon."

"How about after that? Around seven?"

I hesitated. *What's the rush? Making up for lost time?*

"Seven-thirty? I'll pick you up."

"Seven is fine. I'll meet you."

I finished dressing and went to the kitchen, where I grabbed an apple from the bowl on the table and began to sort my mail. Doing anything on a horizontal surface seems to send an irresistible summons to Leo, and the next thing I knew he was mincing around on my electric bill, purring and rubbing his spine along my jaw line. Then he sat down, wrapped his tail around his feet, and stared at me. Jay assumed the same posture, without the tail, and gazed at my face. It was ridiculous, but I felt as if I had to explain myself.

"I can have dinner with an old friend."

Leo blinked. Jay put a paw on my knee.

"Okay, an old acquaintance, sort of. Really more of a classmate. But still."

I lifted the cat onto the floor and told Jay to go chew a bone so that I could sort, open, pitch, and stack the mail without feeling they were accusing me of something. I was just muttering something about being a free and independent woman when the phone sang out again.

This time it was Tom. He said he was going back out to the lake to train for a bit and he thought Jay and I might like to go. I was tempted to call Neil and cancel so I could check out the island, but I had to go see Mom and wouldn't have time to get my brother Bill's kayak in time to have much light left. When I declined the invitation, Tom said, "Okay, I'll grab something when I'm finished and see you then." I should have savored the moment since I couldn't recall the last time two men had asked me out for dinner in the same year, let alone the same evening, but instead I was annoyed that he assumed I'd be available.

"Can't. I have dinner plans."

"Oh. Okay. Dessert?"

"I have some work I really should do when I get back." I felt the sharpness of my tone as much as heard it, but I let the comment lie.

Tom said nothing for a moment, then, "Everything okay?"

A tap at my back door made me turn just as Goldie came in with a huge bunch of fuchsia and yellow gladioli cradled across her chest. Jay greeted her with a wriggly butt and rubbed his body along her leg and she reached down and stroked his cheek.

"Everything's fine," I said. My voice, and my pique, had softened. "I just have some things to do. Gotta see Mom this afternoon after I get some photos ready to send out. And Goldie just walked in, so I'd better go. Have fun."

"Will do. You be good."

I flipped my phone shut and set it down a bit harder than is probably good for it. "Why did he say that?"

Goldie had pulled a pitcher from my cupboard and set it on the table. "Hunh," she said, reaching for the card on the bouquet from the vet clinic. "Nice." Leo hopped up for his share of the attention, so Goldie had to stroke him and then lift him off the table before she could arrange the glads. "I didn't get you a card. Say what?"

"What say what?"

"What does who always say?"

" 'Be good.' "

She looked over her glasses at me. "Let me guess. The doctor called. The anthropology doctor."

"He shouldn't assume that I'm always available."

Goldie stuck the last stem into the pitcher,

filled it with water, and smiled at the flowers. "There you are, children. You look beeyooteeful." She took her glasses off and set them on the table. "Why shouldn't he assume you'll be available? You've been available since you met him. You've been available for years."

"Goldie! You know what I mean."

"I do. But life's too short for that silliness. Games. Just say what you mean and do what your heart tells you and the heck with the rules and shenanigans. And don't pout."

"Not pouting," I said, uncrossing my arms.

Sixteen

The chaos of the morning gave way to a quiet afternoon, and I spent a couple of productive hours on the computer deleting bad photos and organizing good ones. When I had them filed away in folders, I pulled out about twenty shots to send as a sample packet to the editor at *Splash,* a new magazine about water dogs of all sorts. Then I started looking through the photos I had taken at Twisted Lake. Dogs, dogs, dogs. I deleted some and saved the rest into my "To Review" folder. Then I started on the non-dog shots.

I hadn't realized that I'd taken so many photos of the island. Must have been on autopilot. The light had been bad and most of them weren't usable, but I wondered if I might see something new if I manipulated them a bit. I fiddled around with contrast and other elements, fading out shadows and looking for shapes that didn't belong, but I didn't find anything. *What did you expect,* I asked myself at one point, *Colonel Mustard in the bittersweet with poison ivy?*

By mid-afternoon I was not only giddy but my attention had begun to waver and my butt had begun to ache, so I took Jay and Leo out back for a game of tennis ball fetch or, as I imagine Leo thinks of it, "whack the dog's fanny as he races by after the stupid ball and then hide in the bushes." There's probably a word for that in Feline. By whatever name, we all had fun, but after twenty minutes or so I admitted to myself that I could put off my filial obligation no longer.

Don't get me wrong. I'd like to spend time with my mom. In fact, that's the problem. When I saw her two days earlier, she had no idea who I was and was too busy thumbing through her newly arrived *Fine Gardening* to bother talking to me. The time before that she knew me too well and tried everything from tears to threats to get me to take her home, meaning not my house but her own home of sixty years. It hurts like hell when she doesn't know or care who I am, but when she does, she's unhappy enough to give me palpitations. As I pulled on a clean top and thought about my mother's distress, my whole body wanted to topple onto the bed and curl into a fetal lump. As an alternative, I took a bit more care than usual with my makeup and stuck a couple of combs in my hair to subdue its curly rebelliousness.

Mom was in the garden when I got to Shadetree. The semi-resident therapy Poodle, Percy, was lying beside her chair, but he ran to meet me as I walked toward the courtyard. When Percy's previous owner was killed last spring, Jade Templeton, Shadetree's assistant manager, adopted him. Now he came to work with her every day and, judging by the sparkle in his dark eyes, I knew he'd found his calling. The residents loved him.

Jade waved at me from her office, so I veered away from the door to the garden, landed in a chair, sucked up a complaint from my wounded cheek, and pushed the large envelope I was carrying across the desk. "Here you go! And may I say that you look gorgeous. Love your hair. It's really grown out." I was trying desperately to remember when I last saw her. She had been on vacation, but that was only for a couple of weeks, wasn't it? Jade had worn her hair cropped close to her skull in a not-too-flattering style for as long as I'd known her, and now it was done in teensy little braids with teensy little beads at the ends. "Must grow fast! Or have I just not seen you in that long?"

When Jade Templeton laughs, her whole large self laughs, and I defy you to keep a straight face when that happens. "Right, it grows real fast."

I had no idea why that tickled her so, but I was happy to play. "You must have been in the stylist's chair for hours to get those braids done."

That hilarious repartee nearly knocked her on the floor, and I just about lost my own seat when she reached up and pulled her hair off to reveal the familiar close-cropped curls. Her burnt-umber eyes sparkled with mischief. She twirled the wig on her fist, making the beads clack, and said, "Dontcha love it?"

"Oh my God, Jade! I think you've been here too long. You've flipped your lid."

"Girl, that's so bad!" She slapped the top of her desk, then got up and went to a tiny decorative mirror on the wall and pulled the wig back on. "So really, what do you think? Is it me?"

"Completely you. Makes me rethink this mess." I grabbed a handful of my unruly brown mop that always goes berserk in the humidity of August in Indiana. "Anyway," I sucked in a deep post-hilarity breath, "some of the photos are really nice. I think they'll like them."

Jade sat back down and opened the envelope. A couple of weeks earlier I had spent a full afternoon taking photos of Shadetree residents and staff, both posed portraits and candids, and the envelope held prints of the best shots, all five by sevens.

"I have all the digital files, of course, so if anyone wants reprints or a different size, let me know. I'll need the number on the back of the photo."

"Oh, baby, these are *good.*" She drew out the last word. "Aww, look at Myrtle. And Jim Beard." The staff had given the three resident Jims fictitious last names to keep them straight — Jim Beard looked a bit like Santa and would never be confused with Jim Curly or Jim Tall.

Jade called her assistant to help sort the photos for distribution, so I excused myself and walked down the hall to the garden. I was almost there when my phone vibrated in my pocket, telling me I had a message. I pulled it out and signed into voice mail, half hoping it was Neil calling to cancel.

"Janet, it's Anderson. Anderson Billings. Hey, I'm out at Twisted Lake." I wondered for a moment whether this was an old message that had been delayed for some reason since Tom had seen Anderson at the lake the previous Friday. "Great place, as you said. In fact, I was here a few days ago, too." That answered that question. "Saw a friend of yours. So, anyway, I heard a screech owl and came back with my canoe to get to the island, you know, the little island off shore? Pretty sure that's where the bird is. That was Friday night. Well, you know, evening."

I was starting to wonder whether Anderson had a point beyond bird-nerd excitement. Maybe he got a great shot of the screech owl? Maybe he just wanted to thank me for telling him about the place? Then he said, "Janet, something funny is going on out here. On the little island, I mean. I went over there, spent maybe twenty minutes and I saw, well, something happened. So I came back now, well, you know, a little while ago, to have another look around the island. I'm leaving here now, heading over to my mother's house, but I could swing by your place or, you know, somewhere we could meet in, say, half an hour? I'll try you again when I get to Coliseum." Meaning Coliseum Boulevard, one of Fort Wayne's main drags. "I probably should have said something . . . Janet, there's a bird . . . ," and then there was nothing but empty echo, as if whatever was at the end of the connection had been hollowed out, and finally a voice telling me how to save, hear again, or delete the message. I sat down on a bench in the hall and dialed Anderson's number, but it went straight to voice mail. Odd. Maybe his battery ran out, or he hit a dead zone around the lake. It's rolling country, and I've had calls dropped out there. I left a message and turned my phone off.

I found my mother in the garden, as usual. "Hi Mom." I hoped she couldn't hear the quiver in my voice if she was having a good day. If she wasn't, it wouldn't matter. My whole body relaxed when she turned toward me and smiled.

"Janet! How are you, dear?" She gave me the first hug I'd had from her in weeks. "I'm so glad you're here." She pulled off her work gloves and motioned me toward a cluster of chairs.

"You look great, Mom." In fact, she looked happy, and I dared to hope that she wouldn't ask me to take her home.

"Must run in the family." She winked at me. "You look lovely, dear. That rosy top becomes you."

A similarly rosy sense of well-being enveloped me as I looked into my mother's eyes and, for the first time in too long, saw the woman I loved looking back at me. She reached across the table and took my hand.

"We need to talk about a few things." *Uh oh. Here it comes.* I looked at her bony hand folded over mine. *She wants to go home.* "I know what's going on."

My heart gave a little jump. Mom was prone to mildly paranoid notions these days. "You do?"

She laughed and squeezed my hand. "I do. Janet, I know I'm losing my marbles. That's why I want to talk to you now. I'm having a good day, at least so far. So I want you to know a few things." One more hand squeeze and then she let go and pulled a folded set of papers out of her smock's huge pocket. She flattened the creased papers against the top of the table, put her reading glasses on, studied the top sheet briefly, and pushed it toward me.

"Read that."

It was a series of directives of various kinds. What to do about the house. What to do with her property. With her money.

With her.

"As you see, I've signed it, had it witnessed and notarized. My doctor witnessed it."

"Mom . . ."

"No, listen. We have to do this. When your dad died, he left a lot of loose ends, and I won't do that to you and Bill."

"Has Bill seen this?" My brother, Bill, was having even more difficulty dealing with Mom's decline than I was.

"No, not yet." She set her glasses on the table. "Bill isn't as tough as you. Never was."

"I'm not that tough, Mom."

"Yes, you are. And that," she waved toward the tear that was wriggling its way down my cheek, "doesn't mean you aren't. I know, because you're a lot like me." She smiled again. "That's why we fought so much when you were younger."

Sudden anger flared in my brain, snuffed immediately by guilt and a sense of futility. Was my mother opening a conversation about reconciling our long-standing conflicts? Why now, when I couldn't be sure she'd still be with me mentally in ten minutes? Why not ten years ago when we could have enjoyed one another?

"Janet, I've signed a quit claim. It's in there." She waved at the papers in my hands. "The house is yours. Jack Schweyer knows about it." Jack had been my parents' attorney since I was in diapers, which put him at least in his seventies. According to his daughter Alex, who trained her Samoyed at Dog Dayz with me and Jay, he still worked a thirty-hour week. "Everything is yours. House. Furniture." She paused and we sat quietly for a few moments.

"Mom, I don't need the house. Bill should have it."

"The car."

Mom's car was long gone. Bill had seen to that when it became clear that she shouldn't be driving. I looked across the table. My mother was still looking at me, but she had worry lines between her eyebrows and her mouth hung slightly open.

"Mom, you should leave the house to Bill. He loves that house."

She cocked her head. "Who?"

Oh crap.

"Where *is* the car? I need to go shopping."

"You sold the car, Mom, remember? A few months ago."

Something in the musculature of her cheeks shifted and my heart fell into my belly. "No, dear, your dad drove it to work today."

I stayed another twenty minutes, but my mother had already left the building. We walked around the garden and she still addressed every plant by its Latin binomial, but had not a single lingering inkling of who I was. When I got to my car I grabbed my tote bag from the trunk and fished around among dried liver treats, a collar, and a lot of stuff I couldn't identify by touch. I wanted to cancel my dinner with Neil and go curl up with a gallon of Edy's chocolate mint instead, but when I emptied the contents onto the seat, my phone wasn't there. Then I remembered. Pocket. But when I flipped the phone open, it was dead, and I bounced the back of my skull off the head rest a couple of times, berating myself for not charging the stupid thing. Again. I added *charge phone* and *clean out tote bag* to my mental to-do list and floored it out of the parking lot. As I whipped in behind an SUV on South Anthony, I realized that what I really wanted to curl up with was not a frozen milk product at all, but a very warm guy with a fondness for dogs and, I knew with terrifying certainty, for me.

SEVENTEEN

Neil hadn't arrived at *Chez Ma Père* but on a hunch I told the *maître d'* that I was with Dr. Young and I was immediately and unctuously escorted to a table in a quiet corner. I tried not to let on as he pushed my chair in that the hem of my skirt was in the grip of the velvet seat cushion, but as soon as he was gone I squirmed the fabric back down my thighs. The little devil in my mind smirked, *that'll teach you to dress like a girl.*

I considered trying to call Anderson from the restaurant's land line, but his number was locked up in my dead cell phone and I hadn't brought my big bag with my class roster and other sporadically useful things.

I ordered the house white and checked out my fellow diners. All were my age — fifties — or older, well dressed and well coiffed. A local newscaster was holding forth about something on the far side of the room. His face was cloaked in the gloom of what I supposed was ambiance, but there was no mistaking his voice. Since no other voice could compete and the lighting was so bad, I didn't recognize anyone else and decided to preview the menu. I was trying to find my breath, which I'd lost at sight of the prices on the page before me, when a new voice tickled my ears.

"Good evening."

Neil stood beside my chair and laid a hand on my shoulder, the tips of his fingers warm against the bare skin over my clavicle. They stayed just a tad longer than seemed right. I wasn't sure why that bothered me so much and chalked it up to my own nervousness as I watched Neil shed his jacket and drape it over the back of his chair.

"Hi, Neil."

The oily *maître d'* appeared with wine for *monsieur.* Neil greeted him but kept his focus on me, and I saw a twitch at the corner of his mouth when the man spoke. "Eet ees so lovely to see you once more, *monsieur.* Eet has been too long."

It was all I could do to keep my eyes from rolling, and as soon as we were alone Neil leaned forward and said, "So, what part of France do you think François is from?"

"I'm thinking New Haven." Meaning the

small town outside Fort Wayne, not the haven of higher education in Connecticut.

Neil raised his glass, smiled, and said, "Here's to old friends."

"Speak for yourself," I said, laughing a little too loudly. "I'm not that old." At least I assumed I didn't look all that ancient in the dimly lit restaurant.

"Touché." He smiled, but the hardness I had noticed before never quite left his eyes. I searched old memories and was surprised to realize that I just couldn't remember that much about Neil except his high-school heart-throb status. Not that I was in his crowd. I'm sure he thought the smile that curled my lips was a response to his charms, but really I was tickled to realize that the thrill seemed to be well and truly gone. I glanced at my watch.

"I hope you're not in a rush, Janet." He released the stem of his glass, leaned forward, reached across the table, and took my hand away from my menu. I looked up and found him gazing intently at me. "This is a night to savor."

Night? It's not even seven-thirty! I retrieved my hand and took a sip of wine. "Yes, it's a lovely evening. So nice to see you again after all these years. So, Neil, what have you been up to besides doctoring?"

Smarmy François was back. "May I breeng you some *hors d'oeuvres*?"

Without consulting me Neil ordered escargot for two. I started to tell him that I don't like escargot, but his high-handedness ticked me off so I decided instead that I would be paying for my own dinner *sans escargot, merci.* I had intended to anyway, but hadn't been so determined until that moment. A quick scan of the menu told me I'd be having a cup of soup and the free bread, and as we indulged in a bit of small talk, I had a sudden longing for pizza in the backyard with a certain guy in sweatshirt.

François was back with the mollusks. "Would you like to order, *monsieur*?"

"Not now. We're in no rush." Neil leaned back, wine glass in hand.

"Yes, I would like to order." I spoke to the waiter, not Neil. "And these are separate, please. I'd li—"

"No, Janet," Neil interrupted me. "This is my treat. For old time's sake."

"I'll have a bowl of French onion, please. That's all. I'm not very hungry." I was starving, but I could pick up a bag of tortilla chips on the way home. "And the checks *are* separate, please."

I thought I saw a little twinkle in François's eyes, but he kept control. "And for *monsieur*?"

Silence. I knew Neil was staring at me but I worked at closing my menu and smoothing my napkin. He finally ordered, then turned back to me.

"Janet . . ." There was an edge very like anger in his voice, but I had a little snit of my own going so I ignored it.

"Neil, we don't have 'old times.' We barely knew each other in high school, and we know each other even less now. Maybe this wasn't such a great idea."

"Wow. I see you haven't changed much."

"What?"

"You always had a mouth on you." He laughed. "And I always liked that about you. I was too dumb as a kid to let you know, but I did."

"You weren't dumb. You were just wrapped up with being cool."

"Right. Dumb. Have some escargot."

"All yours. I don't like snails."

He raised his left eyebrow. "Why didn't you say so?"

"Why didn't you ask?"

He shrugged, popped one into his mouth, and rolled his eyes. "Mmmm."

François appeared. "To your sateesfaction, *monsieur*?" Without waiting for an answer, he turned to me, "Would you like your soup with *monsieur's entrée*?"

Suddenly his act was unbearable. Maybe it was the wine. I grinned at him and said, "No, I'd like it all by itself. But you may serve them at the same time, please." The smile and bow I got in reply made me sure the man took his cue from David Suchet as Poirot on *Masterpiece Mystery,* so I took a chance and stage whispered, "He's not French, you know. He's a Brit playing a Belgian." I'm pretty sure François winked at me as he turned away.

Neil didn't seem to notice. "Nice dog you had there at the restaurant."

"Thanks. He is a lovely dog."

"Lot of hair."

"Yep."

"I have a bird," he said.

"Really? What kind?" I've photographed pet birds occasionally and find them fascinating.

"Parrot." I started to ask what kind of parrot, but he changed course. "My wife, well, ex-wife, had a dog in the house, but I insisted on no hair."

"So she had, what, laser treatments?"

He looked blank.

"I thought you insisted your wife have no hair."

That seemed to break some of the tension

and we spent the next half hour catching up and eating. Neil showed me photos of his son and daughter, both in graduate school.

"Do you have children, Janet?"

The inevitable question. I understand it, but don't like to answer, because so many people make assumptions about other people based on their parental status. Or they follow up with more questions. Or both.

"No, no kids."

Neil surprised me. Maybe life as a doctor had made him a bit more aware than the average bear about the multitude of possible reasons, but he asked, softly, "By choice?"

"Two miscarriages."

"I'm sorry." He paused, then said, "But you have pets. Show me your pets."

Forgetting that it was dead, I pulled out my cell phone to reciprocate, then said, "Another time."

"Do you have a website?" asked Neil. When I said I did, he typed the url into his smart phone and let me pull up an album of recent shots I had taken at various dog-training sessions. He stopped me at one of a Golden Retriever leaping into the water at Heron Acres. The island where Drake found the canvas bag was clearly in view.

"I know this place."

"You do?"

"Behind Treasures on Earth Spiritual Renewal Center, right? Off Cedar Canyons Road?"

"Right. You've been there?"

"Uh huh. Treasures, I mean."

"But this isn't part of their spread."

"No, I know." He dabbed at his mouth with his napkin. "I walked over during a reception. Too lovely an evening to spend all of it hobnobbing."

That made no sense. The spot where I stood to take the photo was across the water from Treasures on Earth, and from the other side the island wouldn't look the same. "But . . ." I stopped myself.

"But what?"

"Nothing. Never mind." Something clicked in my memory. Neil's lapel pin. That's why it had looked familiar. I picked up my wine glass to give myself a moment to think. The cross with half hearts hanging from it was the same logo that Mrs. Willard had been wearing, but a smaller version. So Neil was involved with that group, too? I was trying to get a grasp on the coincidences that were piling onto one another when he broke in.

"So who bit you?"

It took all my self-control not to spew my wine.

"Oh, shit." My cheeks felt like someone had slapped them with heating pads.

"Aww, she's blushing." And he was grinning and chuckling.

"A kid."

"Clearly. Too small to be your lover."

"I don't think I can tell you who it was. But I think she goes to your church. Or her parents do, anyway."

"Church? Oh, you mean Treasures? Really?"

"Her mom wears that same logo you wear, the cross and broken heart."

"Not broken. It symbolizes . . ."

"I was hoping you didn't know who you were working on."

"I have a memory for tushies."

"Great."

"Besides, your name was on the chart. I just didn't want to embarrass you."

"Until now, you mean."

He laughed. "You can trust me, I'm a doctor. So I'm guessing it was the little Willard darling."

"I neither confirm nor deny. I think she's possessed."

"Why don't you come to a meeting with me sometime?"

"Meeting?"

"Yes. You know, at Treasures."

"I don't think so." I had to admit, strictly to myself, that I was curious, but the last thing I wanted was to be on the receiving end of some sort of cult recruiting session.

"Well, if you change your mind."

We quietly sipped our wine for a moment. The curious little Janet demon in my head wrestled with mannerly good Janet, and of course curiosity won out. "Not saying I will come to any meetings, but I admit that I'm curious. What is that place? Church? Yoga center?"

Neil set his glass down, and although he smiled, his face took on an expression that I could only think of as zealous. "A little of each, I supposed. The Regis teaches . . ."

" 'The Regis'? You mean that's not his name?"

"No, it's an honorific." Neil seemed to realize something for the first time. "I don't know that I have ever heard his first name." I found that pretty odd, but Neil shrugged it off and continued. "We honor the prophets of all faiths and each week our meeting emphasizes a teaching from one of them. We believe that our treasures are here on earth."

I hadn't been to Sunday school in several

decades, but I did remember a few things. “But the major faiths don’t teach that.”

“Yes they do. The Regis has explained that they all teach kindness, generosity, honesty. If we follow those treasure paths, we are led to wealth here and in the afterlife.”

Rather than debate the validity of Regis Moneypenny’s reinterpretation of world religious teachings, I asked about Neil’s parrot, but he didn’t seem to know, or care, much about the bird. “Its not exactly mine. Not for good. I’m just taking care of it for a while. Caring for Earth’s Creatures is part of the treasure path.”

I liked the idea, but the intensity of Neil’s delivery was starting to creep me out, so I steered the conversation back to high school memories. We spent a few more pleasant minutes on small talk, and then I insisted that I really needed to get going. “Early morning tomorrow,” I told him, and didn’t bother to add that it would be one of my rare early morning sleep-ins.

“Right. You photography types like to catch the early light, right?”

I left it at that.

EIGHTEEN

Sleeping in is apparently something I am no longer entitled to do, partly because my friends all "know" that I'm up early and it's okay to call or show up at ungodly early hours. *Why did I recharge that stupid thing?* I asked myself as I stumbled from the bed to the bureau and grabbed my phone.

"Janet. I'm calling from Twisted Lake."

"Uh, okay." I detached the charger cord so I could walk around.

Detective Jo Stevens then startled the bleariness out of my head. "We have a body out here." She paused. "You're awake, aren't you?"

"I am now." *Wide awake.* "Who?" *And why,* I wondered, *are you calling me?* It took a millisecond for the implications of that question to sink in and I felt my knees go weak. Tom took Drake out there to train sometimes in the early mornings. Could he be there yet? I glanced at my wrist but didn't have my watch. *How early is it?* I pulled the curtain open and saw that the sun was fully up. Tom sometimes was there by sunrise. "Jo, it's not . . ." I couldn't finish.

"Look, I'm calling to let you know just so you don't hear it on the news."

My face went cold and my head spun. I leaned against the wall and slid my back down until I was on the floor. Jay hopped off the bed and pushed against me and I whispered "Settle." He lay down and rested his chin on my knee, a worried wrinkle between his eyes.

Jo had paused again, and I held my breath. "Janet, you there?"

My voice didn't want to work, but after a failed try I managed to croak, "Who?"

"Don't know yet. Young guy."

I closed my eyes and let the back of my head clunk against the wall behind me. A voice came from a distance and I realized that I had dropped the hand holding the phone to my lap. I brought it back to my ear.

"Janet? Janet? What's going on? Are you there?"

"You just scared the crap out of me, Jo."

"What?"

"I thought it was Tom."

"Oh, jeez, Janet, I'm sorry. No, no. Jeez, I never thought you'd think that. You okay?"

"I am now." And then suddenly I wasn't. Anderson Billings had called from the lake the previous evening.

"No, I just, well, you were so sure something weird was going on out here and I didn't take you all that seriously, really, well, you know, I was annoyed about having my first date in a thousand years interrupted the other night and . . . jeez, sorry."

"Jo, does he have I.D.?"

"I can't tell you his name until we notify next of kin. Why?"

"Anderson Billings?" Somewhere deep inside knew I wasn't asking.

"You know him?"

I tried to answer but couldn't get anything out. The phrase *it's happening again* chased its own tail through my brain.

"Janet?"

I cleared my throat, then managed, "How?"

"Can't release anything yet, Janet." She paused, then said, "I should have guessed you'd know him. He had quite a camera."

"You found his camera?"

"In his car. One of those ginormous lenses like you have."

Something didn't make sense, but my

mind was too numb to sort through my own confusion and shock. I told her how I knew him, and that he had called the night before. I also told her how his last message had been cut off.

After I closed my phone, I sat frozen for a day or two, or maybe just a couple of minutes. Jay managed to crawl up so that half his body was on my lap, and Leo strolled in and sat staring at me. I opened my phone again and checked the time. Seven fifteen. I pushed number two and the send button, heard two rings and then, "Good morning, Starshine."

"Hi."

"What's up?"

"I . . . Nothing, really. I just wanted to say good morning."

Tom chuckled. "Great morning now. How about breakfast? I'll spring for it."

In spite of myself, I smiled. "You keep feeding me, I'm going to blimp out worse than I already have."

"More to love. And you're not blimped out."

The axis of my priorities had tilted with Jo's call, so despite the pile of work I had waiting for me, I said I'd meet him in half an hour. I fed the fur boys, let Jay out while I dressed, quickly policed the yard and the litterbox, smooched Leo, let Jay back in, and took off.

I managed to keep myself together long enough to order coffee, but when Tom had ordered and the waitress had gone, I fell apart. I finally managed to pull myself mostly together and get the basic story out.

Tom looked stricken. "I had planned. . . . Maybe if . . ." He paused, then went on. "What happened?"

"I guess they can't release that either." I blew my nose, then said, "I thought you were planning to go out last evening to train?"

"Oh, Tommy called and we talked awhile, and then I decided to stay home and read." Tommy, his son, didn't call often. "Jeez, if I'd gone last night, maybe he'd still be alive."

I stared at him but didn't say what I was thinking. *Or maybe Jo would have found your body, too.* As usual, the man read my mind.

"Oh, come on, Janet. It must have been an accident."

The inconsistencies of Anderson's story were starting to line up in my mind. That twinge in my gut told me that whatever had happened to Anderson Billings, it was no accident. Still, I was much calmer by the time I left Tom and headed for the vet clinic to continue the photo essay on "a day in the veterinary life" of Dr. Kerry Joiner. I thought about canceling, but decided that staying home wouldn't help Anderson, and work was probably my best hope for maintaining balance.

The rest of the morning was uneventful and busy enough to keep my mind off Anderson's death. By eleven o'clock Dr. Kerry had given three sets of puppy vaccinations, coached the owner of a fat elderly Basset Hound on canine weight loss, trimmed sixty-four canine nails plus four dew claws, and treated a very unhappy cat with an abscessed tooth. Ava, the most unusual patient of the day, was ushered into the exam room at 11:05.

"What do we have here?" The thrill in Dr. Kerry's voice reflected my own feelings as I looked at the stunning creature on the exam table. She stood about a foot high and cocked her head, obviously sizing up the two of us, then shook out her wings and refolded them.

"Wow. She's gorgeous."

"She is, isn't she?" The woman who had brought the bird in wore a white silk tank top, pale green silk slacks, and expensive-looking white sandals. She was tall and well-muscled, her hair short and chic, and her makeup flawless. “I’ve only had her about a week, but I just love her.” It struck me that her tone didn’t carry the same enthusiasm as her words.

“I can see why,” I said. “Beautiful.” The upper part of Ava’s head was bright crimson, her breast, body, and wings a yellowish green with dark blue peeking out from her folded wings. She made a full turn on the table, fanning her tail feathers as she went, then let out a scream that reminded me why I didn’t want a parrot. “What kind is she?”

Ava’s owner just stared at me, and Dr. Kerry said, “Oh, sorry, I should have introduced you.” Which she did.

“Persephone Swann. Are you related to Giselle Swann?” I asked.

Persephone sniffed. “Cousins. Haven’t seen her in years.”

“Ah. I know Giselle from dog training.”

“She’s an Amazon parrot,” said Persephone.

“Giselle?”

Even though I was smiling, Persephone gave me a look that said I wasn’t as funny as I thought I was. Still, I was curious about Ava. I know just enough about birds to be dangerous, but “Amazon parrot” didn’t narrow the possibilities much. “Right. I just wondered what kind, you know, what species."

The bird bobbed her head at me. Her owner pursed her lips and said, "Just an Amazon parrot." Which struck me as about as precise as, say, "just a Midwestern dog." I remembered reading an article in *Smithsonian Magazine* or somewhere that said there were between twenty-five and thirty known species of parrot in the Amazon, some of them severely endangered by habitat loss and poaching for the pet trade.

Dr. Kerry and I exchanged a look, and then she said, "Let's take a look at this girl."

Ava waddled to the edge of the exam table and looked at the floor, then turned back to the middle of the table and spread her wings. I raised my camera and got several clicks off before Persephone grabbed at my lens and said, "Don't do that."

"Sorry." I pulled my camera out of her reach and capped the lens, making a mental note to check it for fingerprints. I looked to Kerry for help, and she explained about the photo essay, but Persephone was adamant that I not photograph her bird. She also wanted me to delete the photos I'd taken. "I never use photos of people's pets without written permission, so no worries."

"Be that as it may, please delete the

photos you took."

Rather than stand and argue, I deleted most of them while she watched, then excused myself from the exam room and got a bottle of water from the fridge in the back of the clinic. Twenty minutes later Dr. Kerry joined me, shaking her head.

"What the heck was that all about?" I asked her.

"No clue. My fault. I should have cleared it before you met her, but it never occurred to me she'd object so violently. Or at all, really."

Persephone was the first client to object. Most people like to see their pets in published articles and books, or on websites.

"No problem. It would be cool to have a bird in the mix, but no biggie."

"Two more days," said Kerry, twisting the top off a bottle of pop. "Never know what will walk in."

"Didn't it seem odd, though, that she doesn't know what kind of bird she has?"

"Said she's only had him a week."

"Him?"

Kerry laughed. "Yeah. She's not too steady on several details about her new pet. Ava is definitely a boy. I did suggest she consider changing his name."

We chitchatted for a few minutes, then I

gathered up my camera and notebook and headed home where something was, once again, waiting for me on the porch. A bouquet. Another one. I went in through the garage, let Jay out back, and brought my flowers in through the front door. They were stunning — big white daisies, peach-hued roses, blue delphiniums, some kind of pom-pom looking things. I shoved some papers and books out of the way on the dining room table and set the vase down, then pulled the card out of the plastic holder and read, "Thank you so much for the beautiful photos of our Shadetree family. Jade, Percy, and the Rest."

Three bouquets in three days. I couldn't remember when I'd gotten three bouquets in three years. I freshened the water in the other two, brought Jay in, took off my shoes, and linked my camera to my laptop. Only as I waited for all my programs to open did I realize that no one at the clinic had made any rude references to my bitten behind. Maybe I'd escape the ridicule after all. I downloaded the two photos I'd kept of Ava and started a Google image search. Persephone Swann might not know what kind of Amazon parrot she had, but I was determined that I would.

Nineteen

Wednesday evening is one of the obedience practice nights at Dog Dayz, where Tom and I train Drake and Jay. I may forget to comb my hair before I go out sometimes, but I like my dog to look his best when he's out in public, so in the late afternoon I put my laptop to sleep, set up my grooming table in the garage so Jay could watch out the door while I groomed him, and got my box of tools. Jay hopped onto the table and stood patiently while I ground the tips off his nails with a rotary grinder, trimmed the straggly hairs on his tail, ears, and feathers, and brushed him out. When I let him off the table, he shook himself and spun around several times.

"Yep, Bubby, I know you look good." He wriggled his butt like a belly dancer and gave me his goofiest grin.

I still had about half an hour before I needed to leave so I tried to call Bill but got his partner, Norm, instead.

"Hey little sister! Bill's at the gym. Has to keep his girlish figure, you know. I'm here baking peanut butter chocolate brownies to sabotage him. Want to come lick the bowl?"

Norm's peanut butter chocolate brownies are the best worst things in the world. "I'm not coming anywhere near your place until those are all gone."

"I'm crushed." He made little sobbing sounds.

"Hey, I have to get going, but tell Bill I called, okay? I need to talk to him soon. Important."

"Mom?"

Norm had gone through the failing parent thing a couple of years earlier with his dad, and he'd been an emotional rock and a fountain of sensible suggestions and solid information as Bill and I negotiated these waters. "Mom."

"Right. You be home?"

"After about ten."

"Setting the alarm clock now."

"Thanks, Norm."

Twenty minutes later I pulled into the parking lot behind Dog Dayz, grabbed my training bag, and got Jay out of his crate. I spotted Tom's car at the far end of the lot and felt a happy little tingle dance its way through my body. As I walked up to the back bumper of Giselle Swann's beat-up green Yugo, I stopped and stared. Last time I saw that bumper, it was covered with stickers extolling the wonders of Wicca and the superiority of the Maltese, Giselle's dog of choice. *I ♡ my Maltese* and *It's hard to be humble when you have a Maltese* were still there, but all references to witches were gone, a new affiliation in their place. *What the hell?* I asked myself as I read "Treasures on Earth Spiritual Renewal Center" and took in the cross with half hearts dangling from its arms.

Jay apparently decided that we had delayed our entrance long enough and pulled me toward the back door of Dog Dayz. I don't let my dog drag me around, so I had him heel and walk into the building like a gentleman, albeit a wriggly bouncy gentleman. Tom waved from the far practice ring, where he was watching Drake search among six metal dumbbell-shaped articles for the one that smelled like Tom. On the other side of that ring, someone I didn't know was trying to get her Miniature Schnauzer to do a sit-stay, but every time she turned her back, the dog stood up. Just when I hoped that someone would help her, I saw Marietta Santini, owner and chief instructor at Dog

Dayz, walking her way.

Collin Lahmeyer stood in the center of the biggest ring with his Curly-coated Retriever, Molly, lying at his feet. "Okay, people, let's warm up with some heeling," he said. I pulled my fanny pack full of treats out of my training bag, strapped it on, and entered the ring with Jay prancing in heel position at my left side. "Forward!" commanded Collin, and we were off. He followed up with frequent changes of pace — "Fast! Normal! Slow!" — and changes of direction that kept us, dogs and people alike, thinking and moving. After ten minutes or so of the group heeling, Collin assembled us into two lines for recalls. I spotted Precious, Giselle Swann's Maltese, in one of the lines, but I didn't recognize the woman holding his leash. Unlike Giselle, who was three hundred pounds if she was one, this person was more like my size, which is to say she could lose a few pounds. Okay, forty. But she wasn't ungainly, and her black slacks fit well and were slimming. Giselle tended toward baggy or too tight. Besides, Giselle's hair was long, stringy, and usually a day late for a shampoo, and this woman had a nice, shiny, layered bob. Still, I was sure that was Precious. I have a good eye for a dog, and while some people may think that all silky-haired little white dogs look alike, it isn't true. I'd photographed Precious enough times to know his face, his size, and his way of moving on sight.

I figured Giselle must be in the restroom or something, so I got in line behind Precious. I'd been hoping to talk to Giselle ever since the encounter with her cousin Persephone at the vet clinic, and now, after seeing the new Treasures on Earth sticker on Giselle's car, I was even more eager for a chat. Jay and Precious are old friends and, although generally I discourage sniffing and greeting in training situations, I had Jay lie down so that Precious would greet him at his own eye level. Then the woman holding the little dog's leash turned around and I nearly passed out.

"Oh, hi, Janet. Umm, how are you?"

I'm afraid I just stared for a few seconds before I could find my voice, and the woman smiled at me. I couldn't believe that she was wearing soft pink lipstick and carefully applied, subtle eye makeup.

"Have you had a good summer?"

"Giselle!" I raced through my memory files. When had I last seen her? I realized it must have been in May at Greg Dorn's funeral. Three months? Could a person change this much in three months? In any event, there she stood, a changed woman.

My peripheral vision registered a man struggling with a Golden Retriever who wasn't holding his stays. That's what the practice time is all about — reinforcing training in the midst of distractions. They finally managed a short stay at a short distance, and rather than call his dog out of the stay at that point, the man returned to the dog and had her heel to the end of the line. Smart move.

"I, umm, are you okay, Janet?" She squirmed a bit and pushed her hair to the side with her non-leash hand, gestures exactly like those of the Giselle I knew.

I gathered my wits and said, "Wow, Giselle, you look fantastic. How on earth . . . ?"

"I've been away." She smiled, a funny mixture of pride and embarrassment on her face.

The line had moved along and Giselle and Precious were on deck, so I bit back my questions until after they did their recall and Jay and I did ours. When we were all back in line again, I said, "Giselle, really, you look fantastic. How . . . ?"

"My daddy helped me. After, you know, all that happened, I was, you know, in a pretty bad way." I did remember that. Giselle had found a murder victim. "My dad said he was worried and, you know, he offered to pay for me to go to fat camp. So I did."

"I'd say you went to skinny camp, the way you look."

Giselle blushed as red as Ava's feathered forehead and scooped Precious into her arms for a security hug, so I suppressed my amazement at her makeover and changed the subject.

"Giselle, I met your cousin yesterday. Persephone."

"You did? Where'd you meet *her*?" Giselle's tone did not express affection.

I told her about my project at the vet clinic. "I love her beautiful bird. I wanted to take some photos of her but she wouldn't let me."

"Don't know why she had to come back to Fort Wayne."

"Come back?"

"Oh, she lived in, wow, I'm not even sure, somewhere in the East," Giselle spoke slowly, looking at the ceiling. "New something."

"New York?"

"Ppfff. No, silly, I know New York." Giselle giggled. "I haven't even talked to her, really, since she got back," Giselle set Precious back down, then continued, "except, you know, at Treasures, I mean, I say hi, but we don't talk." She giggled again, but sounded more nervous than amused. "At least not to each other." I was going to ask about that when she said, "She's not supposed to let anyone take pictures." She paused, then went on, "I might get a bird, too."

"Really? Wait, Giselle, hold that thought. What do you mean, 'she's not supposed to' let me take a picture of her bird?" Giselle had a way of saying odd things, but that was one of the oddest I could remember.

"It upsets the birds."

My encounter with Persephone flashed through my mind. Ava the badly named bird didn't seem to give a squawk. It was Persephone who was distraught about my camera.

"Giselle?" I thought about pressing the point but I could see that Giselle was beginning to fidget again, so I let it go. "So you're thinking of getting a bird?"

"Maybe. You know, just for a while. Sort of foster it. If they need me too."

"Okay, I'm lost, Giselle. Are you talking about the shelter?" I knew Giselle had volunteered off and on for the county animal shelter for a long time, and they got all kinds of animals, but I didn't realize they had an off-site fostering program.

"Umm, no. I, umm, you know, I go to Treasures on Earth now and, umm, I'm learning to be a Guardian."

I flashed on the parking lot outside the Treasures on Earth Spiritual Renewal Center and tried to imagine Giselle's beat-up old Yugo among the luxury cars there. Or Giselle hanging out with Mrs. Willard or even Giselle's own well-heeled-and-coiffed cousin Persephone. "Yeah, I saw the sticker on your car on my way in. That's quite a shift, Giselle, isn't it?"

"No, umm, not really, not so much? You know, it's all about loving the world and taking care of Mother Earth and her creatures?" Giselle was back to her old habit of making every sentence sound like a question. Still, everything she said echoed what Neil had told me at dinner.

We had reached the head of the line again, so I put my next question on hold, planning to continue after Precious and Jay did their stays and recalls. Precious finished and I told Jay to sit and stay. I had just reached the far end of the ring and turned to face my dog when a half-grown Brittany slipped her collar and zoomed around the place looking for a playmate. She ran up to Jay, licked his chin, backed away, and bowed, an invitation as clear as any you might get in the mail. Jay's fanny was wriggling but he remained sitting. The Brittany apparently decided he was a fuddy duddy and took off again. On her third lap, Tom managed to stop her with a piece of hotdog. He slipped a lead under her chest and let her nibble the meat from between his fingers while her mortified owner got the collar back on her. I walked the length of the ring back to Jay and gave him, one by one, five pieces of homemade cheesie garlic treats to reward him for staying despite supreme distraction. Then I left him again, walked across the ring, and called him to me. He slid to a slightly crooked sit in front of me. I gave him another treat and released him and took him out of the ring for a belly rub.

"Can't ask for a better stay than that," said Tom, leaning over to scratch Jay's chin and confirm that he was, as I thought I'd already made clear, a very good dog.

I stood up and grinned at Tom. "Nice catch there."

"Hey, I'm irresistible," he said, and winked at me.

"Full of it, too." I looked around the room. "Have you seen Giselle since the excitement?"

"I think she left."

"What?"

"I saw her go out the back door with her crate in one hand and training bag in the other," he said. "She looks great, huh? Guess the boot camp she went to was good for her."

"You know about that?"

"I ran into her on campus the other day. I forgot to tell you."

"On campus?" The last I had heard, Giselle was working full time in her father's dry cleaning store.

"She's back in school. I ran into her outside the registrar's office."

"Wow." I told Tom about Giselle's cousin, Persephone, and her bird, Ava, and about Giselle's new affiliation with Treasures on Earth. "What do you make of the idea that they have a bird fostering program?"

"That is weird." He looked thoughtful for a moment, then reached down and stroked Drake's ear. "Let me go do a signal run-through while Marietta is still running utility over there. Then we can blow this joint, huh?"

I took Jay back into the heeling ring, where group sits and downs were up next. People were lining their dogs up along one side of the ring, and I slipped Jay into a spot between a Cardigan Welsh Corgi and a Doberman. Collin Lahmeyer was still in charge, and when we were all in position he said, "Let's alternate sits and downs and do three and a half minutes." He went down the line pointing at each of us for *sit* or *down.* "Position your dogs." I had Jay lie down. "Leave your dogs."

Three and a half minutes may not sound like much, but for a green dog it's interminable. For me, with Mr. Reliable, it was no problem, but the Corgi next to Jay saw the dogs on either side of him lying down and decided he should do the same, although he'd been told to sit and stay. His owner had to go back three times to reposition him. Each time he shortened the distance between himself and his dog, and by the end he was standing two feet from the Corgi, who sat for the remaining time. Collin finally told us to return to our dogs. I had just circled behind Jay to stand at his right side when the front door opened and my eyes went wide.

"Exercise finished," said Collin.

I picked up my leash and snapped it onto Jay's collar. Normally I would tell him, again, what an excellent dog he is, but this time I murmured instead, "Holy crap, Bubby, what is *he* doing here?"

Neil spotted me and met me at the gate

to the ring. "Hi, Janet. My! I had no idea so many grownups like to play with dogs." He was smiling, but I didn't like the condescension in his tone.

"Can't think of anyone better to play with than my dog, actually. What are you doing here, Neil?" *And how the heck did you know to find me here? Did I mention Dog Dayz?* I couldn't remember.

"I was out this way and thought I'd stop in and see what you're up to." He intercepted a long white hair that was floating toward his navy T-shirt and shot Jay an accusatory look, which prompted Bad Janet to whisper an idea in my ear. I resisted the urge to listen to her.

"Come over here and sit down for a minute," I said, and led him to the chairs along the wall. I sat next to him and Jay immediately moved in sideways against both our knees.

Neil scooted his chair back as far as he could and brushed the dog hair off his navy pants.

"Oh, sorry about the hair. He's shedding."

"Clearly." Neil's mouth smiled at me, but his eyes still didn't join in. "Have to admit, she has a pretty coat. It shimmers."

The words were barely out of Neil's mouth when Jay went into a full-body shake, sending a fine cloud of white and silver hairs flying.

Neil jumped up and started madly whacking at his thighs and knees, a horrified look on his face. I had to laugh, but said at the same time, "Oh, jeez, sorry! That's one of his tricks."

Neil gaped at me.

" 'Shimmer,' " I whispered, then in a normal voice, "is his cue to shake. I don't think anyone has ever given that command by accident before."

"So it's my fault." For a guy who didn't much like dogs, he growled quite well.

"I didn't say that." I laughed, glancing past Neil to where Tom stood in the far practice ring with Drake. He smiled at me. I smiled back, then returned my focus to Neil. "I don't think doggy environments are really your thing, Neil."

"I think not." He finally stopped picking dog hair off his clothes and looked at me. "I was going to ask you out for dessert or something, but . . ." He didn't say I was a mess in so many words, but I thought I'd help him out.

"I actually have plans, but thanks anyway."

Looking relieved, Neil said goodnight and left. *Probably the last you'll see of him,* I thought, not unhappily.

"Want to go out for dessert?" Tom stepped up from behind me, and Drake bumped my knee with his nose.

"Oh, I don't know. I'm a mess."

"You are?" He grinned at me. "Makes us a matched set."

I agreed to meet him at Bob Evans for berry cobbler á la mode.

TWENTY

Thursday morning came very early. After the berry cobbler the night before, Jay and I ended up at Tom's house, so I had to get up early to race home, feed Leo and Jay, shower, change, grab my camera, and get to the vet clinic. I wasn't exactly punching a clock there, mind you, but Dr. Kerry had told me they had some interesting clients coming in early. First on the schedule was a twenty-two-pound Giant Flemish rabbit who, at that weight, was a giant even for the breed. After that she had a dog coming in that she thought I would find interesting, although she didn't give me any particulars.

My phone rang just as I pulled into the vet clinic parking lot.

"Hi, Bill."

"Hi, Sis. What's up?"

"I'm just about to start a photo shoot for that article about the vet. Can we meet later? Lunch maybe?"

"Can't do lunch. What's up? Norm thought it sounded important. Something wrong with Mom?"

"No, nothing new with her really, but it is important." I got out of the car and grabbed my camera bag. "Bill, really, I can't get into it now. You don't have any time today?"

He heaved a big dramatic Bill sigh. "I could meet you on my way. Eleven forty-five? Downtown?"

"I can do that." I stopped outside the door to finish the conversation. "Where's your lunch?"

"Parkview Field."

"You're having lunch at the ball park?" Bill is not a hotdogs and peanuts kind of guy.

"New client. Big one. So yes, I'm having lunch at the ballpark."

We settled on the Botanical Conservatory, which is both right next to the ballpark and one of my favorite places. I figured that if I left the clinic at eleven fifteen, I'd just have time to dash home, grab the paperwork on Mom's house, and find a parking place. I turned my phone off, stuck it in my camera bag, and went in.

I found Dr. Kerry in the back room. She was leaning over a big book that lay open on an exam table. Judging by how high she jumped when I said hello, she was so focused on her reading that she didn't hear me come in.

"Sorry."

"Eh, no problem."

"Must be a good book."

"Just brushing up on my leporids."

"Rabbits."

Kerry's eyebrows shot up. "Very good."

I didn't tell her it was a wild guess based on knowing she had a rabbit coming in.

A young man I hadn't seen before came in from the lobby with a folder in his hand and said, "Your first patient is here." He wore blue scrubs, a badge that said "Brian," and a look of astonishment. "It's the biggest bunny I've ever seen!"

Kerry slapped the book shut and laughed. "He's the biggest bunny anyone's ever seen." She introduced us, told Brian he could get things ready for the next client, and headed for the exam room with me in tow.

It was the biggest bunny I had ever seen. His head was as big as Jay's and his ears were nearly as long as my forearm. Dr. Kerry held the backs of her fingers in front of the creature's nose and cooed "Hello, Van Dyke" as he sniffed and then rubbed his cheek against her hand. Van Dyke's owner was a forty-ish man with, appropriately, a Van Dyke beard.

"Janet MacPhail, meet Peter Wills." Then she explained what I was doing there and asked if it would be okay to photograph Van Dyke.

"Oh, my, Van Dyke!" Peter clapped his hands and the rabbit turned to look at him, nose twitching. "You'll be famous!"

The rest of the visit was uneventful and Van Dyke cooperated all the way, especially when Dr. Kerry produced a small carrot from her pocket.

After Van Dyke, we saw a pair of tuxedo cats, sixteen-year-old brothers adopted as kittens from the shelter and still looking spry, and a black tri-colored Aussie puppy in to get his second round of puppy shots and to make me go completely gaga. A lovely morning of routine visits and puppy breath.

"Okay, the next client is the dog I think you'll find interesting," said Kerry. "He's a wildlife detection dog."

For an instant that baffled me, since most dogs seem to detect wildlife with no trouble at all. Then her meaning hit me. "You mean like a drug detection dog, but for smuggled wildlife?"

"Yep." She moved to the sink and

scrubbed for the umpteenth time that morning. That was one of the reasons I used this clinic. They are fastidious about cleanliness.

"In Fort Wayne?"

"Yep." She dried her hands, tossed the paper towel in the trash, and turned toward me. "They've actually intercepted several smugglers in the past few months, here in Allen, as well as Marion and Delaware counties." She was describing a series of counties that coincided with Interstate 69, the fastest route between Indianapolis and the Canadian border.

"What are they smuggling?"

"Monkeys. Reptiles. Birds. Occasionally other things. Mostly tropical, many endangered. Come on." She headed down toward the exam room. "It's horrible. You wouldn't believe how they pack the animals to hide them." I already knew more than I wanted to know, although I didn't like to think about it. I couldn't, in fact, without fighting back tears. Fortunately we reached the exam room door before my mind could dredge up too many articles I had read and photos I had seen. "Anyway," said Kerry, reaching for the doorknob, "Lennen has led to a number of intercepts."

Lennen stood to greet us, tail banging

against the base of the exam table and a big Labrador grin on his face. His handler also stood and offered her hand. "Di Holman. Dr. Kerry tells me you're a photographer."

"Janet MacPhail. And yes. Working on a 'day in the life' photo essay. Okay if I photograph Lennen's exam?"

She hesitated. "You can take the photos. I'll remove his working ID. No photos of me, and no names. Not even Lennen's. And no mention of his job. Just generic chocolate Lab."

I looked the question at her and waited.

"For his safety. He's one of very few dogs who do this job, and he's damn good at it. He's cost the smugglers a few bucks and he's only been working about nine months." She reached down and scratched the base of the dog's tail. "I'll know it's him in the pictures. That's enough." She smiled at her dog, then looked at me. "Dr. Kerry told you what he does?"

"Briefly. He detects wildlife being smuggled in?"

"Right."

"I thought that activity was all through tropical ports. Don't most of the birds come from the tropics?" The long red feather in the bag that Drake found fluttered into my mind. I had never thought that it came from a local game bird. Maybe a parrot, or some other exotic bird. But that didn't explain what it was doing in a canvas bag, on a tiny island in a private lake.

". . . so they're trying new routes, including the Great Lakes." I had tuned out most of what Di said and didn't want to look like a complete birdbrain, so I didn't ask her to repeat the rest. I considered mentioning the bag and feather but decided to wait and talk to Detective Jo Stevens.

Lennen, it turned out, had cut his foot on some broken glass, and a sliver of it was stuck in his pad. While Dr. Kerry pulled it out and cleaned the wound, Lennen smooched with Brian, the vet tech who was holding him. I took photos and Di talked about some of the animals Lennen had rescued. "It's barbaric, the way these sleazebags try to conceal the animals, and sometimes so stupid it would be funny, if not for the cruelty involved."

"I read about some guy who tried to bring a baby gibbon through customs under his sweatshirt," I said. "It was clinging around his waist as it would to its mother." There had been a photo on a website I'd discovered while looking up something else.

"Right. Lennen indicated a woman about a month ago. I wasn't even on duty, and we stopped at a rest stop on the highway. He goes where I go, and we were in the ladies' room. He just insisted the woman had something in a cosmetic case she was carrying, so I detained her, got the state police to come, and they searched her."

"And?" Kerry had finished with Lennen and gave her full attention to his handler.

"So, inside the case was a paper bag with thirteen hair curlers. And inside each curler was a live Guyanese finch."

"Seriously?" I asked, knowing as I said it how dumb it sounded.

"They sell for anywhere from three hundred to a thousand dollars or more."

"But curlers?" I couldn't imagine stuffing a little bird into a plastic tube.

"Right." Di said as she and Kerry lifted Lennen off the table and Di put his official collar back on. "The plastic is more rigid, so more protective, than toilet paper rollers, which a lot of the lowlifes use. And they don't set off metal detectors."

Kerry spat out a string of interesting names for the smugglers, then asked, "What happened to the birds?"

"The live ones were held for evidence at a private, legal aviary in Indianapolis. Three had died. Once the trial is over, the survivors will be returned to Guyana, quarantined, and released. Assuming there are any survivors."

"What?" Kerry and I both blurted.

"Finches live, what, Doc, nine or ten years? Legal wrangling could take a couple of years. And who knows how old the birds were when caught. Just sayin'."

Just when I thought things couldn't get any more depressing, Peg came in to say a dog that had been hit by a car was on its way in. Di and Lennen left, and Brian and Dr. Kerry went into high gear preparing the surgical area. They were all set when the distraught driver arrived with the dog. "I didn't see him, he just ran out from between parked cars, going like hell, I didn't see him, will he be okay, I was only going twenty-five, he doesn't even have a tag or collar." She stopped to take a breath and, as soon as the little dog was out of her arms and in Brian's, she burst into tears. Peg, the receptionist, took charge of the driver and I followed Brian to the surgical area where they were already setting up for x-rays.

I stayed out of the way but managed to get a few shots. While Dr. Kerry waited for the radiographs she examined the dog, who was now panting heavily but remaining calm. He whimpered softly when Kerry touched his thigh. "Broken, I think." She kept one hand lightly on the dog's shoulder. "Janet, could you get me the microchip scanner from that drawer. Let's see if this little guy is chipped." He was, and Kerry asked me to take the scanner to Peg and have her look up the dog's microchip identification and, if possible, notify the owner.

When I returned, the dog had been anesthetized and his back leg shaved from hip to hock, the joint above the foot. I took more photos as Kerry set the leg. "You don't wait to be sure the owner will pay for this?" I asked.

Dr. Kerry gave me a look that suggested I'd lost my mind. "Why would I leave an animal in pain?" I didn't have an answer for that. "We hope they pay, but the dog comes first." She rubbed her nose against her arm. "Why does my nose always itch when my hands are busy? Anyway, this doesn't look too bad. Clean break, not displaced. He's going to be a sore little puppy from the bruising, but I think he'll be fine."

Peg appeared in the doorway. "Dog's name is Mike. Owner's on his way. Said the plumber accidentally let the dog out. How is he? The guy is frantic. Asked me to call him back." Kerry filled her in.

By the time I left, the owner was pacing the lobby waiting for Mike to be completely out of the anesthesia and the driver who hit him had calmed down. She had offered to pay the bill. The owner said no, but after considerable discussion he agreed to let her pay half, which I figured was good therapy for her.

Twenty-One

Bill was waiting for me in the lobby of the Botanical Conservatory, although I didn't see him at first. He was partially hidden by a flock of some fifty plastic flamingos and a humongous multicolored beach ball.

"What's all this?" I asked as I wove through the plastic birds.

" 'Beach Days.' More inside." He started to laugh. "Remember when we stuck fifty of these guys in the yard for Mom's fiftieth birthday?"

We reminisced for a few minutes about happier times with our mother, and then Bill checked the time and asked me what was going on. I told him about my conversation with Mom about the house, and felt a sad little twinge as I watched him fight to keep the emotions off his face when I said she had given it to me.

"Here." I handed him the envelope I had brought.

"What's this?"

"I know you love that old house. You helped put in those gardens and you helped Dad finish the basement. To me, it's just a house. Lots of memories, sure, but I like the house I'm in. Better yard for the dogs. So it's all yours."

Bill stared at me as if I were speaking Martian.

"Mom gave me a quit-claim making the house mine, and I want you to have Norm draw up another for me to sign. If you want it, it's all yours."

"Janet . . ." Bill cleared his throat.

"If you don't want to live there, you could rent it out, or you can sell it. Whatever you like."

My brother is a sweet guy, but he's not a hugger. At least I haven't seen him hug anyone except Norm in years. Imagine my surprise when Bill stood, pulled me to my feet, and wrapped me up in a big bear hug. I tried to hug back, but he had pinned my arms to my sides, so I just stood there for a couple of minutes with my nose pressed into his fine summer-wool jacket and the faint scent of his oh-de-so-subtle cologne swirling around my nostrils.

I meant to go home after my meeting with Bill, but my emotions were running wild, and as I drove east on Coliseum I had an overpowering urge to see Tom. I parked, all the while trying to convince myself that I was there to talk about the strange happenings at Twisted Lake. Nothing more. A little internal jab to the conscience made me give that up, though, and as I scurried up the sidewalk to the building's entrance I admitted to myself that I wanted to see him and hear him and breathe him in.

When I turned down the social sciences corridor, I could hear Tom's voice from several doors down, and he did not sound happy. "I've been bringing him in here for years, John. He barks less than you do, he's a registered therapy dog, and my students come to see him more than to see me."

"He's a therapy dog?"

I hung back just outside the door to Tom's office.

"Yes, he is. Tested and registered with the largest therapy organization in the country."

Whoever was in there with Tom sort of harumphed, and said, "What do *you* need a therapy dog for?"

There was a moment's hesitation, and then Tom said, "John, did you know that it's illegal under the Americans with Disabilities Act to ask a person why they need a service animal?"

A short, balding man backed out Tom's door, so I tried to look as if I had just arrived. He glanced at me, then said to Tom, "You should have said he was certified to begin with. We could have avoided all this." And then he was gone.

I stepped into the doorway. Tom was petting Drake, who was lying in front of the file cabinet on a plaid doggy bed. "That *man* is certifiable, doncha think?"

"What exactly *do* you need a service dog for, Professor Saunders?"

Tom looked up at me and his expression changed from royally annoyed to surprised and delighted. "Hey, it's my favorite photographer!" He stood and gave me a hug. "I need him to help me meet women. Regular chick magnet, you know?"

"Good for you. What was that all about?"

"I didn't say he was a service dog. I said therapy. Not my fault if that pompous a . . . , uh, administrator doesn't know the difference." Yet another reason I'm nuts about this guy. "Come on, let's go outside. Drake could use a little walk."

"Can't stay long. I was just driving by."

Tom pulled the door shut behind us and waggled his eyebrows at me. "Ah, the old 'I was just in the neighborhood' ploy."

We walked across the parking lot to the

grassy bank of the St. Joseph River and I told him about my encounters with Mom and Bill. He asked how my morning session at the vet clinic went, and that led us to Lennen and wildlife smuggling. "I can't help thinking there's more to that red feather than we know," I said.

"Have you heard the news about Anderson?"

I stopped and took Tom by the arm. "What?"

"I heard it on the radio. He drowned."

"No he didn't."

Tom looked at me, questions all over his face. "Janet?"

"It doesn't make sense." My cheeks were burning and I wasn't sure whether it was the August heat, my anger, or a hot flash. I pointed to a big maple a few yards off the path. "I need to stop a minute."

"You're flushed," Tom said, looking at me even as we headed for the patch of shade. "You really okay?"

It seemed about twenty degrees cooler under the tree. I leaned back against the trunk and gazed at Tom for a moment without speaking. He pulled a handkerchief from his pocket, wiped my sweaty face, and waited.

I told him about the message Anderson

had left me Tuesday. "He had already been to the lake, Tom. He was back in his car, leaving. Not arriving. *Leaving.*"

"Maybe he went back for another look?" Ever the voice of reason, but he didn't sound convinced either.

"He had already loaded his canoe onto his roof, or whatever. He was on his way. Said he'd be on Coliseum in half an hour."

Tom tilted his head back and looked into the maple's wide arms.

"He didn't go back out on the water, Tom." Then I remembered something Jo Stevens had said. "They found his camera in his car, Tom. He wouldn't have gone back to the island without his camera."

Tom told Drake to lie down, then tried to put his arms around me. I pushed him away, then stood very still, eyes squeezed shut, listening to the blood in my ears beat like bass drums. I thought the top of my head might blow off as rage thick as magma bubbled up inside me. I have no idea how long I stood like that. Everything else had stopped, and I was mildly surprised when I opened my eyes and saw Tom watching me. I don't know how he managed it, but he looked concerned and angry and thoughtful all at the same time.

"It's all connected. Somehow, it's all connected."

"Maybe." Tom looked thoughtful. "I bet a bird guy could identify that feather, or get close anyway."

"A 'bird guy'?"

He grinned and squeezed my hand. "Yeah, you know, like I'm a plant guy, and you're sort of a dog-hair-and-pixels guy. Bird guy. Ornithologist."

"Is there anyone here?" I asked, tilting my head toward the buildings of the Indiana-Purdue Fort Wayne campus.

"No, but let me ask around. There has to be someone at one of the main campuses." Meaning Indiana University in Bloomington, or Purdue in West Lafayette. By then we were almost back to the building. Tom ran the tips of his fingers along my cheek. "You okay?"

"Not exactly." I pushed my fury and grief out of my throat. "Anderson was a really nice young man. I want whoever did this held accountable."

"Janet, let the police do their job."

"Right."

"Janet! Don't do anything reckless. I don't know what I'd do . . ."

I didn't realize what he'd said, or started to say, until I was almost home. For the moment I was just too angry about Anderson Billings to pay attention.

TWENTY-TWO

The light was flashing on my answering machine when I got home. It was Neil, and he began by saying he had left a message on my cell, but wanted to be sure I got it. I scratched Leo's chin while the message continued. It didn't make much sense. "It was great to see you last night." *No it wasn't,* I thought. *You hated being in a building full of dogs and,* I smiled at the memory of Jay "shimmering" all over Neil's pants, *dog hair.* When the message finished, I hit "Erase" and headed out the back door with my critters, thinking about the rest of the message. Neil hoped he could see me again soon. "How about a walk on the River Greenway or something when the heat breaks," he'd said, "say around seven? You could bring your dog if you want." That made me laugh out loud. *As if I'd go for a walk on the Greenway with you and without Jay, you boob.*

I picked up the hose, turned on the water,

headed for my thirsty flowers, and forgot all about Neil Young and his hifalutin message. As I watched puddles form where the water was slow to soak into the ground, I could almost see Twisted Lake. I needed to get out to that island. Of course, whatever Anderson saw might be long gone by now. Or maybe he didn't see anything. But what did he mean, "There's a bird"? There are lots of birds out there. And then I thought of the red feather in the bag that Drake found. Long red feather. Persephone Swann's beautiful parrot had long red feathers like that.

Mayhem in the yard derailed my train of thought. Leo had initiated a game of "ambush the dog" and Jay obliged by running from him, then turning the tables and chasing Leo into shrubs. And my flower beds. "Hey guys! Outta the flowers!" I had just finished watering the last of the pots when a flash of neon pink caught my eye from across the fence. It was Goldie, kneeling on a pad in the herb garden on the far side of her yard. Her "witch's garden," to be precise. She had put it in last spring, and it was filling in nicely three months later. I was surprised that she hadn't come over to say hello. It wasn't like Goldie to ignore us.

I shut off the water and went out my gate

and in through hers. I called her name as I approached but she had her back to me and didn't respond. Odd, I thought. Is she losing her hearing? I didn't want to startle her so I arced around and entered her peripheral vision from the side.

"Oh! Janet!" Goldie jumped, then laid a hand over her chest.

"Sorry!"

"No, no!" She reached for her ears and pulled out a pair of ear buds. I could just hear a gravely voice coming from them.

"Dylan?" I asked.

Goldie grinned at me. "Leonard Cohen." She pulled an MP3 player from her pocket, turned it off, and returned it with the buds. "See, I've joined the twenty-first century." She stood up and pushed the sleeves of her faded blue shirt to her elbows.

Leo wandered over, and Goldie plucked a bit of catnip from the garden and tossed it on the ground. A hint of its minty scent mingled with the mix of bergamot, sage, and thyme already held in the humid garden air. We left Leo to his ecstasy, and Goldie went to the fence and said hello to Jay.

"Have a few minutes, Goldie?" I asked, thinking maybe I could finally pin her down on whatever was going on with her health.

"Sure. What's up?"

"Say, I made some lemonade last night. Let's go sit with Jay and have some."

She looked a little suspicious, but agreed. When we had settled into my Adirondack chairs and spent a few minutes on small talk, I said, "Goldie, really, you have to tell me."

"Tell you what?"

"I saw you at the hospital. Nuclear medicine? And all those supplements you've been buying for months? And you've lost weight, and . . ." I set my glass down hard enough to splash lemonade onto the tangerine tabletop and was surprised to find I was angry.

"Don't be angry." Goldie reached out and touched my forearm.

"Why not?" I glared at her. "You told Tom."

She looked surprised. "What are we talking about? Told Tom what?"

"At the co-op. He said he saw you there, that you two had a talk."

"Oh." She did a little hand-washing motion. "That."

"So?"

"I'm fine. Now I'm fine."

"No, you're not." I felt my eyes fill with tears, and then I felt a warm furry chin on my lap. Goldie isn't the only one of my friends who is psychic. Jay is, too, and always there when I need him. I stroked the top of his head and looked at Goldie. "You've been saying that all summer. Stop dodging me. Whatever it is, just tell me, damn it."

"Okay. I had a scare. A big one. Had a funny mammogram last spring. In May. But . . ."

"May," I said, my voice flat with disappointment.

"Right. And I had to have another, and then other tests, you know, and it's gone on more or less all summer."

"And?" By then my anger was giving way to the fear that had been lurking behind it all along. She started to speak, but I cut her off. "And what? Goldie, you've lost weight and . . ."

"I know." Now Goldie looked a bit angry. "Look, you're not the only one that was scared, Janet. And it's my life. My body. Private."

I gaped at her. "Private? Goldie, I'm your friend. Your, I don't know, your more than friend. I should have been there for you."

"But Janet, you were." Her face settled back into its usual gentle calm. "Look, I always knew you were there. You, and Tom, too." She leaned toward me. "You and Tom."

"But . . ."

"You and Tom, Janet. Stop fighting it."

"Don't change the subject. So what about now?" I wanted her to say it straight out, either way.

"I'm fine. You saw me at the hospital for the final consultation. All clear. Well, almost. I have to go for some final blood work, but that's it. Much ado about nothing."

"But the supplements? Your weight?"

"All coincidence, I guess. Okay, not all. I did up my antioxidants. Just, you know . . . ," she hesitated. "I was scared."

"When do you go for the blood work?"

"Tomorrow. No biggie, I just need to pop into the lab at Parkview."

"I'll drive you," I said. She seemed ready to argue, but stopped and nodded. "But you look so thin, Goldie."

"Oh, that. I decided to go off wheat for a while to see if I felt better. Lost twenty pounds." She gave me a devilish grin. "Maybe you should give it a try."

"Thanks a lot." And to my horror I burst into tears.

"Oh my, Janet! I'm sorry, I was teasing!"

"No, no, not that." It wasn't her suggestion that I could lose a few pounds that tipped me over the edge. It was an overwhelming wave of relief and anger and loss. Goldie was okay. Anderson was dead. And it was Goldie's turn to listen as I told her about Anderson, his message, and my certainty that he had been murdered.

TWENTY-THREE

Friday morning I was up way too early after a long Thursday and another restless night. It was the last day of my week-long photo shoot with Dr. Kerry Joiner, and she started surgeries at seven-thirty. I wanted a few shots to round out my photo essay, so I was there, at least in body. Kerry was in surgery for two hours, then had a series of routine appointments. Two kittens, a Pug puppy, three Labs, and a guinea pig later, I had photos of one and all. No one snarled or snapped. Even my bitten behind had no complaints.

I left the clinic a few minutes before eleven, but even so, by the time I got to my car, my stomach was disturbing my peaceful day with loud growls. I'd had to scramble to get to the clinic on time and had made do with an apple for breakfast, so I was famished and I knew exactly what I wanted to eat, and who I wanted for company. I hit

Tom's quick-dial number.

"Can't wait to see me, huh?" he answered, chuckling. The night before we had seen one another at agility practice, and Tom had asked me for "a real Friday night date with all the trimmings." At first I thought he meant our usual walk with the dogs followed by take-out and beer in the backyard, but he clarified. Dinner, movie, nightcap, the works. I was equal parts excited and terrified, his "expand the family" comment still bouncing around my brain. The last thing I wanted was to lose Tom. The second-to-the-last-thing I wanted was for him to do something silly like propose. At least I didn't think I wanted that.

"You're actually an afterthought."

"I'm crushed."

"I'm starving. I thought first of grilled cheese and tomato at the Firefly. Then I thought of you."

"Ah, hard to compete with that." I told him I also wanted to talk to him about some things.

"You're snooping around again, aren't you?"

"Not snooping. Thinking." *Thinking about snooping.*

He met me at the Firefly, and once I had several bites of the best grilled-cheese-and-tomato known to humanity, I told him what I was thinking. "Anderson saw something out on the island that had to do with birds, and I think parrots are tied somehow to Treasures on Earth or Regis Moneypenny." I reminded him about Persephone Swann's beautiful if badly named bird Ava, and Giselle's comment about becoming a "guardian" to "sort of foster" birds for Moneypenny's organization. "Anderson said 'there's a bird,' which didn't make sense to me because the place is full of birds. That's why I told him about it in the first place," I said. "But if he meant a strange bird, an exotic bird . . ."

"That would make more sense," Tom agreed.

"Remember that dog I told you about, the wildlife smuggling dog?" I asked.

Tom had just taken a bite of his sandwich so he nodded, cheese ecstasy lighting up his face. He swallowed and said, "Detection. He's a detection dog, not a smuggling dog."

"Thanks, Professor."

He grinned and popped the last bite of sandwich.

"Tom, what if they're smuggling parrots? Rare parrots? Expensive parrots?"

He wiped his mouth and said, "Possible, I guess. But why let anyone know about the birds? I mean, besides potential buyers?"

"I don't know." I thought about what little I did know. "I'm not sure they mean to let people know anything except that they foster them and find them homes. Persephone was none too happy that I took photos. Made me delete them."

"Too bad. We could have tracked down her bird's species."

I grinned at him.

He grinned back. "You kept some."

"Just one. But it's a good shot." Then a conversation with Neil Young sprang into my consciousness. "Oh, my God, Tom. I completely forgot. Neil said he has a bird, but then changed the subject."

"Neil? Oh, the pretty doctor?" Tom's tone took me by surprise, but when our eyes met he just grinned at me and said, "Man doesn't like dog hair much, does he?"

"You saw that?" I chuckled, and started to remind him that Neil was just someone I knew in high school, but Tom interrupted. "So, he has a bird?"

"I, uh, yes. A parrot. But that's all he told me. Come to think of it, he changed the subject when I asked about it."

"People usually like to talk about their pets."

"But these people don't. Maybe they're

not supposed to, but they're people, so they slip up. Maybe Moneypenny is using his followers to hold his birds pending sale." Goldie's comments about Treasures on Earth's building permits came flooding back. "Tom! They're planning an aviary! We're definitely on to something. I need to call Jo."

"Speaking of calls, I have a call in to someone at Cornell vet school. Send me the photo and I'll send it after I hear back. I bet he can identify the bird, or knows who can." He stood and put a twenty on the table. "I have a departmental meeting so gotta run." He started to leave, but turned back and said, "We should send a picture of the feather, too. Maybe Jo would let you photograph it. You do need to call her. But Janet," he took my hand and looked into my eyes. "please let the police do this. If you're right, if these people did kill Anderson, they're dangerous."

I agreed, but fell a bit shy of a promise.

When I got home, a florist delivery truck was just pulling out of my driveway. "Great," I mumbled, "another bouquet." I parked in the driveway and retrieved a stunning arrangement of orange and blue gladioli from the porch. It was from Bill. The note attached said, "The door is always open," and a house key was tied to the card with a blue satin ribbon.

As soon as I had let Jay out, found a place for the glads, and changed the water in my other three bouquets, I left a message for Detective Jo Stevens to call me, and then called Goldie. I grabbed my keys and bag and met her in the driveway.

Twenty-Four

"I just don't understand why you're fighting it," said Goldie. We weren't exactly discussing my relationship with Tom. She was discussing it, and I was listening. "Look how well you two get along."

I pulled into the Parkview Hospital parking garage entrance and pulled a ticket from the machine.

"Not to mention how hot he is." She tried to elbow my ribs, but couldn't quite make it with her shoulder belt fastened. "You know, Janet," she suddenly sounded thoughtful, and I feared something philosophical might be coming, but then she said, "I don't believe I ever saw a photo of good ol' what's his name."

"Who?" I found a space across from the entrance, so we continued the conversation on our way to the lab.

"Chet. I have no idea what he looked like."

Like a jerk. "He was pretty good looking.

That was part of the problem." I laughed, although I was wondering why the mention of his name still made me want to kick something. "That, and his unwillingness to take a job that didn't fit his elevated self-image. And there was the gambling, of course."

"What kind of good looking?"

"Who cares, Goldie?" I asked, but she apparently really wanted to know. "Okay, I don't know, sort of dark and handsome good looking. Think, I don't know, young Tom Cruise-ish."

"Whereas now we have mature Harrison Ford-ish." She opened the door to the lab and ushered me in. "Progress!"

"Why are you asking about Chet, anyway?"

"I don't know," said Goldie as we reached the door to the lab. "He just popped into my head."

We were in and out in ten minutes, a medical miracle of sorts. As I approached the kiosk at the parking garage exit, I noticed a set of big green fuzzy dice in the window facing us. I pulled up and handed my ticket to the attendant, a slightly scruffy guy with a gray comb-over and an impressive beer belly. He checked the voucher stamp and said, "Thank you. Have a nice day." In the half-second between the end of his "day" and my car's response to my foot on the gas, we made eye contact. Twenty feet later, I stopped before turning onto Randallia and burst into screamy laughter.

"What's going on?" asked Goldie, looking around for the joke.

"Goldie! Do you know who that was?"

"Who *who* was?"

"Chet! That was Chet!"

She whipped around in her seat as I pulled onto the street. "Go back! Janet, go back, I didn't get a good look."

I pulled over to the curb and put the car in park, and Goldie and I laughed until we had tears running down our face.

"Nice career move, Chet," I said. "Oh, jeez, I have to call Bill. He'll love this!"

"Do you think he recognized you?"

I shrugged. "I barely recognized him. It didn't click until we were moving again." I fished a tissue out of my tote bag and wiped my eyes. "Oh, man, that was great."

Laughter really must be therapeutic because I felt better than I had in days. We were both still grinning when we parted ways at home, and I spent a few happy minutes throwing a ball and running around like a nut with Jay. Then I went in. I still had a couple of hours before I needed to get ready for my dinner date, so I linked my camera to my computer and began downloading photos.

I'd been at it for about half an hour when Leo strolled in, hopped onto my desk, and yawned at me. Mid-cat-smooch I sat straight up and swore. I'd forgotten all about getting Bill's kayak, and I was planning to go to Twisted Lake the next morning with Tom. Partly it was a snooping around mission, and partly a training session. Several members of Tom's retriever training club would be there. I could take some photos, and check out the island with lots of people and dogs around for safety. If I had a way to cross the channel.

"Come on, Jay," I said, grabbing my keys and his leash. "Car ride!" You'd think from his bouncing around that he never got to go anywhere.

Norm was mowing the lawn when I pulled up in front of their place. He waved, then disappeared around the side of the house. I found my darling brother in the garage, overhead door up, clearing shelves of old paint cans and loading them into boxes.

"Hi, Bill. What's all this?"

"Taking these to the toxic county dump. County toxic dump. Whatever." I must have looked perplexed, because he said, "We have a Realtor coming Wednesday to put the house on the market. We're moving to the new place, you know, the old place, as soon as we can get in there and do a few things." He sat down on a box. "What's up?"

"Thanks for the flowers. They're gorgeous."

Bill mock saluted. "Here for the kayak?" He studied my face for a moment. "What canary did you eat?" He reacted to my story about seeing Chet pretty much the way I did, and we had the best mutual laugh-fest we'd had in years. When we finally settled back down, Bill said, "Okay, then, the kayak!"

We decided I should take Norm's, which was small enough to maneuver into my van if I folded the crate down and Jay rode loose. I prefer to have him in his crate in case of accident, but it was a short drive so I figured it wouldn't hurt for once. When the kayak was loaded, Bill gave me a hug. It was getting to be a habit. "Careful out there."

"I'll be fine."

"Not worried about you. That's an expensive kayak."

I smiled all the way home, thinking it was nice to see Bill so happy. When I got there I had just enough time to take Jay for a short walk before I needed to tidy myself up, and that gave me a chance to call Giselle. I wanted to find out more about the Treasures on Earth bird fostering program, and Giselle might be my best source. Hell, she might be my only source, since I wasn't inclined to cultivate Neil Young any further. Giselle agreed to meet me for coffee on Sunday.

When we got back home I fed Jay and Leo and was just about to take a shower when the doorbell rang. "Crappola," I said, pulling my T-shirt back on. As I reached for the doorknob, I glanced out the front window. "Oh no," I whispered, then to Jay I said, "Down." He lay down and watched the door, eyes sparkling with anticipation. You'd think they were delivering dog food. When I thought about it, I realized that a dog-food delivery would make me happier, too.

But no, it was not a dog-food delivery truck in my driveway. It was a florist's delivery truck. I pasted a happy look on my face. It was not, after all, the delivery man's fault that I already had four bouquets in my house and didn't need another.

Bouquet number five was gorgeous, if redundant. The sweet fragrance of the pink roses was intoxicating. Jay and I retreated to the kitchen and I set the bouquet on the table and reached for the card. "Hope this makes you as happy as you make me. Love you. See you tonight! Tom."

"Where am I going to put this one, Bubby?" Jay wriggled his nub and grinned. "Okay, no room in here. How about the living room?" I cleared a space on top of an end table, inhaled the intoxicating scent once more, and headed back to the bathroom with Jay at my side. I sat down on the edge of the tub and took Jay's head in my hands. "What am I going to do, Jay-jay? Tom wants to expand his family. You want to live with Drake?"

At the sound of his buddy's name, Jay whirled and raced to the living room. No doubt he'd be watching out the window until his friend, and mine, arrived.

TWENTY-FIVE

"Holy mackerel! That's a lot of flowers!"

Tom stood in the doorway between the kitchen and living room looking from one bouquet to another. The one from Goldie was on the kitchen table. The other four were scattered around the living room. Shadetree Retirement Home bloomed from the table behind the couch and the one from the vet clinic sat on the coffee table. Bill's and Tom's bouquets flanked the couch, one on each end table. "I don't have any more horizontal surfaces in the public part of the house, so I hope that's it for a while."

"If I'd known, I'd have sent chocolates instead."

The instant our eyes met we both burst into laughter. It was the kind that won't stop, and we ended up sprawled side by side on the couch, the dogs half in our laps, Leo leaning toward us from the armrest, tears running down our cheeks. My ribs were beginning to complain about all the crazy laugh-fests, but the rest of me was glad for the chances to purge other emotions, at least for a little while. When the hysteria had run its course, I pulled myself up and my skirt down and scurried off to repair my hair and makeup. We told the doggy and kitty boys to be good, locked the doors, and left.

Maybe the laughter had cleared my brain, because I managed to keep all the crazy goings-on of the week in a shadowy corner of my mind through dinner. By the time we left the restaurant, the sun had set, the temperature had dropped, and we were both much more relaxed. Tom checked his watch and said, "We should get going if we're going to make the movie."

"Why don't we just go for a walk? It's so nice out now. We can see movies in January."

Tom draped his arm over my shoulder and steered me down the sidewalk. "Works for me." There was an oldies concert in Headwaters Park, so we wandered around the well-lighted, well-populated area for about half an hour, then Tom guided us to a bench from which we could hear the band and watch kids splashing in the fountain.

"They're playing our music." They had

just wrapped up a Credence medley and were slowing it down with Scott McKenzie's "San Francisco."

"Goldie's music," I said, and he smiled. "I talked to her today. Finally got it out of her. I still don't understand why she didn't want me to know she was having all those tests, but at least it was a false alarm."

When I felt him straighten his back, I knew the truth and felt the blood drain from my cheeks.

"She lied to me," I said as much to myself as to Tom. My voice was steady in spite of my roiling emotions.

Tom held my hand in both of his and said, quietly, "She doesn't want you to worry. But yes, I guess she lied. She had surgery in June . . ."

"Surgery! She had surgery and didn't let me help her?" I pulled my hand away and started to get up, but Tom put a hand on my shoulder and I stayed in place. "June . . . She told me she went on a retreat."

"Janet, none of this is about you."

"Wha . . ." I felt as if he'd slapped me, and shrugged his arm off my shoulder. He grabbed my hand before I could get up and held on tight.

"I don't mean it that way. I mean that Goldie is . . . was . . . ill, and her decisions about how to manage her illness and her life are hers. She feels pretty strongly about her privacy in this."

Anger gave way to hurt feelings. I was ashamed of them, but there they were. I said, whining more than I liked, "But she told you."

"Only because I saw what she was buying, all the supplements. I saw that the day last May when you introduced us at the Co-op, and again when I ran into her there last Saturday." I realized that Tom, an ethnobotanist, would have known the significance of the supplements as soon as he saw them piled in Goldie's cart. He knew his herbals.

"Why didn't you . . ."

"I was going to tell you on Sunday, remember? But then Goldie showed up. I left hoping she might tell you then."

I fished a tissue from my purse and wiped my eyes and nose. "So tell me now."

"They caught it early and it looks like they got it all. She wasn't lying about that part, she is fine. Or will be. At least that's how it looks."

"Or so she says."

Tom squeezed my hand and chuckled. "So she says, but I think she told me the truth once she got going."

I couldn't believe my probably best friend

hadn't told me her life was in danger. "But . . ."

"Really, Janet, she didn't want you to worry. She told me that you didn't need to know she was sick to be there for her, because you are always there for her, and that she would tell you when she was either cured or incapacitated."

I couldn't think of anything to say to that.

Tom went on, "She's okay with whatever comes, you know." He pulled me into a hug and whispered in my ear, "You have to trust her with this."

I don't think of myself as spiritual, although something in me moves when I look into my dog's or cat's eyes or when I watch a sunrise. But Tom has worked with shamans, and that's how he often refers to Goldie, and something in the warm night air wrapped itself around me, and I knew he was right. I had to trust her with this.

I leaned into Tom and felt the steady rhythm of his breathing for a few minutes, then said, "I need to walk it off." We took the trail around the park along the river, walking in silence at first. Then I asked, "What do you think is going on with Treasures on Earth and their parrots?"

"It's odd, that's for sure. I can't imagine they're into avian worship. Maybe a sort of 'practice,' as in Buddhism? Maybe they do good by fostering homeless birds?"

"I have a bad feeling about it. There's a lot of money in tropical birds." I had known that for years, and in light of all that had happened, I'd been reading up a bit on the Internet. I told Tom about a few recent cases involving exotic birds brought into the U.S., then asked, "Did you find your bird guy?" Tom had said that he would check around for an ornithologist who might identify the feather in the bag Drake pulled out of Twisted Lake.

By that time we had circled the park and were back at Tom's car. As he unlocked my door, he said, "Sort of. Ornithologist at Cornell gave me the name of a parrot specialist at Florida State, so I have a call in to him. Never guess his name."

"Nope, I never will."

"You're no fun."

"Oh, gee, okay, how about Robin?"

Tom grinned. "Not bad. But no. George Crane." He chuckled, then said, "I actually knew a guy named Bass. Fish guy."

"Well," I said, sensing a contest coming on, "I once met an emergency vet named Bassett."

Tom grinned. "I'm hoping to hear back from Dr. Crane on Monday." When he'd settled into the driver's seat he leaned over and kissed me, then said, "And that's enough of all that for the rest of the night, my love." Then he pulled something out of his pocket. "I was going to do this in a more romantic setting, but it's burning a hole in my pocket," he laughed, and pressed a small black velvet-covered box into my hands.

Oh shit. An almost irresistible urge to bolt swallowed me up, but I closed my eyes and held my breath for a few seconds. Tom had been talking about expanding his family. Was this his way of proposing? My thoughts were racing around like a flock of flighty sheep, and that image led naturally to Jay and our sporadic adventures in herding, and that led to a vision of Tom sitting on his couch reading with his dog snuggled under one arm and mine under the other. And that, I thought, was a lovely image.

"Aren't you going to open it?"

I opened my eyes and opened the box.

Twenty-Six

Saturday morning we loaded the kayak onto Tom's van and the dogs into crates in the back and were on our way to Twisted Lake by six thirty. There was a nice breeze but something about the texture of the early sunlight promised serious heat later in the day, so it was good to work the dogs early. A few of Tom's retriever-training friends would be there with their dogs, and Jay would likely be the token herding dog.

We stopped for a traffic light and Tom glanced at me. "So really, you like it? You can exchange . . ."

"I *love* it!" I patted the pendant that lay an inch above my sternum. It was a gold disc, about an inch and a half across, with an Australian Shepherd moving in profile at a trot. "You must be psychic. I've wanted a nice Aussie necklace ever since I got Jay."

"Yeah?" He smiled and drove on. "Glad you like it. Never know about women."

I snorted, and thought about my mixed emotions ever since I opened that box and realized that he was not proposing. How could I feel disappointed when I had been telling myself I didn't want him to up the relationship ante?

Tom went on. "As I started to say the other night, Drake and I are tired of living alone . . ."

It's scary how often the man does that. And now that he had misdirected me with the necklace, he really *was* going to propose. I closed my eyes and held my breath, trying to figure out what I was going to say.

". . . so I'm going to start looking for a puppy this week."

My whole body relaxed and I started to laugh.

"What's funny about that?" Tom looked at me as if I'd lost my mind, which I very nearly had, and then looked back at the road.

"No, not funny. It's great! A puppy! Perfect."

We talked puppies the rest of the way to the lake. When we got there, Collin Lahmeyer was already there, along with three other local members of the Northern Indiana Hunting Retriever Club. This was an unofficial session, and Collin had invited just a handful of dogs and handlers. Tom had told me that everyone here had a dog entered in the test the following week. Besides Drake, there was one more Lab, a yellow bitch named Annie, plus a Flat-coated Retriever and a Golden Retriever I'd never seen before, and Eleanor, a Golden I did know from training at Dog Dayz. As I expected, Jay was the token herding dog, but Collin had told me to bring him along for a swim. Besides, like most Aussies, he's up to just about any sport you ask him to try, and he was a terrific retriever in water and on land.

"Do I have time to go to the island now, before the dogs are out there?"

"Don't see why not," Collin wiped his sunglasses and put them on. "Dogs won't be out there anyway. We're working water and upland retrieves, so no reason to have them on the island at all. Help yourself."

I *can* manage the kayak myself, but not gracefully, so I let the men use the advantage of several extra inches of height to lift it off the car for me and told them that I could take it from there. I got Jay out of his crate and switched his nice collar with license, I.D., rabies, and microchip tags for an old ratty one with just an I.D. I keep that one for wet, muddy outings. "Let's go, Bubby,"

I said, and Jay executed several vertical bounces to look me in the eye.

It took me longer to lug the kayak to the shore and get in it, which I don't do gracefully, than to paddle to the island. I offered Jay a ride, but as usual he preferred to swim alongside. He shook himself on the island's grassy bank while I hauled the kayak out of the water, and we set off to explore.

The island was three or four amoeba-shaped acres in size. Toward the middle, a small rise in the ground pretended to be a hill but didn't quite make it. There was only one real tree standing, a ghostly old sycamore that from a distance appeared to be dead. Up close, I could see that a few branches had live leaves, but the tree probably wasn't long for this world. Most of the ground was covered with thick brush and skinny saplings, thigh-high grasses and wildflowers. Everything had that beat-up look of late summer, except for the purple asters and ironweed and gold-petaled black-eyed Susans. A few saplings, mostly maples as far as I could tell, were taking hold, but only a couple of them even reached my chin. The remains of several good-sized trees lay rotting among the herbaceous plants. Something must have happened out here to strip the place of trees. Wind? A tornado? It wouldn't have been recently. I made a mental note to ask Collin.

I looked back at the main shore, trying to locate the spot where I had stood with my camera the previous Sunday. If I could see where I was when Drake swam out here, I might be able to figure out where he found the bag, or the general area at least. I knew I had been about halfway between the little peninsula where Collin had stood with his shotgun and the short beach where Tom had waited with Drake. And I knew I had been near a beech tree, because I had used its smooth trunk to block the sun for some shots.

I spotted the tree on the shore opposite me and thought about Drake's trajectory through the water and then on the island. Jay was rustling around in the brush, lifting his head every minute or so to check my whereabouts. I walked to a spot by the water that seemed about right for Drake's line of travel the previous week, and I thought about how he had all but disappeared into the grass and weeds. Slowly I made my way in that general direction.

My nose was starting to run, probably from mold spores on the rotting vegetation, and I reached into my pocket for a tissue. My fingers found something else, and I pulled out a business card. Anderson Billings' business card. I must have worn these jeans to the final meeting of my photography class. I flashed on an image of Anderson handing me his card when I asked where I could see more of his photos, and that numbing sense of loss wrapped itself around me again. I was getting very tired of losing friends.

I looked at the image on the card, a bluebird in flight, and reached for my cell phone. What had Anderson said? "There's a bird?" Something like that. I pulled up his voice message and listened again, focusing on the important parts. "Janet, something funny is going on out here. On the little island, I mean. I went over there, spent maybe twenty minutes . . . I'm leaving here now, . . . but I could swing by your place or, you know, somewhere we could meet in, say, half an hour?"

I stopped the recording and thought about his words as I walked, making my way west between the tangled vegetation and the water. Anderson must have been on his way if he wanted to meet me in thirty minutes. So how could he have drowned? And why were he and his canoe found in the lake while his camera was in his car? It just made no sense. I realized that Detective Jo Stevens hadn't returned my call, and I hadn't tried to reach her again. I needed to do that when I finished here.

I played the message again and focused on the next part. "I'll try you again when I get to Coliseum." Meaning Coliseum Boulevard. "Janet, there's a bird . . ." Did I hear a thump this time? I played it again, but I couldn't be sure. Why was the message cut off like that? I wondered, and then my own reveries were cut off when Jay began a deep rumbling growl.

TWENTY-SEVEN

Jay stood in an area of low grass between me and a stand of wild roses. He had drawn himself up tall and rigid and a deep low growl filled the air around us. His eyes were locked onto the far bank of the lake, or perhaps the fence just beyond it that separated Heron Acres from the Treasures on Earth Spiritual Renewal Center spread. Jay took several steps forward and growled again. His hair stood out all over his body as if he'd taken on an electrical charge.

I walked to my dog and knelt beside him. "What is it, Bubby?" He turned his head and slurped my face, then turned back to whatever he saw or heard, his nose raised slightly and twitching. A shiver went up my arms, but I said, "Whatever it is, it's a long way away, right, Bub?" I was talking to myself as much as to my dog, but I scratched behind his ear, then stood up and continued walking. Jay came with me and I asked him, "What did you see? A fox or something?" He stayed between me and the lake, glancing across the water every few seconds, but finally dropped his guard a few minutes later. I didn't realize how tense my own shoulders were until Jay went back to sniffing around the brush and my muscles relaxed.

We made our way slowly around the perimeter of the island, zigzagging between the low grass along the shoreline and the shrubs, grasses, and weeds toward the interior. There were remarkably few signs of human visitors — an old blue sweatshirt, a couple of empty beer bottles, a broken fishing pole. Jay chased up a rabbit. First I wondered how in the world it got out there, and then I hoped it wasn't alone. *Alone isn't good. Alone is lonely.* Just as I was feeling very sorry for the rabbit, I caught myself and squeezed out a different line of thought. *Alone is independent. Alone is free.* I watched Jay nosing through some tangled bittersweet vines and said out loud, "I'm not alone." Jay raised his head and looked at me, tongue hanging out the side of his mouth. "I have you and Leo."

A shotgun blast made me jump, even though I knew they were using blanks for the training session. It was followed by a loud squawk that seemed to come from the old sycamore on the island. Crow? It didn't sound like a crow. I couldn't see anything at that distance. I couldn't see the mainland where the dogs and their handlers were, either. Too much island in the way and even without trees, the shrubs and lower-growing plants blocked my view.

Jay went back to his exploration, and I continued walking. More blasts followed at irregular intervals, but I didn't hear any more squawks, just the occasional tweet of a sparrow and the complaints of a very vocal blue jay. My own blue Jay and I walked on until I could finally see the action. A dog was swimming away from the shore, a wake fanning out behind, but the shadows cast by the trees offshore made it impossible to see who it was. It took me a moment, but I finally spotted the training bumper bobbing in the murky water. Jay saw it, too, and made a move to go after it. "Jay, down," I said. He hesitated, but lay down and watched. As the dog emerged from the shadows, the sun hit her golden head and I was pretty sure it was sweet Eleanor, the Golden Retriever I knew from doggy school. She snatched her "bird" and turned back toward the far shore.

I squinted into the sun and looked at the

staging area for the practice retrieves. Something was going on over there. I tried to make out what all the movement was behind Rhonda Lake, Eleanor's owner. There seemed to be two people, one of them with a television camera on his shoulder, trying to get close to the water. Then a man intercepted them, arms outstretched to form a barricade to keep them from getting too close to Rhonda and her dog's landing spot. Collin Lahmeyer. His long-legged stride was impossible to mistake. I wondered what that was all about, but turned my attention back to Eleanor for the moment. She was a strong swimmer, and she burst out of the water and shook herself. "Look at her shimmer," I said to no one in particular, and then I started to laugh at the memory of Jay "shimmering" his lovely white hair all over Neil Young's expensive dark slacks.

We were in sight of the kayak when Jay let out a yip and dove into a stand of Queen Anne's lace and asters, his nub wagging a hundred miles an hour. I started to follow, caught my foot in a tangle of bindweed vines, and stumbled forward several giant steps, dragging the broken vine behind me. "Shit!" I reached down to unwrap the vine from my foot and snatched my hand back, swearing again. My shoelace was covered with burrs. They weren't yet dried to the razor sharpness they would take on later in the fall, but they were nasty enough.

Jay barked again. "Quiet!" I said, looking up from the tangle around my feet to see what he was up to. He's not a silly barker, and I've learned to pay attention when he sounds off. He let out a muffled brffff and turned to look at me, as if to say, "That wasn't a bark, okay?" and then he stuck his head back into the brush and began pulling at something.

"Hang on," I said, and bent to unwind the rest of the bindweed from my foot. Jay looked at me and whined, which I understood to mean, "But really, you gotta see this!"

When I was free, I stepped more carefully through the nest of intertwined vines and tall grass, mumbling, "Better not be a dead rodent." Jay has a knack for finding dead squirrels and chipmunks, the rottener, the better. But when I reached my dog and looked at the ground in front of him, I sucked in my breath.

A pile of crimson feathers with a few turquoise ones mixed in lay at the base of a wild rose bush. What made me hold the air in my lungs was that most of the feathers were still attached to a body. A lifeless eye gazed back at me. The short crimson feathers on the bird's head stood out in haphazard directions, rather like a punk rocker with a red hot dye job. The beak hung slightly open, as if its owner had been surprised by death. A curved beak. Parrot. I thought of Ava, Persephone Swann's lovely bird. But this was not, I thought, the same species. Despite having half its breast gone, I could see that it had been a slightly smaller bird, and I didn't recall Ava, or whatever he was called now, having yellow feathers in his tail, nor the stunning splashes of turquoise on his back that this little creature had.

Jay made a move toward the bird but I blocked him with my arm and whispered, "Down." He sank to the ground beside me, head thrust forward and nose twitching. I fished a plastic bag out of my pocket, inserted my hand, and started to reach for the bird when another squawk assaulted my ear drums. "What the . . . ?"

I stood and scanned the island, trying to locate the source of the racket. I'm not a real birder, but I do photograph enough birds and other critters in the wild to be familiar with most of the local voices, and this did not sound like any I knew. In fact, if I had to guess, I'd say it sounded like a parrot. *That's just nuts,* I thought, and then glanced at the little body at my feet. *Parrots?* As I continued to scan the island, and particularly the old sycamore, I fast forwarded through the past week. *Parrots,* I thought again, but this time I wasn't asking. Something weird was going on involving parrots. First, the red feather in the bag that Drake found on the island. *This* island. Then there was Ava, Persephone Swann's lovely "Amazon parrot," which I had yet to identify more precisely. And Giselle's comment about becoming a "parrot guardian," which I took to mean foster home. Was Regis Moneypenny running a parrot rescue program though Treasures on Earth? The conversation with Di Holman about her dog Lennen's discoveries of smuggled birds ran through my mind. Persephone's insistence that I not photograph her parrot. Anderson Billings' message had said, "Janet, there's a bird . . . ," followed by that thump and then a terrible silence.

A flick of red against the sky pulled me out of my dark thoughts and I watched a bird fly toward me from the sycamore. Details and color were lost to the bright cloud behind it, but it seemed to be about the size of a crow with a longer tail. As it closed on us, the colors blossomed. This was no crow. It was a parrot, vivid scarlet with flashes of gold and turquoise. It flew directly over us, low enough that I could hear air moving through its flight feathers, then circled out over the water and back to the semi-cover of the tree. "Janet, there's a bird . . ." Had this been what Anderson meant? A parrot?

I looked at the dead bird again and decided to leave it where it was for Jo Stevens. To make it easier to find, I tied my plastic bag to a chin-high clump of ironweed to my right and another to a shrub to my left. *What if something messes with it?* There were plenty of crows and other scavengers on the island that might be tempted. At first I couldn't think of anything to cover it up without messing up the site, but then the image of an old sweatshirt came back to me. I thought it was pretty close to where I'd left the kayak. I pulled my phone from my pocket and dialed Jo's number while I ran for the sweatshirt, Jay bouncing at my side. The call hadn't gone through by the time I got to the shirt, and I checked my phone. No bars. "Crap!" I shoved it back in my pocket, grabbed the shirt, and scurried back to the dead parrot. I debated for a moment, then decided that draping the shirt over the body wouldn't hurt much and might keep scavengers away for a few hours. Before I did that, I took a couple of photos with my cell. *Better than nothing,* I thought. I covered the bird, weighting the shirt edges with rocks.

"Let's go," I said. "Time to get off this island and get some help, Bub."

Twenty-Eight

The training session had wrapped up by the time Jay and I got back to the mainland, where wet-and-muddy owners were throwing sticks and balls for their wet-and-muddy dogs to retrieve. Jay flicked his gaze from them to me to them and whined. "Go," I said, gesturing toward the furry mayhem, and he was off. I pulled Bill's kayak well out of the water and joined Tom and Rhonda and a woman I didn't recognize.

"This is my frie . . . whoa!" Rhonda lurched into me as two dripping Golden Retrievers tugging at opposite ends of a float toy ran into the backs of her knees. "Hey, you two!"

The dogs stopped cavorting and looked at her, still holding onto the toy. The other woman took the middle of the length of rope between the two plastic end grips in her hand and said "Out" very softly. The dogs let go, attesting to the many hours of training they'd had. Every muscle in their bodies spoke to their hope that she'd fling the thing back into the water so they could do it all again.

"Who's this handsome guy?" I asked, looking at the Golden I didn't know.

"This is Pilot," the woman said, wiping her hand on her jeans and holding it out to me. "Stephanie."

"Janet."

She turned back to the dogs and pitched the toy into the water, and they were off.

Rhonda joined in. "We've been planning a visit for ages and finally have a good excuse." She went on to explain that they had met at the Golden Retriever National Specialty Show a couple of years earlier and had stayed in touch ever since. Now Stephanie and Pilot were visiting for a few days before all four of them headed off together for this year's Nationals in St. Louis.

"Oh, so you don't live here?" I asked.

"New Jersey."

We chatted another minute or so, but I was antsy to tell Tom about the parrots, so I excused myself as soon as was marginally polite. As I walked toward Tom I pulled my phone out and dialed Jo Stevens' number again, expecting to get her voice mail. When she answered in person, I stopped walking and told her what I'd seen. She said she'd be there in half an hour and asked whether there was a boat available to get to the island. I told her yes, hoping Collin's boat was still there but figuring Jo could take the kayak and I could swim if necessary.

When I told Tom I'd found a dead parrot and had seen a live one on the island, he stopped mid-stick-toss and stared at me. Jay bounced up and down as if to say, "Throw it! Throw it!" and Drake sidled over and whacked his tail over and over into the side of my knee.

"Don't Labs have nerves in their tails?" I asked, moving away from Drake and rubbing my knee joint. "Jeez, it's like a billy club!" I took the sticks from Tom's hands and threw them into the lake for Jay and Drake, then said, "You think that feather, you know, in the bag, you think that might have come from the dead bird?"

"Wow."

"Is that yes?"

"Did you have your camera with you?" Tom asked.

"In the car. But look at this." I flipped my phone open and showed him the pictures I had taken of the dead bird. They were dark and grainy, but he could see enough.

"Get your camera. Take some decent

photos of those birds and we can send them to the guy in Florida." He called the dogs to him. "In fact, we can probably I.D. them ourselves from photos and confirm with him."

He walked with me to the road and pulled his x-pen out of his van while I got my camera. "We'll put the dogs in here and take Collin's boat to the island."

"Collin's boat is here?"

"Yeah." He gestured toward the bank, but I couldn't see anything but grass and weeds from where we stood.

"We should wait for Jo."

"She can use your kayak, or I'll come back for her with the bass boat." He set the x-pen up in the shade, filled a water bowl and set it inside, ushered the dogs through the parted sections, and clipped it closed. Jay and Drake sprawled in the grass, dripping and grinning as only tired, mucky dogs can.

I checked my watch. "Tom, it's been twenty minutes since I called. She'll be here before we even get to the island. Let's just wait for her."

He started to say something, then shifted his gaze from me to something behind me. "Yeah, she will."

I turned.

"Hiya." Jo wore tan chinos and a short-sleeved white shirt. Her clothing did not say "cop," but something about her screamed, "Do not mess with me." When she reached us, she pulled her sunglasses off and wiped them, then gestured behind her. "Hutch'll catch up. He's changing his shoes." Hutch was Deputy Homer Hutchinson, Jo's partner. Jo put her glasses back on and grinned at me, "He's upgrading his wardrobe and doesn't want to go wading in his new shoes."

We resumed walking and the boat came into sight. "How many of us can that boat take?" I asked, eyeing a not huge rowboat pulled half out of the water and tied by a very long line to a small pin oak. I didn't wait for an answer. "I'll meet you there," I said, and headed down the beach to the kayak. The Goldens were still playing, and Pilot ran to me with two tennis balls sticking out of his mouth, did a little happy dance, and ran toward the water with Eleanor in hot pursuit.

I got to the island before Tom and the two detectives, so I checked my camera settings and scanned the old sycamore for signs of the parrot, using the telephoto lens for a closer look. At first, I saw nothing. Then a flash of scarlet caught my eye, but I lost it as quickly as I'd seen it and had to pan back and forth very slowly a few times before I found it again. And there he, or she, was. Definitely a parrot, and almost as definitely the one I had seen earlier. How many parrots could there be on this little lake island in northern Indiana? Then again, I'd seen or heard about more parrots in northern Indiana in the past few days than I would have thought possible, so who knew? I brought the image in as close as I could and took several shots, then shifted my position and took a few more. The landing party had arrived and were tramping toward me, so I recapped my lens and made a mental note to try to get closer to the tree after the others left.

Twenty-Nine

The makeshift cover I'd made with the old sweatshirt was still in place, and when I pulled the shirt away, the dead parrot didn't appear to have been touched or moved.

"Where'd that shirt come from?" asked Hutch.

"Oh, uh, over there somewhere." I gestured vaguely.

He and Jo exchanged a look I couldn't read and Hutchinson pulled a plastic bag from his fanny pack and put the shirt in it, then wrote something on the bag.

"Never occurred to me that it was connected." I was mildly embarrassed, although I wasn't sure why I should be. "Uh, there were, are, a couple of empty bottles over there where the shirt was. I did think it odd . . ." I looked at Jo but she seemed more interested in the dead bird than in my thoughts. "I could probably find them if you think they're, you know, if you want me to."

"You think this is the bird that feather came from?" Jo looked at Tom.

"No idea. I'm a plant guy." He grinned, but she didn't get the joke, so he told her about the parrot specialist in Florida. "Hoping he'll call here, or there will be a message from him when I get home."

"Janet, can you get some photos before we move this bird?" She laid a ballpoint pen near the bird for scale.

I set the date marker to "on" and took several close-ups, then moved away to get a view of the area where I had found the bird. I was walking back toward them when that now-familiar sky-ripping squawk rang out from the lone island tree. We all turned that way. The little parrot was in full view, standing far out on a branch. As if in slow motion he unfolded his wings and glided into open air, seeming to move slowly at first, then swooping our way like a scarlet missile. He rocketed toward Tom and Jo where they hovered over the little body on the ground. They both raised their arms and ducked, but he cleared them by ten or twelve feet, then disappeared toward Moneypenny's place.

"Holy . . . ," said Jo.

"Wow!" said Tom.

"Holy wow is right," I said, still staring

after the bird.

"Is it attacking?" asked Hutch.

Jo looked at the bird at her feet and said, "If I had to guess, I'd say it's protecting a friend."

"Guess I won't be getting any more shots of him, or her, today," I said, and explained that I had hoped to take some photos for identification purposes.

Jo and Hutch pondered the best way to pick up the corpse, which wasn't in great shape, and Tom and I set out to look for the beer bottles.

"Don't touch them," Jo reminded us. Or me, probably.

I more or less remembered where I had landed the kayak on my earlier trip, so we started there and walked in the direction Jay and I had taken. Although I wanted to find the bottles, I couldn't help watching the sky and checking the tree every minute or so. A movement on the shore toward Treasures on Earth caught my eye, but Tom distracted me with a "There they are!" and when I turned to look across the water again, whatever it was had vanished.

"What?" Tom asked.

"Thought I saw something. I think Jo was right."

"Widowed bird?" he asked.

I looked at him to see if he was trying to be funny, but knew right away that he wasn't. "Something like that." I heaved a big sigh, then turned toward the beer bottles and took a few photos, figuring Jo was going to want them.

"Nice out here," said Tom, looking around. "I wonder what happened to the trees."

"I don't know. Storm? Tornado?"

He gestured toward a big trunk partially hidden in the tall grass. "Not that one."

He was right. I hadn't noticed before, but the tree had been cut down, not broken. I started to say something when Tom jerked his head around and signaled me to be quiet. He was staring across the water toward the fence that separated Heron Acres from Treasures on Earth. Moneypenny's place.

"What?" I whispered.

Softly he said, "I thought I saw someone over there. I heard voices."

"Not Jo and Hutchinson?" I asked, nodding toward the two detectives, who were crunching their way toward us through a pile of dry sticks.

"Maybe. But I'm sure I saw someone."

"So?" Hutch was swatting bugs away with one hand and picking little green burrs off his slacks with the other. "Can we just do this and get back to civilization?"

Tom led them to the bottles. When I said I had already taken pictures, Hutch turned a plastic bag inside out, picked up a bottle, and pulled the plastic up around it. The maneuver was so familiar in an earthier, doggier context that the image of it broke through my tension and I started to laugh.

"What?" Hutch wiped at his face with his arm.

"Nothing." I stopped myself, but then he did it again with the other bottle and my lips blew an involuntary raspberry that morphed into one of those squeal-laughs. Even as I cracked up, I knew I was laughing harder than I should be but I couldn't stop myself, and then Tom watched Hutchinson finish bagging the second bottle and he started to laugh. Before long we were completely out of control, and the two detectives were staring at us as if we might need straight jackets. When we finally seemed to be recovering our senses, Jo looked at Hutch and they shrugged at each other, and it took everything I had not to relapse into more squealing and giggling.

Hutch slapped at his own cheek and said, "I'm outta here."

Tom mock punched my arm and then led

Jo and Hutch back to the boat. Hutch stooped to pick something up on the shore — the dead bird, I supposed — and I turned back to the kayak. As I started to push off, something made me turn to look again at a stand of shrubs near the old sycamore. The sun was in my eyes and at first I didn't know what I was looking at, but then I made out a man standing just in front of the shrubs. A big man, with light-colored hair lifting in the breeze — blonde, or maybe gray. I sat very still as the kayak drifted into the lake, paddle poised but quiet in my hands. I felt a chill in my cheeks and relief that I was on the lake and putting deep water between him and me.

I tried to call to Tom and the others, but couldn't make my voice work. In any case, they were out of sight and probably wouldn't hear me. I dipped my paddle into the lake and turned the kayak away from the island, away from the man in the shadows. I kept paddling, gaining some speed, then turned for another look. He stood in the open now, in the light. As I watched, he raised his hands and held them as if he were holding something. I saw his finger move up, down, up, and I got it. An imaginary camera. I went back to paddling, then looked one last time. Another gesture. He held his hand up, index finger pointed at me, and his thumb flicked down and up. Then he raised his finger to his lips and pursed them as if blowing.

My first instinct was to get out of there as quickly as I could, but that impulse immediately gave way to rage. Not stupid rage. Not the kind that would have sent me back to the island to find out what the hell was wrong with the guy. I have been known to do reckless things like that, but something about the guy's body language scared the recklessness out of me. I pulled my camera from where I had stashed it in the cockpit and slipped the strap around my neck. I knew the jerk wasn't going to pose for me and I wouldn't have time for manual settings, so I flipped on the auto setting for athletic action, hoping the camera would do the work for me. I dipped my paddle just enough to turn the kayak parallel to the shore and laid it across the cockpit. He was still there, closer now to the water, and he seemed to be dragging something behind him. A rubber raft, maybe? I raised the camera and clicked off a series of shots. The first couple caught him full on, but his reaction time was fast and he turned away, arm up to hide his face. "Too late, you son of a bitch," I said. I stowed my camera again and then I got out of there as quickly as I could.

Thirty

Jo and Hutch had almost reached their car when I caught up with them. After my adrenaline-driven paddle back from the island and run across the field to catch up, I could hardly speak, but I finally managed to tell them about the man on the island and his bizarre gestures. I'd had the presence of mind to grab my camera, and I showed them the images, but they were too small for any detail other than his general build and clothing, and the fact that I had not imagined him. As I told the story, though, I started to feel a little silly, and said, "Maybe he was just trying to be funny?"

Jo gave me her "have you lost your mind" look and gestured at my camera. "Email those to me as soon as you get home." She was already moving back toward the boat. Hutch was ahead of her and looked like he was planning to rip the guy's head off if he caught up with him. Hutch and I had not gotten off to a great start, but he had grown very fond of Jay and I was sure he'd shoot anyone who threatened a hair on his furry body. Jo stopped, turned toward me, and said, "Go home, Janet. Now." She turned and ran after her partner, phone to her ear, but paused and said something to Tom as she passed him.

I bent over with my hands on my knees, still catching my breath and wondering if I was going to be sick. It seemed as if I stood that way for an hour, but it couldn't have been more than a few seconds before I felt Tom's hands on my shoulders.

"Janet?"

"Okay. I'm okay." I collected my camera from where I had set it on the grass and stood up. "Just that post-adrenaline barfy feeling."

"What the hell?" Tom asked. "Jo told me to take you home. What happened?" I told him, and he started to turn toward the lake, as if to follow the deputies.

"Tom, Jo told me to go home." I knew she was concerned for my safety, but I didn't want to admit that out loud. Instead, I said, "I took some photos of the guy. She wants me to send them to her."

Tom turned toward me, hesitated a moment, then said, "Okay, let's go." Ten minutes later we had the kayak, x-pen, and dogs loaded. I took a last look across the field and lake but other than the bass boat resting on the island's shore, I couldn't see any activity out there. Jo and Hutch must have walked to the far side, beyond the sprawl of bushes.

By the time we turned onto Coldwater Road and headed toward town, the nausea had passed. It was replaced by a more considered fear, and various parts of my body began to tremble, first my stomach, then my hands, then my lower lip. *Aw, shit, Janet, don't start crying,* I thought. If I were honest I'd have to admit that I felt safer with Tom there beside me, but I didn't see any need to say so, especially with tears. I tried to force myself to breathe deeply, but my stupid nose sniffed without my wanting it to.

Tom reached over and took my hand but remained quiet for a few minutes. Then he asked, "What else happened out there?"

I had told him a man was out there, but had not told him about the pistol gesture. I finished up the story just as we turned onto Coliseum. "I think you should stay with me until Jo finds that guy."

"What are you talking about?"

"I don't think you should be home, especially alone. Come to my house."

I made a rude noise. "He was just a nut."

"My point exactly."

"I need to go see Mom. Haven't been there since Tuesday."

"Love to see your mom."

"I need to change."

He squeezed my hand and turned his gaze from the road ahead for a quick ogle. "Don't change, Janet. You're perfect as you are." I made another rude noise and he checked out my mucky clothes and grinned. "Okay, on second thought . . ."

My focus was drifting, and unlike my camera lens, my brain isn't easy to twist into clarity. It works at times more like a fast-motion auto setting, readjusting constantly, but it's not nearly so clever as my camera at keeping a single subject in focus. This was one of those times, and my thoughts hiphopped back and forth from my mother's losing battle with Alzheimer's to the weirdo on the island to Anderson Billings' odd message to the pleasure of watching a group of frolicking dogs to the weirdness of seeing parrots by a lake in northern Indiana.

"I think I need Ritalin or something."

"Why is that?"

"What the hell do you think is going on

out there?"

Tom chuckled. "Wow. Can't even focus on not being able to focus, huh?"

"It's all interconnected. I'm sure of it now. What the heck could Moneypenny's group be up to? I mean, parrots?" We had just pulled into my driveway. "We'll have to leave the dogs here while we visit Mom. Too hot in the car."

Tom was shaking his head before I finished the question. "We don't know who that creep was or what he might know about you, so I think my place is a better bet." He parked in the shade, rolled down all the windows, popped the back of his van open, and opened his door. "Let's just grab what you need to take the boys to my place. They'll be safer, and you can clean up there."

My thoughts kept bouncing around while I grabbed some clean clothes and my laptop, and took five minutes to refresh the water in the five vases and remove a few droopy blossoms. When we were back in the car I said, "If someone is out to get me and knows that much, then they know about you, too."

Tom frowned. "Maybe."

"I'm not leaving Leo here alone."

"Of course not!" Tom's a big fan of my

brave little cat.

"Let's leave the three musketeers with Bill and Norm while we visit Mom. If it isn't safe enough for me . . . Unless you don't want to g . . ." He held up a hand and stopped me before I finished the last word.

I made the call and Norm was delighted to have "the boys" for a couple of hours. I ran back in and got Leo, and to sweeten the deal, we swung by the Cookie Cottage and got a mixed box. Norm was a sucker for the animals, and Bill was a sucker for cookies. It runs in the family, but I managed to control my white-chocolate-macadamia lust, breaking off a smallish piece and giving the rest of the yummilicious thing to Tom.

THIRTY-ONE

Shadetree Retirement Home looked like I remembered Elmhurst High School on prom night. The lobby was decked out with crepe paper streamers and helium balloons, and big band music filled the air.

"Wow!" I said as we approached the door to the dining cum recreational event room. The music was much louder here, and, it turned out, was live. The singer appeared to be about sixteen, but he was doing a reasonable cover of the old Bing Crosby classic, "Swinging on a Star." I knew it from *Going My Way,* one of my mother's favorite old movies. The crepe-paper-and-balloon theme was repeated here, with strings of tiny white lights making everything sparkle, including more than one pair of elderly eyes. Several couples were dancing, while others occupied chairs and a few wheelchairs around the perimeter of the room. One or two appeared to be asleep. A long table held finger food and a punch bowl.

Jade Templeton waved and grinned from the row of chairs to my right, where she was talking to a resident who didn't seem to be as happy as the others were. I looked around for my mother and finally spotted her on the far side of the room, dancing with a white-haired man in white slacks and shirt and a startling purple jacket. I elbowed Tom and pointed, and he grinned.

The band struck up a new number, an instrumental, and Tom leaned toward my ear and said, "In the Mood."

I couldn't stifle a giggle. "Not here, Tom. I mean, most of them won't remember by tomorrow, but still . . ."

"The song, Janet, the song, although . . ." He chuckled as he draped his arm across my shoulder and steered us toward the punch bowl, then spoke low into my ear. "How long did you say we have to stay?"

I handed him a cup of what appeared to be sherbet-and-ginger-ale and said, "Here, let me punch you."

A short fellow I had seen before at Shadetree was reaching for the ladle, and Tom passed his cup to the man. Then he bowed slightly and gestured toward the dance floor. "Shall we dance, m'dear?"

"Oh, I, uh . . ." *Holy cow, I really am at the*

prom, I thought, recalling that less-than-stellar event of my teenhood. I glanced down at my wide-soled running shoes, fluorescent-green anklets, and denim capris. "I don't know, Tom. I forgot my dancing slippers and frock."

He just grinned at me and held out his hand.

"Oh, why not," I said, and we joined the other dancers just as the tune ended. I tried to turn back but the vocalist said, "Now we're going to slow it down a bit, so grab your sweetheart," and Tom did just that.

He pulled me close and I was once again astonished at how easily our bodies fit together. A reasonable rendition of "Unforgettable" coiled like audible smoke around me. I closed my eyes and let everything go except the movement, the music, and the man. When the music stopped, we just stood like that for a moment. Then the band launched into "Rock Around the Clock" and broke the spell. I declined to jitterbug in my clodhoppers, so we turned back toward the punch bowl.

Neil Young was standing with an elderly woman in a lovely floor-length pink gown and firmly sprayed blue hair. He was speaking to her but looking at me. Tom said, "My, your friend gets around, doesn't he?" He sounded almost as annoyed to see Neil as I was.

"Let's go see Mom," I said, changing course and circling the dance floor.

She had disappeared.

"Back to the punch bowl," said Tom, nodding in that direction. My mother was standing by the table, loading finger food onto a little paper plate. The woman in pink had vanished and Neil was beside my mother, smiling his high-school-heart-throb smile. He leaned in to say something. By the time we got there, she was giggling.

Neil nodded at me. "Janet," he said, and held his hand out to Tom. "Neil Young."

"Tom Saunders."

I couldn't tell whether they were squeezing the feeling out of each other's hands, but the grip seemed to last a long time. Or maybe time was just losing its shape and oozing around like a Salvador Dali clock. They reminded me of a pair of male dogs posturing. The body language was right, both standing as tall as they could. And the direct stare. I almost looked around for a chair to set over one if a fight broke out. I saw Marietta Santini do that once at Dog Dayz when a couple of dogs got into a squabble. She pinned one down with the rungs under the chair while somebody pulled the other dog away. I watched the men's faces, hoping one of them would give in and feeling a little tremor of hope that it would not be Tom.

It wasn't. Neil retrieved his hand and turned toward me. "So what are you doing here, Janet?"

"Visiting my mother." I nodded toward Mom, who was busy loading her plate with olives. I was sure I had told him she was living at Shadetree. "What are *you* doing here?"

"I came to see my aunt."

Something about that bothered me, but I couldn't think what, so I focused on my mother. I touched her arm and said, "How you doing, Mom?"

Her mind might be flickering on and off, but her reflexes still work. She let out a screech that rattled my earrings and whacked at me with her paper plate, launching a dozen olives into the air. One of them hit Neil square in the silk hankie and another lodged in my hair.

"Ma! Calm down!" I made a move toward her and she backed into the table.

"Get away from me! I don't know you!" She sidled along the edge of the table, then looked blankly at Tom and spoke to Neil. "Do you know this person?"

I'd like to say I was getting numb to the impact of having my mother react as if I were an axe murderer, but I'm not sure that will ever be true. My heart was pounding in my ears and my eyes stung. I felt strong hands moving me a step away from the direction my mother was headed and I heard Jade Templeton's soothing contralto. "It's okay, Janet. I've got her." And she did. She put her arm around Mom's shoulders and said, "Mrs. Bruce, let's go sit down for a minute, okay?"

Mom looked sideways at Jade and pursed her lips and stiffened her backbone, but she let herself be led to a chair by the wall. A young woman who looked to be about sixteen appeared with a whisk broom, dust pan, and towel, so the rest of us moved out of her way. Tom extricated an olive from my frizzy hair. "You okay?"

"I'm great."

Neil folded his olived handkerchief and put it in a pants pocket. "Sorry, Janet. That's tough. How long has she been like that?"

"A while. She's been here since May, but it started, I don't know, a year or so . . ." My voice petered out under the weight of recent events and I changed the subject. "Neil, what is going on at that Treasures on Earth place?"

Tom cleared his throat and a look like he had been slapped moved across Neil's face, but he recovered almost before I saw it. "What do you mean?"

"Janet, maybe this isn't . . ." Tom started, but I cut him off.

"The parrots, for one thing, Neil. What's with the parrots?" I heard my volume rising but couldn't seem to reach the controls. "You people all have parrots, Neil. What's up with that?"

Neil took a step back and looked around, but no one seemed to be paying any attention. That's one advantage to raising your voice in a nursing home, I supposed. Half the residents can't hear you.

"Janet," said Tom, gripping my elbow and trying to turn me toward the exit. I tried to pull away but he tightened his grip and whispered, "Janet! Not here, not now."

I craned my neck for a last look at Neil, but the good doctor had already bolted for the other door, so I went with Tom, shrugging him off my arm when we got to the building exit. I pointed toward the other side of the parking lot. Neil was unlocking a car. Black. Beetle-like. "Tom, is that the car we saw on Tappen Road last week?"

"Probably not. Come on, Janet, why would your doctor friend . . ."

That hit me all wrong and I snapped, "What, you don't still know any women you knew in school?"

"That's not what I meant, and you know it. But why would Neil be skulking down Tappen Road like that? There are lots of black cars." We watched Neil pull onto South Anthony and Tom said, "I don't even know what that is."

"You didn't know what the one on Tappen Road was, either."

We sat in the car without speaking for a long couple of minutes, but glaring through the windshield so hard I half expected it to crack. Tom broke the silence.

"Come on, let's take Leo to my place and then take the dogs for a walk. Then we can all go to Zesto's for a cone. I'll save some for Leo even."

I was a little steamed that he thought he could distract me with ice cream. I was more steamed at myself that he was right.

Thirty-Two

We had planned to sleep in Sunday morning for once, but a bright flash followed by a roar that sounded like a mountain being dragged across the roof landed two dogs on us when there was just enough light to see shapes in the room. One of those shapes was Leo. He was hunkered down on Tom's dresser.

"Drake, you big weenie," said Tom, but he wrapped his trembling dog in a securing arm and pulled him in close. He lay his chin on top of Drake's head and grinned at me. "He doesn't even flinch when we're outdoors in a storm. I think it's an excuse."

Jay wasn't bothered by storms, but he knew an opportunity when he saw one. He had squeezed in between Drake and me and rolled against me into belly-rub position. Of course, I obliged.

An hour later the storm had passed and Tom's backyard radiated summer scents of wet grass, mulch, and a chorus of flowers. I breathed it all in so deeply that I could almost taste the roses, lavender, flowering tobacco, sweet alyssum, and more that fringed the back of Tom's house. Jay and Drake were getting noses full, too, although they were more interested in following some sort of track across the grass and under the fence.

A flash of red in the air made me jerk my head around. The image of a scarlet parrot flashed through my mind, but was quickly replaced by the male cardinal that had landed on a feeder in the neighbor's yard.

"Open the door, please, ma'am." Tom was inside the sliding screen holding a tray with two steaming mugs and two plates bearing whatever he'd been heating in the oven. More inspiring morning scents hit me when I liberated him. Coffee, cinnamon, and yeast.

"You baked cinnamon rolls?"

"Sure," he said, pulling a kitchen towel out of his pocket to dry the table and chairs. "Was up at four mixing and kneading and working my fingers to the bo . . ."

"Frozen, right?"

He held my chair out for me and said, "Refrigerated."

When we had finished eating, Tom took

the dishes in and brought more coffee and I cranked up my laptop. We had already emailed my photos of the three parrots — Persephone Swann's lovely Ava, the dead bird on the island, and the live one — to George Crane, the ornithologist Tom had contacted. We were both eager to see what he had to say, but first I checked my own emails for anything critical, then passed my computer to Tom. As he signed into his account, he said, "It's too soon to expect anything, you know. His auto reply said he was gone for the weekend."

Jay and Drake raced onto the deck, a floppy flyer in one mouth and a tennis ball in the other. Dogs and toys were all sopping wet, mucky, and very close. "Not now, guys! Off! Off!" I waved them away, curling my legs up into my chair to keep from getting slimed. They looked so disappointed in me that I almost caved in, but the sound of Tom's phone saved me from having to do a load of laundry before I could leave.

Tom got up to answer the phone and handed me my laptop. "You could leave more clothes here, you know, in case of wet dog attacks," he said, touching my shoulder and grinning.

"Stop that," I said.

"Stop what?"

"Reading my mind."

He was still laughing when he shut the door behind him.

I looked at the dogs. They were still on the deck, Jay lying in sphinx position with the floppy on his paws, Drake sitting, his lip bubbled out where it was caught between tennis ball and tooth. "He does, you know. He reads our minds," I said. They wagged their tails in agreement.

The door slid open behind me and Tom said, "Janet, come here. Bring your computer." When I turned I saw that he was gesturing for me to hurry, and seemed very excited. "Hang on," he said into his phone, and pressed the mouthpiece against his shoulder. "Set it up and open my email again. Here." He re-entered his password and opened his account, then spoke in the phone again. "Okay, downloading now."

There was an email with photos attached, and he opened the first one. It could have been a portrait of Ava, I thought, although I'd have to see the photos side by side to be sure. The lovely creature was perched on the shoulder of a grinning, bare-chested child with the bowl haircut characteristic of Amazonian Indians. Tom opened the second photo, then the third. Two more parrots, or possibly the same bird. In one shot, the crimson bird was perched on a branch, and the photo was obviously taken at considerable distance from beneath, meaning it was a very tall tree. The third photo showed a parrot in flight, and aside from the forest in the background, it might have been the bird flying around Heron Acres. But one small red parrot in flight looks pretty much like another to me.

"What are we looking at?" asked Tom.

The voice on the other end of the line was speaking fast and sounded agitated. I couldn't make anything out, but Tom's forehead had puckered up in his worried-and-potentially-angry look. I'd have to settle for the retelling, I guessed, so I went into Tom's office and turned on his printer. I'd loaded the printer software onto my computer a week or so earlier when I needed to print something. I found some photo paper on a shelf, so once I slipped it into the feed tray we were all set. I went back to the computer and sent all three photos to print, then opened my own parrot photos and printed them. At least we could compare them side by side.

"No, really, plenty of room," Tom was saying into the phone. "In fact, you can have the house to yourself if you like." He winked at me. "Great. See you Tuesday." He paused, then said, "Right. Nothing until then. Thanks a lot."

I retrieved the photos and spread them on the counter.

"Wow," said Tom, frowning and shaking his head.

"He's coming here?" I was leaning over the pair of Avas. "Do you have a magnifying glass handy?"

"He wants to see the birds for himself, but he's pretty sure . . ." He disappeared down the hall and came back with the magnifier.

"Sure of what?"

"Two endangered species," he said.

I raised my head and gaped at him. "What?"

"That's what he thinks. This one," he said, pointing at the photo of the bird that looked like Ava, or whatever his name was now, "is an endangered Amazonian parrot. He's emailing us the names, but wants us to keep it to ourselves until he gets here. And these," he pulled the other photos toward himself, "are, he thinks, a critically endangered African species."

"So Anderson was right. Something is going on out there." I looked at the photos, trying to take it all in. "You know, that dog I met at the vet's, the wildlife dog, his handler said bird smuggling is pretty active around here."

"Some greedy s.o.b.'s will do anything for money."

"No wonder Persephone didn't want me to photograph Ava. Although come to think of it, I think she said 'they' didn't want the birds photographed."

" 'They' means whoever is placing the birds with people. Treasures on Earth. Moneypenny." Tom got up and let the dogs in. "Janet, if they *are* smuggling endangered birds, there's a lot at stake — money, possibly big money, and criminal prosecution if they get caught. They have a lot of territory to defend." He stood in front of me, put his hands on my shoulders, and looked into my eyes. "Please don't go snooping around out there alone." He paused. "Or at all. Leave it to the cops."

"Okay."

"At least be careful, will you?"

"Okay." I started to collect my things, preparing to go home.

"You're coming back, right?"

"I hadn't really thought about it. I have a lot to do at home. Laundry, mowing, fun stuff like that." *And besides, I'm terrified to give up my autonomy, so back off, Bub!*

As he does so often, I think the man read

my mind. "I know, you need your space." There wasn't a trace of snark in his tone, but I looked at him to double check. He just grinned at me and said, "That's one of the many things I love about you. But if you change your mind, the door is always open."

A few hours later, I decided that being alone might not be such a hot idea, so I loaded the critters up and went back to Tom's house for the night.

Thirty-Three

Monday, Monday. The Mamas and Papas were rocking it out when I stepped out of the shower. Maybe it's because I work for myself, but Monday doesn't seem any less trustworthy than any other day to me. Mondays do tend to be busy, though, and this one promised to be a doozy. I had a lot to do, including some of the things I had planned to do the day before, and I had to go home to do a lot of it. First, though, I needed some exercise to fight back at the white chocolate macadamia cookie I'd eaten on Saturday. Okay, that was just a mouthful, and if I stuck to just a mouthful of things I like, I wouldn't be constantly trying to drop twenty pounds. I had eaten too well over the weekend and I needed a long walk.

Tom was starting breakfast when I got to the kitchen, but I declined. "I'll get something later. Want to go for a jog before it heats up." I gave him a kiss, keeping a hand on his chest to make sure that's all it was, and left. A quick stop at home to drop Leo off, and ten minutes later Jay and I were jogging east on the River Greenway along my favorite stretch of the muddy Maumee. There's a bend there in the river, and the path descends into a shallow dip maybe forty feet across before it rises again. The elevation loss is no more than three feet, but it's cooler there, more moist, and on a bright day the early sun through the leaves colors the air a warm gold-green. I always breathe a little more deeply as I pass through what I think of as "the green bowl."

As we came out the east side of the green bowl I caught motion in my peripheral vision and turned to look toward the river. A great egret rose from the near bank, almost indistinguishable from the strings of mist rising from the water to dissolve in the air. A few strides later we reached the two-mile mark and I slowed to a walk, then stopped for a drink. I took a couple of swallows from my bottle, then pulled Jay's folding water bowl from my pocket and poured some water. Jay took three polite laps and quit. His tongue hung out the side of his mouth as he watched me, eyes sparkling with pleasure.

"Okay, let's go back," I said, and we began

the walk back to the car. At that slower pace, Jay got to sniff the grass and brush alongside the paved path and I got to watch the river and field for interesting wildlife. In the forty-five minutes it took us to reach the parking lot I saw a pair of mallards, two rabbits, a chipmunk, and, by dumb luck, because I almost never see snakes, a lovely common garter snake. And lots of those ubiquitous sparrows and finches and the like that my birder friends call "LBJs." Little brown jobs. Lovely term.

My phone rang just as I started my car. It was Peg at my vet's office.

"Can you pop in today? You have a delivery."

"A delivery?" That didn't make any sense.

"Yep."

"This isn't a butt joke, is it?"

"Nope." I think she snorted. Hard to tell on a cell phone. "No, something was just delivered for you, so if you can come by . . ."

I remained suspicious, but the fact was that I did need to drop off copies of the photos I'd taken the previous week. The good ones, anyway. I had them ready to go at home. I told her I'd be there in an hour or so. "But if this has anything to do with my posterior . . ."

"Can't guarantee that," she said, and I'm

sure she was laughing when she hung up.

When I pulled onto my street, a pink delivery van was parked in front of my house and a middle-aged man was walking across my lawn toward the front door. *Oh no,* I muttered. *No no no.* But yes, he was indeed delivering flowers. To my house. I got out of my van just as he reached for the doorbell.

"Mrs. MacFall?" he asked, stumbling over my name.

Close enough, I thought, wondering if I could get away with claiming to have moved away. But it wasn't his fault that I already had five big bouquets in my house. I took the flowers in through the garage and went back for Jay. Once I had refreshed his water and filled a glass for myself, I focused on what to do about the latest floral invaders. Leo was on the table checking the flowers, and Jay was flopped in the middle of the kitchen. They both seemed to be eager to learn who sent the latest fragrance blast, this one a mix of pink and white snapdragons, big white daisies, and a blue flower I didn't recognize. I pulled the card off the little plastic holder and opened it. "That's a surprise," I said. Leo licked his paw, a maneuver I recognized as a ploy, and I told him so. "You are too curious." Jay was openly interested and cocked his head in anticipation. "They're from Jo Stevens." Jay's cocked head swivelled the other way and Leo set his foot down and stared at me. "It says, 'I have news, but in the meantime, thank you for getting me back in touch with dogs. Tell you soon. Jo.' " I looked at Leo, then at Jay. "What do you suppose this is all about?" We all just looked at one another for a moment, and then I set about finding a place for the flowers. In the end, I moved Goldie's garden bouquet to my bedroom dresser and kept Jo's bouquet on the kitchen table. Then I headed for my vet's office.

The parking lot was crowded, which wasn't unusual on a Monday morning. In fact, as I recalled all too clearly, it was on just such a crowded Monday morning that I was bitten by dear Tiffany Willard. My *gluteus maximus* contracted at the thought.

Peg grinned when I walked in. I could hardly see her behind a big bouquet of candy-colored lilies on the counter.

"Nice flowers," I said.

"They're for you."

"No!" It came out much too loud. Two vet techs turned to look at me and a Corgi in the waiting room stood and started to bark. "Sorry," I said, and then leaned over the counter toward Peg. "What do you mean, they're for me? You already sent me flowers last week." *You and practically everyone else I know.*

Peg handed a file to one of the vet techs but she was looking at me. "That box goes with it. All I know is that the delivery guy said it was for you. Arrived just before I called you."

"Oh my gawd," I groaned as I picked up a white box shaped like the gift boxes my dad's Christmas ties always came in. I split the tape holding the lid shut and opened it. Inside was a lovely braided leash. "Oh my!" I picked it up and repeated myself. The leash was about four feet long and made of leather as soft and pliant as velvet, three strands of it braided into a strong and elegant piece. I opened the envelope that was inside the box. It held a beautiful if schmaltzy get-well card, and inside that an engraved card of some sort. I read the handwritten note at the bottom of the get-well card first while my other hand continued to play with the buttery leather. The note was written in a tiny, tight hand and said,

> We hope you have recovered from your accident, and are feeling as well as ever. Please accept this invitation as a token

of our friendship.

Sincerely yours, Mr. and Mrs. Floyd
Willard and Tiffany

"Oh, man, this is bizarre," I said, staring at the writing.

"Let's see," said Peg, holding out her hand.

I gave her the get-well card and looked at the smaller insert. It was an invitation to a reception at Treasures on Earth Spiritual Renewal Center. It was for two. "Now that's just weird."

"It is," said Peg, handing the greeting card back across the counter and pointed at another card in the box. "What's that?"

I picked it up. "Free pass to visit the art gallery at Treasures on Earth." The pass turned out to be two passes. Just when I had been wondering how I might sneak into the place I suddenly had two opportunities. Three, if I didn't give one of the gallery passes away.

Peg gestured for me to lean close and then whispered, "My brother lives in the subdivision across the street from that place, and he says there's a lot of activity there really late at night."

"They do seem to have a lot of services, or events, or whatever. The parking lot is always busy when we go swim the dogs."

"Late at night, Janet! Like delivery trucks in and out."

"So they have to get food and stuff," I said.

"At midnight?" She said that in a normal voice.

I focused on what she was saying. "No, that doesn't make much sense."

"Don't go," she said.

"Oh, I'm going. I've been wanting to get in there."

Her eyes closed and reopened in a long blink, and she said, "Don't say I didn't warn you."

"You want to go with me, don't you?"

"I'm off tomorrow." She scribbled on a sticky note and handed it to me with a big grin on her face. "Cell number. Call me."

Thirty-Four

My cell phone rang just as I reached my van with the invitation and my beautiful new leash clutched in one hand, keys in the other. I had talked Peg into keeping the flowers. I had more than enough at home and didn't really want another reminder of Tiffany dear. I remembered her well enough whenever I sat a certain way. The leash was too sweet to pass up, though.

A fog of sadness settled around me when the caller identified herself as Anderson Billings's mother. Sadness well-seasoned with rage. "I'm so sorry, Mrs. Billings."

"I just don't understand what happened," she said. "He was a good swimmer. I just don't . . ."

His drowning didn't make sense to me, either, although I knew nothing about his swimming ability. It was just that he must have been in his car, or getting in, when he left his message on my phone. Mrs. Billings didn't need that tidbit added to the load she was carrying, though, so I kept it to myself and said, "What can I do to help?"

She was slow to speak, but I knew she was there so I waited, pressing my fingers against my chin to stop it trembling. Finally she said, "I was going through some things he left . . ." Her voice trailed off again but she recovered more quickly this time. "He left some things in his car. I found something in his jacket, in the little pocket at the back, you know, I think it's for a music player or something?"

"For an MP3 player?" Electronically challenged as I am, the only reason I knew to make that guess was that my new rain jacket has the same feature. I had to read the tag to figure out why I would want a teensy pocket at the back of my collar.

"Right. MP3. But I don't think that's what this thing is."

"What is it?" *And why did you think to call me?* I was surprised that she even knew who I was.

"Well, I thought at first it was a toy. It's Tweety Pie. You know, from the cartoons?"

Anderson had a Tweety toy in his MP3 pocket? "Okay."

"Anderson loved Tweety Pie when he was a little boy. I guess he still did." I heard a huge sigh. "So I just sat here and held it for a while, and then I noticed that Tweety Pie has a line around his neck, so I pulled his head off . . ." She paused long enough for me to form a macabre image of poor Tweety having his cute little head yanked off. ". . . and it's one of those, what do you call them? Thumb drives? For the computer?"

"Thumb drive. Right." I had seen cartoon and action figure thumb drives. I almost bought one of Marmaduke but it didn't have enough memory for my purposes. "Mrs. Billings, why are you calling me about it? Is there something on the drive?"

"I don't know. I haven't tried it. But the thing is, there was a tiny slip of paper tucked into Tweety's body, you know, the cap. It had your name and number on it. So, I don't mean to be rude, but who are you?"

I explained how I knew Anderson and asked if I could drop by to get the thumb drive.

"Anderson called me from the lake that day. He . . . he was supposed to drop by and he called to tell me he'd be later than planned. He had to see someone first. Was that you?"

"Maybe. Probably." I told her about the message he had left me.

"I have to go to the . . . to make arrangements. I . . ." She choked a little and I waited, not wanting to rush her. "My daughter is here. We're going to the funeral home. Family . . ." Another pause, then she told me where she lived and said she'd leave Tweety in an envelope inside the screen door.

I checked the time. Mrs. Billings lived across town in a lovely older part of the Aboite area, and the trip there and back would eat up most of an hour. I considered picking Jay up and going for a walk at Fox Island Park, but the thermometer at Times Corners said it was already ninety-one degrees, confirming that he was better off at home. I cranked up the AC and the radio. Springsteen was dancing in the dark. Perfect. But maybe whatever was on Anderson's thumb drive would shed a little light on whatever was going on out at Regis Moneypenny's place.

I found the house with no problem, and liberated Tweety Pie from the big manilla envelope that was propped between the doors and asked him, "What do you have to tell us, little guy?" In its ever-convoluted way, my mind flitted from Tweety's perky little face to birds of the flesh-and-blood variety, and from there to Dr. Crane, the ornithologist who was interested enough in "our" parrots to fly up from Florida. I decided to call Tom to find out if there was any further news.

"Dr. Crane will be in tomorrow afternoon. He's getting a car, so I gave him directions. He'll come to my office and wants to go to the lake right away. You want to go with us?"

Are there parrots flying around northern Indiana? "Of course I want to go." I told him about the thumb drive and promised to call him if there was anything important on it. I started to tell him about the passes for the Treasures on Earth art gallery, then decided to wait until I saw him at Dog Dayz in the evening. He was going to ask me not to go, and I was going to go anyway. Maybe I wouldn't tell him until after the fact. Avoid the argument.

It took about twenty minutes once I got home to do a few things and make a pot of coffee, but I finally pulled Tweety's head off and attached it to my laptop. A series of jpg files appeared. Photos. I opened my photo handling program and put up an array of images. The thumbnails were too small to show much so I started through them one by one. The first three didn't seem very interesting but I had a hunch that they had been taken in fairly rapid succession and that Anderson had been slowly panning across the island as he took them. Had he been trying to follow a bird in flight? If so, he missed. Then something in the fourth photo caught my attention. A shadow where I wouldn't expect one, knowing as I did the dearth of fat-trunked trees out there. It was at the top right of the photo frame. I was sure Anderson had been using a telephoto lens, so whatever made the shadow was fairly far away.

I went on to the next photo. Nothing. I jumped back to the previous photo and compared the two. Anderson had definitely been panning from right to left. I kept going. The shadow reappeared, and this time I could see what made it. A leg, clad in dark pants standing between two scraggly shrubs. The next photo showed legs and torso, and based on height, I was pretty sure it was a man. The photo also had a date and time imprint. Anderson must have turned the marking feature on for some reason. I clicked through to the next shot.

I stared at the photo on the screen in front of me. The figure stood in the brush in front of a clump of maple saplings, turned a quarter turn to my left. He — or she? — was holding something out with both hands. The position of hands on an object made me flash on an image of my mother emptying her big canvas tote bag of garden clippings. I zoomed in on the face, but the lighting was bad and I couldn't make out the features. Maybe the same creep I had seen on the island on Saturday. I moved the photo so that I could see what was in his hands.

It was a canvas bag. In fact, I was pretty sure it was the bag that Drake had found out on the island, the one that had started this whole strange adventure. The figure held it by the bottom corners as if shaking it. Anderson had caught the exact moment that its contents fell from the opening, and suddenly at least one question was answered.

I zoomed back out to the full picture and clicked to the next one. The figure was kicking the thing on the ground, maybe to push it into the brush. The canvas bag hung slack in his left hand. The next picture was zoomed in farther. The shot over-reached the lens's capability and the focus was fuzzy, but it still showed that what had fallen from the bag was the body of a bird. A bright red parrot.

There were two more photos. The first of them showed the figure walking toward the far side of the island, left arm flung up and out, the canvas bag flying toward a stand of brush. The final photo made my shoulders tighten up. The person had stopped and turned toward the camera, toward Anderson Billings, mouth open as if to yell. I've photographed thousands of animals in action and I know the posture of impending motion. Knees bent, upper body leaning into a sprint. But which way? Which instinct took over? Flight? Or fight?

Thirty-Five

I leaned back in my chair and tried to clear my mind, and suddenly the memory I'd been trying to tease out of the tangle popped into view. The man in the photos, the man who made the creepy gestures at me, had been at our training session the day Drake found the bag. I remembered now, I had seen him talking to Tom and asked later who he was, what he wanted. "I just wondered what all the dogs were doing here." Wasn't that what Tom had told me the man said? And something about the guy really liking dogs? He hadn't stayed more than about five minutes, which didn't exactly scream "dog lover" to me. But now it was starting to make sense. Was he the mysterious figure in Anderson's photos?

If he was dumping dead birds and bloody tote bags on the island, he must have been surprised to see a bunch of dogs swimming around, and Drake's little discovery must have really shaken him up. But how did that make sense? Anderson was out there on a Friday, the Friday before last, and the retriever training session was the following Sunday. *Think, think.* I grabbed my phone and found Anderson's message. He left it last Tuesday, so I was clear about that. I listened again to the message. "I was here a few days ago, too. Saw a friend of yours . . . came back with my canoe to get to the island . . . That was Friday night. Well, you know, evening."

The dates on the photos. I checked them. Why hadn't I noticed that they were dated more than a week ago, the day before Drake found the mysterious bag? *Oh, Anderson, why did you wait so long to say anything? Why did you go back there alone?* Then it hit me that if someone had killed him, they would have looked for the photos. Especially if the killer was the man *in* the photos.

I dialed Jo Stevens' number. As usual, I got her voice mail, so I left a message about the thumb drive and the photos. I closed with a question. "Jo, what images were on Anderson's camera? I know it was in the car, but he had it on the island earlier. At least, I think he did." I had almost hung up when I thought of something else. "Jo, was Anderson's laptop there, in the car?" It must have been, I thought. He needed the intermediate step of a computer to move the photos from his camera to Tweety.

I was about to get up when Leo waltzed into the room. Jay was sacked out by the wall, but he opened a sleepy eye when Leo sniffed his ear before coming to me. Leo sat down in front of my feet, yawned with all his might, made a couple of passes over his paw with his tongue, and stared at me through half-closed lids.

"Whatcha doing, Leo *mio*?"

He hopped into my lap, sprawled across my torso, and pushed the top of his head into my chin. The rumble that rolled out of his little body sounded like a motorcycle trying to rev up.

"I have things to do, Mr. Cat."

He squinted at me as if to say, "What's more important than this?"

I scooped him around and cradled him, and he snuggled against me, then reached with one paw and laid it, soft and warm, against my cheek. He was right. Everything else could wait a while. Or at least until the phone rang. I might have let it go to voice mail, but Leo scrambled out of my lap at the sound, so I went ahead and answered.

"Do you want to go to Michigan the end of the week?" It was Tom.

"Is this a rhetorical question?"

"Puppy search question." I swear I could hear the grin in his voice. "I talked to a breeder near Ann Arbor. She says she has the perfect obedience prospect, eight weeks old."

I couldn't think of a single reason not to tag along to see eight-week-old puppies.

"I wasn't really planning to get a puppy quite yet, but if this little bitch is as nice as she says . . ." The excitement in his voice made me want to run right over and hug him. "We can take the dogs with us. She said she has shade we can park in and we can open the van . . ."

"You don't have to convince me, Tom," I said, laughing. "I'm in." I thought of my plans to visit Treasures on Earth. *You mean snoop around,* whispered the prissy little voice in my head. "Not tomorrow. I have something I need to do."

"No, too much going on this week, and Dr. Crane is coming in. I'm thinking Friday."

That settled, I told him about the thumb drive and the photos.

"You called Jo, didn't you?" Tom's question irritated me even though I knew he was just looking out for me, and I didn't answer right away. "Janet?"

"Yes, Dad."

"Aw, come on. That's not fair." Now he was the one who sounded irritated.

For some reason, my eyes filled up with tears and my nose started to run. I decided to blame it on hormones and took a deep breath in hopes of a counterbalance. "Sorry."

Silence on the other end.

"I called her. Left a message." Then I told him about the bouquet she had sent, and her note. "I wonder if she's getting a puppy, too?" If she was, I wondered when she would ever have time for it. Not that I'm the boss of other people's relationships with their pets.

"See you tonight?" Tom asked.

"Ha!" I couldn't remember the last time I had missed Monday night obedience practice at Dog Dayz. Then I asked, "Hey, what color is she?"

A non-dog person might have wondered what I was talking about, given the nonlinear direction of the conversation, but Tom didn't hesitate. "Yellow." I knew it was said with a smile, and, picturing a baby yellow Labrador Retriever in my mind made me smile, too.

Jay woke up restored. Bouncing off the walls, really, so I took him out back for a game of "tennis ball that way, frisbee this way" in hopes of taking the edge off before Dog Dayz training. Goldie waved at me from her kitchen window, so when Jay's tongue seemed to hang reasonably far out of his mouth, I refreshed his water bowl and walked through the two gates, mine and hers, and up the steps to Goldie's back door.

"Come in, come in! Just making iced tea," she called. "Want some?"

"What's in it?" Goldie's summer teas nearly always feature fresh herbs from her garden, and love Goldie though I do, some of her concoctions don't appeal to me.

"Green tea, fresh spearmint, and johnny jump ups." She plopped ice cubes into two jelly jars and, when I nodded at her, poured the tea.

We carried our glasses out to her covered porch and I told her the summary version of what was going on. She peered over her glasses at me. "You're at it again?"

"I'm not at anything." I tried to out-stare her but knew right away that it wouldn't work. "Okay, yes, I want to find out what happened to Anderson and what the heck is going on out there at Treasures on Earth. And I don't like being threatened by creepy guys."

"You don't know that he's connected to

Moneypenny's place," she said.

I hadn't mentioned the photos Anderson had taken of the man and the dead bird. For a moment I debated whether I should, because I knew that any mistreatment of animals would light a fire under Goldie, and she was no stranger to taking a stand on issues. In the end I told her about the photos of the man, but left the bird out of my story.

When I had finished, Goldie took a long drink, set her glass on the table, and said, "You're not telling me the whole story. That's okay. I'm sure you have your reasons." In anyone else, I would take such words as pure peevishness, but that's not what I heard, and when I looked at Goldie and saw the love in her eyes, in the soft lines of her cheeks, something almost tangible drained out of me. I thought back to my conversation with Tom and my hurt feelings when I learned that Goldie had lied when she said she wasn't ill. What was it he had said? That I wouldn't need to know she was sick to be there for her, because I was always there for her.

Fear. That's what left me in that moment. I had been terrified and hadn't even known it.

Thirty-Six

Dinner was an English muffin with cream cheese and grape jelly, which I calculated to cover my grains, my dairy, and my fruit. All my dishes were in the dishwasher but I'd forgotten to turn it on, so I ripped off a stretch of paper towels and made that my plate. I grabbed a bottle of diet root beer and plunked myself down on the couch to watch the six o' clock news, which was the usual uplifting mess. When the national news finished, I went to brush my teeth, and sat back down to put my running shoes on just as the local news got rolling. I stopped mid-tie of my right lace and stared at the screen.

The reporter was talking about Anderson's death; the backdrop was Twisted Lake and a bunch of wet dogs and their mucky owners. The reporter led her cameraman toward the shore and asked one of the dog owners to explain what they were doing. Tom. And behind him, hanging back from the group, was the creepy man whose face was becoming much more familiar than I wanted it to. He was looking toward the camera, at Tom, it seemed to me. *Don't give your name,* I thought, just as the reporter asked, "What's your name?" Of course he answered. He explained that it was an informal meeting of the Northern Indiana Hunting Retriever Club, and the camera panned toward the water and zoomed in on one of the Flat-coated Retrievers bringing back a bright orange bumper.

Jay was hopping around in front of me. I swear he checks the calendar for dog-training nights. "Yeah, yeah. Let's go." As I loaded him into his crate in the back of the van, I said, "I really wish he hadn't told them his name." Jay replied *brrffff.* "I don't know. Just makes me nervous."

Tom wasn't there yet, but I spotted Giselle and Precious as soon as I walked into Dog Dayz. I still couldn't get over how great Giselle looked. Made me wonder if I might be able to wangle a photo assignment at the fat camp she went to, but I dropped the idea in about three seconds. I would never go away for a month without Jay and Leo. Even a week was a stretch, although I did that occasionally. I started toward Giselle, but a voice calling my name changed my course.

"Sylvia!"

"Hi, Janet. Long time!" Sylvia Eckhorn pushed a blonde curl out of her eyes and gave me a quick hug. We both executed body blocks to keep our dogs apart while we greeted each other, then let Jay and Tippy, Sylvia's lovely multi-titled champion Cocker Spaniel, say hello. They've played together many times, so we were careful to keep the greetings subdued so they didn't rile up any less mannerly dogs — or owners — with their antics.

"Mama!"

"Mama Mama."

Two little voices piped up from behind Sylvia. Meg and Liz, Sylvia's twin daughters. They were playing on a quilted comforter spread out and anchored under an exercise pen, the dog-person's equivalent of an old-fashioned play pen.

"Wow, Syl, they're getting big!" I had Jay lie down and took a step closer to the twins. "Hi, girls." Meggie giggled and said, "Ha." Lizzie blew a raspberry and threw a teddy bear in my direction.

"Yeah, they are. Fourteen months almost, if you can believe that. Lizzie is walking, running almost, all over the place. Meg's happy to crawl." She sighed. "Guess I should be glad for an extra week or two with just one on her feet!"

There was a time when I desperately wanted kids, but now I was exhausted just thinking about keeping up with these two. I said, "They'll be showing in Pee Wee Handlers pretty soon."

"What's that?" Sylvia had the full attention of Jay and Tippy and a few other dogs nearby as she filled the treat pouch she wore around her waist.

"Oh, right, I always forget that's pretty much an Australian Shepherd Club thing. It's a handling class for kids under five. Mostly with really kind dogs that take charge of their peewee handlers." Also the cutest, funniest classes I've ever had the pleasure to photograph.

"How fun! But we don't have an Aussie, so . . ." She looked genuinely disappointed.

"The dog doesn't have to be an Aussie." I told her a bit more about that and promised to get her information on Pee Wee classes when the girls were ready.

"So how's your mom, Janet?" Sylvia was a nurse and had helped deal with my mom when we checked her into Shadetree Retirement Home. It was no longer safe for her to live without supervision and care, but that didn't mean she wanted to leave her home.

"Off and on." I told her the latest, and then she shifted to a direction I didn't expect.

"I saw Tom on the news tonight." Sylvia suddenly looked very serious. "He isn't hooked up with that Treasures on Earth bunch, is he? Because if he is . . ."

"Heavens, no! Why would you think that?"

"Oh, thank goodness." Sylvia's face relaxed slightly. "It's just that I saw, well, oh, never mind."

"Oh no no no, Syl," I said. "You can't get away with that. Why did you think he was?"

"There was someone in there, in the news clip. He seemed to be with Tom, but maybe he was just interested in the reporter and camera." She pushed her treat pouch around to the small of her back so Tippy wouldn't be staring at it during training. "I just, well, I kind of know him. Not a . . . Never mind."

"I know who you mean, Syl. The creepy guy in the background." I told her about my encounter with him, but stopped short of mentioning the photos.

"Be really careful, Janet," she said. Her bright blue eyes were open wide and a little wrinkle drew a line just above her eyebrows.

"What do you mean?" I laughed when I said it, but felt a chill set in at the base of my spine.

She shook her head, checked that the twins were okay, and gathered the leash's slack in her hand. "Just be really careful." Then she and Tippy joined the group already heeling around the ring and I was left staring at the moppets. Lizzie was sprawled on the comforter, sound asleep. Meggie was trying to feed a plastic ball to her teddy bear. And I was wondering what in the world Sylvia was talking about. More to the point, who *was* that guy and what was he up to?

Jay was getting antsy so I pulled myself back into dog training mode and we stepped into the heeling mob just as Marietta Santini, Dog Dayz owner and drill sergeant, called, "FAST!" I couldn't have chosen a more effective way to clear my thoughts and focus on the task at hand. More than one bruise in my past bore witness to the need to pay attention when running with a dog on a leash and twenty other dogs and people doing the same in a confined space. Jay was delighted with the chance to move a little faster, even if it only lasted a few seconds.

Tom and Drake showed up just as Marietta called out "Normal!" to bring us all back to a brisk walk. He set his training bag down, changed Drake out of his every-day collar to his training collar, a lovely tooled black leather job with no tags to get in the way. Tom draped his leash over his neck, told Drake to heel, and stepped into the ring behind Judy Herschel and her well-behaved Boxer, Corey, and in front of Elmer Bruebaker and his not-well-behaved Lab, Beeswax.

It's not the dog's fault. Elmer rewards her for every behavior. *Bark bark bark,* says Beeswax, and Elmer strokes her head, tells her she's a good girl, and shoves a treat in her mouth. *Pull pull pull,* Beeswax drags Elmer across the room to jump all over someone else's unamused dog, and Elmer says, "She just wants to say hello," strokes her head, and pops another treat in her mouth. She's been snapped at a couple of times, but Beeswax is nearly as oblivious to the unhappy reactions of the dogs she accosts as is Elmer, so most of us have learned to just watch for them and body block Beeswax to protect her, and our own dogs, from her lack of social graces. I was a little surprised that Tom chose to step into the crowd in front of the blonde bombshell, since she's particularly fond of Drake.

Marietta directed us to halt, then to line up for stays. Tom looked at me and lifted his eyebrows, and we moved to the mat where people were setting up their dogs and found an opening big enough for Drake and Jay. I removed the leash and set it down behind my dog, as we would do in an obedience trial, and pulled a large folded index card from my training pouch and unfolded it.

"What's that for?" asked Tom.

"Remember when he," meaning Jay, "got up and grabbed my arm band during stays in the last two trials?" In obedience trials, each handler wears an armband with an entry number. When we do the stay exercises, we take off our armbands and set them behind our dogs so that the judge can see who is who. I had come back into the room at our last two trials to find Jay where he should be, holding my number. That meant that he had moved out of position to pick up the card-stock armband and then had returned to the place and position I had left him in. Clever little trick, but it meant a non-qualifying score. "This is a set up," I told Tom as I set the card behind Jay and slightly to one side so he could see it if he turned his head.

"This will be a five-minute stay. Position your dogs."

All along the line commands could be heard to "sit" or "down." The more experienced trainers chose the position most challenging to the individual dogs, or created a challenge of another sort. As we often do, Tom and I gave our dogs different commands, so when we walked away Jay was sitting and Drake was lying down. I noticed that Rhonda Lake had her lovely Golden Retriever, Eleanor, facing the opposite direction from the rest of the dogs. Pilot, the Golden I had met with Rhonda at the practice session on Saturday, was lying down next to Eleanor but oriented like the rest of the group and wearing an ear-to-ear doggy grin. I wondered whether I could sneak out to my van for my camera. Pilot's smile was definitely photo-worthy.

"Are you going to hide?" asked Tom, meaning go somewhere the dogs couldn't see us.

"I can't. I need to see that he doesn't grab the number." I'm working on out-of-sight stays, but Jay finds them a bit stressful. "We need to fix this if he's going to get his CDX," I said, referring to the mid-level obedience title. "You can go. We can talk later."

"Nah, doesn't matter. Rather be with you." He winked at me.

"Wow. I win out over a musty storage room," I said, referring to the glorified closet where the out-of-sight handlers crowded together and stressed out over whether their dogs were staying put. Then I shifted to more serious things, telling Tom what Sylvia had said about the man in the news clip and in Anderson's photos. "I'm more interested in what she's not saying, but this didn't seem the time and place to ask her."

"No, she doesn't get to spend quality time with her dog very often anymore," said Tom. "Cute kids, those." He nodded toward the x-pen where both of the toddlers were now asleep on the comforter.

I agreed, and fought down a twinge as an old, painful memory tried to surface. "I don't think she gets a lot of help with them, but I can't think of a more cheerful, competent person to manage two lively little girls. So, any news?"

"Funny you should ask. George Crane called. He got an earlier flight to Indy and is driving in from there."

"Tomorrow?"

Marietta called, "Back to your dogs," so we had to shut up for a moment. We repositioned the dogs so that Jay was lying down and Drake sitting, and walked away again when Marietta called, "Leave your dogs."

Tom picked up the conversation again,

saying, "Tonight."

"What's tonight?"

"Bird guy is tonight. George." He looked at his watch. "Should be here any time. He called from north of Anderson just as I pulled into the parking lot."

I knew that he meant the town of Anderson, but Anderson Billings's young face seemed to hover before me and that sense of loss that had been simmering inside me burst into flame. Tom usually picks up on my little shifts, but he was watching Elmer try to get Beeswax back into the line of dogs. Again.

"Think I should offer to help him?" Tom asked.

"He won't listen." I paused. "Then again, you're a guy, and you have a Lab who complies with your every whispered wish. Elmer might think you know a little something."

Tom turned to me with his here-comes-trouble grin and waggled his eyebrows at me. I couldn't help but laugh, and said, "Uh oh." He leaned toward me and whispered, "How about we get together later and see if you will comply with my every whispered wish." Then he turned with a throaty chuckle and left me for Elmer and his cute and wild Labby girl.

Thirty-Seven

After we finished the stays, Tom took Drake to the other ring to practice directed jumping. Maybe it's all the retriever training, which requires Drake to work at a distance from Tom, but they make it all look easy. As I watched them, I wished again that I had brought my camera in with me.

Tom stood at one end of the ring with Drake sitting at his side. Then he gave a command that I couldn't hear, he spoke so softly, but I knew to be "fly out." Drake raced straight ahead, running between two jumps set up halfway down at right angles to the side of the ring. One, the high jump, consisted of three wooden boards held edge to edge by the standards to form a solid obstacle. The other was a single wooden bar set into cups on the standards. The ends of the two jumps stood about twenty feet apart.

When he reached the far end of the ring,

Drake spun around and sat down, his tail whipping back and forth and his face alight with anticipated fun. Tom stayed still for a couple of seconds, then raised his right arm toward the high jump and said, "Over!" Drake took off, veered to his left, and cleared the twenty-four inches he was required to jump with plenty of air beneath him. He was already turning toward Tom when he landed, and he slid into a sit right in front of the man. Again, I wished I had my camera to catch their matching grins.

Tom was setting Drake up for the other jump when I saw a man I didn't know walk in the front door. That wasn't unusual. But he didn't have a dog with him, or a woman with a dog, and the only man I'd ever seen come in here unaccompanied by one or both of those was Neil Young. This guy was about Tom's size, five ten or so, but a good decade younger, maybe more. He was clean shaven and had his hair pulled back in a ponytail. He scanned the room, then started our way. When he got close I realized that although he nodded at me, his smile was for Jay. But he did have the grace to greet me first. "Janet, I presume?"

"I'm going to take a wild guess. Dr. Crane?"

"George." We shook hands, and he nodded toward Jay and asked, "May I?"

"Wow. Thanks for asking, and yes, of course."

He knelt and held out the back of his hand. I released Jay from the down-stay and he was up in a flash, wriggling like a hula dancer and pushing his shoulder into George, who quickly had his fingers deep in blue-merle fur.

"I'm going to take another wild guess. You know about Aussies and their affinity for butt scratches?"

George said, "I grew up with them. Just lost my old dog a few months ago." He stood back up and looked at the action in the ring. Drake sat at the far end from Tom again. "That must be Tom and Drake."

Tom signaled Drake to take the bar jump, and once again Drake was nearly perfect. Tom finished up the session by giving Drake a jackpot of treats, handing him five or six of them one right after the other. Then he pulled Drake's special training toy, a five-inch stuffed mallard with one wing and evidence of several "surgeries," from his back pocket and tossed it. Drake pounced on it, tossed it in the air, caught it, and shook it.

To George I said, "Male bonding. Could go on for hours." Then I called, "Tom."

Drake ran to the edge of the ring and showed me his duck, and Tom followed. Once the introductions were out of the way, Tom suggested we go to his house so George could settle in. I pulled Tom aside in the parking lot and said, "I'll come over for a while, but then I have to go home."

"It might be easier if you stay the night at my house. I think George wants to get out to the lake early to see if we can spot the parrot."

I hadn't told him about my plans to snoop around Treasures on Earth with Peg, but I had told him I had an appointment the next day. "I can't go in the morning. I have an appointment."

"But I thought you wanted to be in on this?" Tom looked into my eyes. I know he was reading my mind. "You are, aren't you? You're up to something."

Offense being the best defense, I dodged a direct answer and said, "I didn't think he would be here until tomorrow. I kept Wednesday open, but made an appointment for tomorrow morning."

Tom leaned back against my van, folded his arms across his chest, and looked at me through half-closed lids. "What are you planning?"

"What do you mean?"

"Janet . . . Never mind. Do what you want."

"I will."

"I know."

We stared at each other, and something passed between us. Not anger, not resignation. It seemed more like understanding. After a moment, I sighed and said, "Look, I just have a lead . . ."

"A lead? A *lead*?" Tom stood up straight and I couldn't be sure in the yellow-tinged light of the parking lot but I thought his face darkened a tad. "The only lead you should worry about is the one attached to your dog."

My own face heated up at that. "Excuse me?"

"Janet, whatever you have, give it to the cops. You said yourself that something very weird is going on. It isn't safe. Don't be st . . ." He caught himself before he said "stupid," and his voice softened. "Janet, let Jo and Hutch look into things. Just give them what you have and leave it."

"Look, Tom, I'm not going to do anything dangerous. But Anderson was my student, my friend. I sent him out there. Someone killed him, and I think the autopsy will show that, somehow. Even if it doesn't, I *know* it." My voice cracked, but I recovered. "And something is going on with those birds."

"But you don't have to . . ."

I cut him off. "Don't tell me what to do, Tom." I signaled Jay to hop into his crate and took the opportunity to take a deep breath while I filled his water bowl and shut the hatch. I considered going straight home, but I wanted to hear what Dr. Crane had to say about my photos of the parrots and about the birds themselves. "Shall we?"

George entered Tom's address into his GPS in case they got separated.

"Anybody else hungry?" I asked. My cream cheese muffin was long gone, and it turned out George hadn't eaten. I called our favorite pizza place and said I would swing by there on my way. I checked my messages, too, but didn't have any. I thought that was odd since Jo was usually quick to get back to me, especially about potential police business. She did say she had something big going on, though, so I decided to wait until morning before I pestered her. I was just setting my phone down on the seat when it rang and scared the bejeebers out of me. *Note to self: what were you thinking when you reset the ring to "Vintage Telephone"?*

It was Peg, verifying our early morning rendezvous outside the Kroger store at

Coldwater and Dupont. Before we hung up I asked, "Peg, do you have a camera?"

"Sure."

"A little one? You know, point and shoot?"

"Yes. Nice little one. Fits in my pocket. Oh, I get it. That's what you want, right?"

"Right. One that fits in your pocket. Charge it, okay?" Common problem among my beginning students, forgetting to charge their cameras. One reason I prefer regular batteries.

The pizza was just coming out of the oven when I got to the carry-out counter and Jay and I walked in Tom's door a quarter hour later. Drake, always a perfect gentleman, ushered us in with a smile on his face and a wag in his tail. Tom and George gave me back-handed waves but kept their noses pointed at Tom's laptop. I set the pizza down and looked over Tom's shoulder.

An array of six parrot photos filled the screen. They were all basically red, but the shades varied from a deep red approaching purple to a bright tangerine-red. "How true are those colors?" I asked George, knowing that photos don't always show colors as we see them in real life, and that the screen settings would further affect their hues and intensity.

He glanced at me and nodded as he

answered. "Reasonable. At least the colors. But seeing them here is nothing like seeing them in the open, in the sun. This one, for instance," he pointed at the tangeriney bird, "practically glows in the flesh. Or the feather, I guess. And this one," he clicked on another photo and it filled the screen, "is almost iridescent." He clicked the mouse again and the photo array reappeared.

"Okay, let's feed the man," said Tom. He put his laptop to sleep and cleared the table, pulled three Harps from the fridge, and opened the pizza box.

I grabbed some plates and napkins and told the dogs to lie down. "So, what did I miss? George, what are you thinking?"

"The birds in the photos are not common parrots." He stuffed most of a pizza slice into his mouth and rolled his eyes and groaned. Both dogs cocked their heads, and when I looked toward the movement I saw that Drake had strings of drool hanging to his paws and Jay had little drops of saliva dripping from his dangling tongue like a leaky faucet.

"All of them?" I asked. "They're all rare?"

George swigged some beer and studied the bottle as he set it down, as if considering his response. "Okay, the parrot in the veterinary office, he's not rare. Not exactly.

But he's not a common pet species either, and he'd be expensive to buy. South American species, doesn't breed well in captivity. So his owner must really be into parrots, or into conspicuous possession." He seemed to be waiting for an answer.

"Possibly conspicuous possession," I said, remembering Persephone Swann's expensive duds and jewelry and her pulled-together chicness. "But I don't think she had a clue what kind of parrot Ava was, or is, whatever his name is now. She didn't even know he was male."

Tom joined the conversation. "Could she have forgotten? I mean, we run into that with dog owners all the time. People who can't remember what breed the shelter told them they were getting, or they never check it out and realize the I.D. was wrong."

It's true. I remember a woman who came for a beginning obedience class at Dog Dayz. She had an Australian Cattle Dog, probably purebred and a pretty nice example of the breed. Unfortunately, the shelter had misidentified the dog as an Australian Shepherd, and the woman held tight to that claim despite the obvious differences between her dog and Jay. I wasn't sure the comparison worked for Persephone and her bird, though.

"I don't know. Remember what Giselle said about becoming a foster home, or, what did she call it? Guardian?" Tom nodded but George needed an explanation. "She made it sound like some sort of fostering program. Like they farm the birds out to members to take care of, but I didn't get the impression it was meant to be permanent. Tom, remember what Goldie said? That Moneypenny was planning to build an aviary of some sort out there? Big fancy one?"

George leaned back and closed his eyes, letting his head fall forward and nod up and down a few times. I waited until he seemed to come back to us, then asked, "What about the other birds? The loose one and the dead one?"

"Ah, yes, a whole different matter with them," George said. "A whole different matter."

"Endangered, you said?" asked Tom.

"Critically endangered."

"What does that mean, in terms of numbers?" Tom again.

"We don't know how many are left in the wild," said George. "Hard to get accurate counts in Congo. This species has been documented only in one remote valley. It's hard to get to, and dangerous. I know one field researcher who studied them there several years ago, but she got out when the fighting got too hot. I have a call into her, but she's on sabbatical, in the field. In the Malagasy Republic. Might be a while."

We all sat silent for a moment, then George said, "So what do I think? I think you have some black-market trade in very rare, critically endangered, expensive parrots going on here."

"Why would anyone let a bird, two birds! like that loose?" I knew as soon as I said it that it was dopey. "Or more to the point, how would they get loose?" An image of the dead bird and the flight of the bereaved mate or friend came back to me like despair itself. "And the one that died. Sad enough, but sadder yet for an endangered species."

"Tip of the 'berg," said George. "The numbers of animals killed in the illegal trade, the smuggling, is obscene. Not just birds, of course. Trade in live exotics, trade in pelts and body parts and eggs . . . To the poachers and middlemen, dead and injured and diseased animals are just part of the cost of doing business. To the animals . . ." He lifted his beer bottle to his lips but put it down without drinking. "To an endangered species, it may mean the end of their road."

"And not only for the individual species

in question," said Tom. "Whenever you remove an entire species, or reduce its numbers so much that it may as well be gone, you affect all the other species around it. Plants as well."

I can only take so much of this topic at a time. It makes me roiling mad, but more, it makes me feel I'm drowning in sorrow with no hope of ever surfacing. So I changed the subject, although not to a happier one. "Tom, did you tell George about Anderson Billings?"

Tom looked like I felt after the previous few minutes. "Right. Let's fill him in. You start. Be right back." He picked up the empty pizza box with one hand and the two bits of crust he had saved with the other and turned toward the kitchen. "Janet, you want to release the boys?"

George seemed to have just realized that the dogs had stayed where I told them all through our dinner and conversation. "Impressive. They're really good."

"Free!" I said, and Jay and Drake were on their feet and crowding into Tom's legs faster than you could say "pizza bones!" To George I said, "Consistency. That's about all it takes."

Tom had the dogs sit and handed a piece of crust to each of them. From the looks on their faces you'd think he had given them each a haunch of venison. Then Tom pulled a towel out of a drawer and wiped each slobbery canine chin and said, "Good thing we didn't have a four-course dinner. They'd have drowned themselves."

We moved out to the back patio and filled George in about all the strange goings-on — Ava's visit to the vet, the bag that Drake had found with the red feather and blood inside, Anderson Billings's photos of the man on the island disposing of the dead bird, my gruesome discovery, and the dead bird's companion. I told him that several people associated with Treasures on Earth seemed to be getting involved with parrots. I'd heard that from Persephone Swann and then her cousin Giselle, from Dr. Neil Young, from Mrs. Willard. Tom told him about the creepy guy and his not-so-subtle apparent threat.

"You have the picture?" asked George.

"What picture?"

"The guy. You said you took a photo of him?"

"I do," I said, and went into the house for Tom's laptop. I'd sent all my photos related to the strange goings-on to Tom, partly so he would have them and partly for backup. I'm sloppy about my house and my hair and makeup, but fanatical about backing up my work. It's all backed up automatically every evening to on-line storage, but I had decided on an extra measure of safety in this case. I set the computer on the patio table and pulled up my photos of Mr. Creepy, then turned the screen toward George.

"Zoom in on him," he said, and I filled the screen with the man's face.

"Cold-looking bird," said Tom.

George turned away from the screen and looked first at Tom, then at me, and said, "I know him."

Thirty-Eight

"You know him?" I thought I must have heard wrong. How could George, an ornithologist from Florida, know the weirdo who had been skulking around Twisted Lake and dumping dead birds out there?

George continued to stare at the screen. "I do. Or did. Name's Rich Campbell."

"Is he a bird guy?" asked Tom, apparently assembling the pieces more quickly than I was.

"Yep, he is. Raptors. At least when I knew him."

"So what's he doing with dead endangered parrots?" None of this made a featherweight of sense.

George seemed to be weighing his words.

"How do you know him?" asked Tom.

"Grad school." George finally turned away from the face on the screen and looked at Tom, then at me. "Haven't seen him in twelve years. Not too pleased to see him now."

My stupid phone rang. "Hold that thought, would you? I want to hear this, but I need to take this call." To Tom I said, "Jo Stevens."

I walked into the living room to take the call and told Jo that the ornithologist had arrived and identified the birds and the creep at Twisted Lake. "Where you been, anyway? I thought you'd call back hours ago."

"Right. Sorry."

"Actually, I thought you were going to drop by Dog Dayz."

"I had to go to Evansville."

Jo had family there. "Everything okay?"

"Yep! Everything's fine." She sounded fine. She sounded buoyant, in fact.

"Jo?"

"Long story. I want to tell you in person. How about I drop by late morning?"

"Okay. Oh, wait." Peg and I were planning to go to Treasures on Earth midmorning, but I couldn't be sure how long we'd be there. "I can't. Later?"

We made plans to touch base early afternoon and I went back to the kitchen to hear what George had to say.

"Sorry. Go ahead." I sat down at the table.

"So, he was a year ahead of me. Had a couple of classes with him my first year, then didn't see much of him for a couple of years. He did his fieldwork in New Guinea, or that's what he said, while I was finishing course work and taking exams, and when he came back, I left for the field."

Or that's what he said sort of rattled around my brain, but instead of pursuing that odd comment, I asked, "Where was that?" It wasn't particularly relevant, but I'm always fascinated by where academics of various stripes choose to do their research. I would love to travel. On the other hand, I won't leave Jay and Leo for longer than a week, so I won't be going anywhere exotic any time soon. There's nothing to stop me having some vicarious adventure, though.

"Southern California and the Baja."

Tom and George had a brief academic bonding moment when they found that their research stomping grounds overlapped. The objects of their interest may have as well. Birds and plants. Then I butted in again to ask, "What kind of birds were you studying?"

George looked surprised. "Parrots, of course. Mexican red-heads to be exact. *Amazona viridigenalis.*"

"Red-head?" asked Tom. *"Viridi?"*

"Right," said George. "Also known as the green-cheeked or red-crowned Amazon. We online?" he asked, gesturing toward the computer.

Tom signed into the Internet, and George pulled up the California Parrot Project and showed us a photo of his bird, at least for his doctoral research.

Thank goodness for the scientific names, I thought. How else would anyone be sure they were talking about the same species?

"So they're in California?" I asked.

"Not native. Introduced there. They're established around L.A. and farther south. Other places, too. Hawaii. I've seen them in Florida. Texas."

"But they're native to South America?" asked Tom.

"Mexico. They're native to the northeast coast, but are considered extinct in most of their native range. Like a lot of parrots. Loss of habitat is responsible for a lot. And the pet trade is a huge problem. They're endangered, and their numbers are falling."

That numbing sense of loss was filling me up again, and I said, "That must be hard. Studying something that's disappearing."

George looked at me, then down at his hands. He said, "There are times when I think about doing something else. But," he looked at me, then at Tom, "maybe we can learn enough to save them, or maybe what we learn with one species will save another. I have to hold that hope, you know, or what's the point?"

Tom steered us back from the brink, back to the problem at hand. "So, George, I don't think you finished the Rich Campbell story."

George cleared his throat. "Right. So Rich was there in Storrs when I got back from California."

"Storrs?" I asked.

Both men answered, "University of Connecticut."

"So Rich was there, on the list to graduate, dissertation defense scheduled, even had a couple of job offers, as I recall. All sorts of buzz about his work. Groundbreaking field data on the New Britain Gray-headed Goshawk. First-ever field study of them."

Tom said, "New Britain. They found a new species of orchid there in 2011. Blooms for one night. First night-blooming orchid we know of."

"Yeah?" said George. "So, see, it can happen. New species, new sub-species."

"So I'm guessing that in Mr. Campbells' case, something was amiss?" I asked.

"Oh, yeah," said George, drawing out his words. "He hadn't been there."

Tom and I blurted at the same instant, "What?" in my case and "Oh, man" in Tom's, followed by, "How did it come out?"

George chuckled. "Rich had a girlfriend. They lived together, had for a year before he left, and another year when he got back. M.A. student in linguistics. She was planning to surprise him with a trip to the Greek islands to celebrate his doctorate and his job offers. She needed his passport number to buy the tickets. I saw her a couple of days later, and she said she couldn't find it at first. You know, she thought it would be in his desk or filing cabinet but she didn't see it. She was getting desperate because she wanted the tickets to be a surprise, to give them to him at his defense party."

Suddenly I was flashing on my jerk of an ex-husband, and I could almost see what was coming. "He was playing around on her, wasn't he?"

George nodded. "He carried a sort of messenger bag around, you know, to the library, whatever. So she thought maybe it was in his bag, although carrying his passport around all the time didn't make much sense."

Tom must have picked up on where my

thoughts were going. He touched my arm and winked at me. Such a small gesture, such a humongous whoosh of good feelings.

"So Liesl, his girlfriend, looked in the bag." He looked thoughtful. "Liesl . . . Can't remember her last name. Anyway, she didn't find the passport, not then, but she found a photo."

"The other woman." I said.

"The other family," said George. "Woman, two little boys. And Rich."

I gasped, and Tom said, "He was married?"

"He was."

"I knew he was a creep." That may have come out as a growl, because Jay and Drake both raised their heads to look at me.

"What happened?" asked Tom.

"Liesl was livid. But also very controlled. Smart, really. They had a joint bank account, for one thing, her only account. So she didn't confront him right away."

"Wow," I said. "I threw his stuff out on the lawn and changed the locks." I realized as soon as the words were out that I was merging Campbell's story with my memories of Chet.

George turned a confused expression my way but Tom came to my rescue, saying "You probably would have." He took my hand, laughed, and looked at George. "Janet is nothing if not direct."

George went back to his story. "She moved her money to a new account, and kept looking for his passport and ticket receipts. She never said so, but I think by then she was out for revenge."

"Did she get it?" I asked.

"Oh yeah. She finally found his passport, along with the ticket stubs from his flights. You know, back in the days of actual tickets. He'd never been to New Guinea."

Now Tom sounded angry. "So he fabricated his field data."

"He did."

"So what happened?"

"The ticket stubs showed a round trip to Lincoln, Nebraska. And I guess there was a note on the back of the photo. Something like, 'The boys wanted you to have this, love' whatever her name was."

"How did Liesl know it was current?" asked Tom.

"Good question. I wondered that, too," said George. "Liesl said he was wearing a shirt that she gave him for his birthday a couple weeks before he left."

"Nice." Tom doesn't often sound sarcastic, but he made up for a long dry spell in his delivery of that one word.

"So Liesl had a place and a name." I laughed out loud at that, although not without a pang for Rich Campbell's wife.

"She did. She actually found her, then decided it wasn't up to her to shatter the woman's life. She thought Rich should have to do that himself."

"And she told the university?" asked Tom.

"Oh yeah. She waited until the day of his defense. Friend of mine was there in the department when it happened. He said Liesl showed up just as Rich and his committee members were getting ready to go in for the defense. She smiled at Rich and asked Alan Milcourt, the committee chair, for a word." George sort of snorted and smiled. "I guess she finagled Milcourt to a spot where Rich could see them. Then she handed Rich's passport to Milcourt, along with a copy of the photo, and copies of the ticket stubs."

I burst out laughing, then had a frightening thought. "Rich is a scary guy. At least he is now. Wasn't she afraid he'd come after her? I mean, she just blew up his life."

"She left. She had already taken her share of the bank account, and I guess she went straight from the department to the airport. I actually ran into her a couple years later in New York. In transit at JFK, actually. She was teaching English in Kuwait, home for a couple of weeks."

"Did she tell his wife?" I asked.

"Didn't have to. His wife showed up unexpectedly the same day. To surprise him and celebrate his doctorate."

"Oh my," I said. "Poor woman. I hope the little boys didn't have to see whatever came next."

"Yeah, I guess the wife got to his place, you know, his and Liesl's, shortly after Rich got there. My friend, the one who was in the department when Liesl showed up, followed Rich home. He didn't know Liesl had left, and he was afraid for her."

"I would think so," said Tom.

"Burkhardt. That was it. Liesl Burkhardt. Anyway, it took Rich's wife about half a second to realize that he had been living there with a woman. And of course Rich was in quite a state already. Milcourt and the committee were not gentle. The way I heard it, when his wife showed up at the apartment, Rich was ranting one minute and crying his eyes out the next, asking her to forgive him. My friend, Joe Doyle, said that Rich's wife didn't seem surprised. Said she calmly took off her wedding ring and walked into the bathroom, and then they heard the toilet flush. When she came back, Joe said she looked at Rich and said, 'You think your life just went down the crapper? Just wait,' and then she walked out."

Thirty-Nine

Tom wanted me to stay the night. "I'm worried about you being home alone, especially now," he had said. "You can take off early in the morning. We'll be up anyway. But that guy, that Rich Campbell, I don't like it, Janet."

But I wanted to go home. I needed to run a load of laundry, which I hadn't done in too long, and I didn't want to have to rush home in the morning to get ready to meet Peg. Or, more to the point, to go to Treasures on Earth. I wanted to look reasonably put together for that. In a place full of coiffed and polished people, I knew I'd learn more if I seemed to fit in, or nearly so.

"I won't be alone," I had told Tom. "I'll have my bodyguards." Meaning, of course, Jay and Leo. And then Jay and I went home. Leo met us at the door, twined around my legs and then Jay's, and then curled up on the recliner in the living room, which is probably where he was when we arrived. I emptied my pockets, pulled off my jeans, tossed them into the hamper, and carried it to the laundry room. I started to turn the light on to walk through the kitchen but decided I should pull the blind down over the window on the back door first. I set the hamper inside the laundry room and looked out the window, my hand on the cord to drop the shade. My backyard was dark, but Goldie's deck light was on, and the white and pale pink flowers she had planted around its edge seemed to emit a light of their own. They made me smile.

I closed the shade and flipped the light on and was stuffing the last of the laundry into the washer when my phone rang. I nearly tripped over Jay when I turned to go to the kitchen. "Do you have to follow me everywhere, Bubby?" I asked him. He wagged his butt at me as I reached for the receiver. "Of course you do," I said, stroking his cheek with my other hand. "You're an Aussie."

Goldie had seen my light come on and wanted to know what was happening. I filled her in on the basics and declined an invitation for hot milk and spicy Mexican chocolate-and-cayenne cookies. "By the way, someone was there earlier this evening.

He looked familiar but I can't think where I've seen him. Maybe on TV. I think he might have been there at the lake with Tom."

My stomach nearly dropped on the floor. *Rich Campbell?* I couldn't imagine who else "maybe from TV" might be looking for me, and the thought that he really might know where I lived propelled me across the room to check that the deadbolt was fastened. The phone cord stopped me halfway there. "Goldie, hang on," I said, and set the receiver on the counter with a thunk. All the doors were locked. I would have armed the alarm that Tom thought I should have installed, if I had actually had it installed. For the first time, I wished I had done so. I closed the rest of my blinds and curtains, then picked up the phone again. "Okay."

"Something wrong?" Goldie asked.

"No."

"Tell me."

"No, nothing."

"You shut your curtains. You checked your locks, didn't you? Who was that man?"

"What, I can't shut my curtains?"

"Janet, you never shut the curtains in your office. You're afraid someone may look in. What's going on?"

I told her about creepy Rich Campbell. Not the whole story, just the part on the island. And I didn't tell her he pretended to shoot me, just said he made a gesture.

"He gave you the finger for being on the island? Your friend's private island?"

I left it at that. She wanted to know if there was any news about how Anderson Billings had died, and she wondered what was taking so long. "It's not like they can just fart around forever to do the autopsy."

"Autopsy is done. But the lab results won't be back for a while." Which reminded me that I hadn't heard anything about the funeral. "Goldie, do you have today's paper?"

"Right here."

I had her check the funeral notices, but there was no mention of Anderson. I'd have to remember to find out in the morning. I wasn't keen on funerals, but felt I should be at that one.

Just as we were wrapping up the conversation, Goldie said, "Come sleep over here, Janet. The boys can come with you."

"I'm fine here. Got all kinds of security, and I have the best watch cat in town." I wasn't kidding, either. Leo had shown his mettle when it mattered. "And you know Jay isn't about to let anyone hurt me."

She wasn't happy, but she let it go. *She can't exactly scold* me *for being stubborn,* I thought, and smiled. It was getting late, but I couldn't get Rich Campbell's girlfriend Liesl out of my mind. What was her last name? Baker? Brubaker? I sat down at my computer, woke it up, and typed "Liesl" into the search engine, then stared at the screen. *Burkhardt,* that was it. You wouldn't believe how many Liesl Burkhardts came up in my initial search. I added "Kuwait" to the terms, doubting that she would still be there but hoping that might narrow the field to a Liesl Burkhardt who had at one time taught English in Kuwait. Nothing. So I deleted "Kuwait" and typed in "University of Connecticut." Bingo. I read the article, dated 1995, twice through.

"We're coming to visit," I said when Goldie answered. I pulled a pair of shorts on, fastened Jay's leash to his collar, shoved my keys and my cell phone into my pocket, lifted Leo out of the recliner, and moved the whole kit and caboodle to Goldie's place, where I told her about the article I had just read.

"She drowned. Goldie, she drowned in a lake in November."

"What a shame," said Goldie.

"Doesn't that strike you as odd?"

Goldie shrugged, but her voice said she wasn't so unfeeling. "People drown."

"How many people have you known who drowned, Goldie? And two people connected to this guy drown?" My pitch was rising so I reeled myself in a turn. "In strange circumstances, too."

Goldie nibbled a cookie and asked, "Where was this again? The girl, Lisa. And when?"

"Liesl. Massachusetts. A pond on Cape Cod. In November." Goldie's cuckoo clock chirped midnight. I considered calling Tom despite the hour, but I knew he and George planned to get up at o-dark-thirty in hopes of seeing the parrot. George thought their chances were better if they were there shortly after sunrise, which was around six forty-five these days. Besides, how would it help for them to know about Liesl tonight?

"You're right. Makes no sense, unless she was suicidal. I mean, we don't know much about her. That's possible."

"But I knew Anderson, and he wasn't suicidal," I said.

"So what do we do now?"

"Sleep, I think. I have to be up early." I told her what Peg and I were planning.

"I'll go with you. Been wanting to see what's going on in there anyway." For the first time in I couldn't remember how long there was a fire in Goldie's eye.

"I only have two tickets to the exhibit," I said.

Goldie would not be deterred. "I'll buy one at the door."

"Not sure you can do that."

"I'll ask. Besides, they're not going to turn away an old lady whose two friends have passes." She laughed and said, "Don't worry, I won't wear my Land Trust T-shirt." Leo waltzed back into the kitchen, apparently having completed his investigation of Goldie's house. She picked him up and snuggled her face into his neck. "You going to sleep with me tonight, Mr. Leo?"

"He doesn't like to sleep in the bed." I should know, I've been trying to get him to sleep in mine for the past two years. There's nothing so soothing as a cat. Except a dog. Or one of each. Which reminded me — time to hit the sack.

"Ha! Show's how much you know!" said Goldie. "He always sleeps with me when he comes for a visit." Which he had done a couple of times when I had to be out of town for a few days. I don't like to leave him alone, even with food and extra litter boxes, so he goes to "Aunt Goldie's" or, the last time, to Tom's place.

"Fickle pickle," I said, standing and running the backs of my fingers down Leo's cheek and neck. "Okay, see you in the morning." Jay was on his feet, sleepy looking but ready to follow wherever I led. I leaned down and hugged him. "At least one of you is loyal!"

As I walked away I heard a thump behind me and Goldie said, "Janet."

I turned. Leo was following me and Jay, his eyes wide and very focused on me. "Aww, Leo *mio.*" Whether he understood my words, who knows? But I couldn't help thinking he knew what they meant, and I felt a stab of remorse. The last thing I would ever do is saddle my animals with guilt. I scooped him up and he shoved his head into my chin. Ten minutes later I fell asleep in Goldie's guest room with my dog pressed against my legs and my cat purring on the other pillow. Safe.

Forty

I jolted wide awake in the morning, figuring I had overslept and cursing myself for setting my cell phone alarm incorrectly. Again. I always seem to miss some little detail and end up with p.m. where I want a.m. or Off where I want On. But when I flicked my phone on I saw that it wasn't quite six a.m. I hadn't planned to get up for another hour and even that wouldn't give me my usual sleepy-bye quota, but after five minutes of trying to grab another hour, I got up. Leo was gone. I figured he had gone off to Goldie's room. Jay stood on the bed, grinning and wriggling his fanny at me.

"Okay, hang on, Bubby," I said. When we emerged from our room a few minutes later, all was quiet, but Goldie's bedroom door was open and her bed was made. I called, "Goldie?"

No answer. I grabbed Jay's leash from the kitchen table and opened the back door.

Goldie was deadheading flowers by the light of a headlamp, dropping the cuttings into a little basket that I knew she would empty into her compost pile at the back of the yard. She looked up and smiled. "Morning, sleepy head."

"It's barely six, Goldie. It's not even light yet."

Jay ran to Goldie for a quick good-morning kiss, then went off to do what he needed to do. I kept an eye on him but didn't need the baggy in my pocket yet.

"I'm going to go feed him," I said. "Okay if the boys stay at your place, though, when we go out? I hate to admit it, but I'm just the tiniest bit nervous about leaving them home alone."

"I was going to suggest it. I already put some food on the washer for Leo." Goldie kept a litterbox at the ready, as well as a supply of cat food, the kind I bought, and dog treats.

Once we were cleaned up and dressed we still had plenty of time, so I offered to treat Goldie to breakfast at Panera Bread, using its proximity to Coldwater Road as an excuse. "You get that bear claw because it's close to Coldwater Road, too?" asked Goldie, who had limited her carbosplurge to a chocolate chip bagel with one pat of butter.

"Yes."

"Say, isn't that your doctor friend?" Goldie was looking past me toward the cash register.

Without turning around I said, "Oh, crap, really?" She nodded at me and I said, "Maybe if I don't turn around . . ."

"Maybe, but he's coming this . . . no, false alarm. He left."

I leaned forward from my little corner and looked out the window. It was indeed "my doctor friend," Neil Young. He had a Panera Bread shopping bag that, judging by the way it moved, seemed to be loaded. "Goodies for the staff lounge, I guess," I said. He folded his long legs into a little red sports car and pulled out onto Coliseum. "Jeez, one big-ticket car isn't enough for him?" I muttered, and told Goldie about the black sedan he had been driving the last time I saw him. I watched the car, vaguely interested and expecting him to turn right onto Parnell to drive to the hospital, but he moved into the left lane and made a U-turn instead. "That's weird. He's not headed for Parkview."

We both watched the car go by in the far lane and turn north on Coldwater. Then Goldie looked at me. "Maybe he's going where we're going."

"Great." Just what I needed, two weird guys around.

When we had finished our breakfast goodies, I snapped the lid onto my coffee and said, "Let's go. I'd just as soon sit around in the Kroger parking lot as here, and if Peg is early we can swing by Heron Acres and see Tom and George. They might be on the island, but . . ."

Peg was already there, reading something on her e-reader. We climbed into her car and I introduced Goldie. "Oh, you're the one who drove Janet to the emergency room after she was mauled at the clinic," said Goldie.

"Oh, great, here we go," I said. "Must I remind you that we wouldn't have these tickets if not for my misfortune?"

"Did you bring your Tiffany deflector in case the little darling is there?" asked Peg.

"Why would *she* be there?" Goldie asked.

"She won't be." Why *would* she be? "Her family is involved with Treasures on Earth. Her mom wears a pendant with their symbol, you know, the cross with the two heart thingies? And Neil knows them. But there's no reason for them to be there on a weekday morning." I hoped not anyway. I'd forgotten my chain-mail undies.

Goldie and Peg chattered away for a bit,

discovering that they had several friends in common, which is not unusual in Fort Wayne. I let my thoughts go where they would. I didn't really want to think about death and loss, but every time I tried to steer my mind toward something happier, it fought me and won.

It was obvious that something very shady was going on at Treasures on Earth. Was that Moneypenny's game? Smuggling rare tropical birds and selling them for big bucks? Between what I had read and what George had to say, I knew there were profits to be made. Big profits in some cases, assuming the birds survived long enough to make it to a buyer. But how cynical would someone have to be to run a group that claimed to be dedicated to spiritual renewal while exploiting endangered species behind the scenes? And what was a "spiritual leader" doing hooked up with someone like Rich Campbell? Campbell had proven himself a liar and cheat long ago, and he might even be a killer. Then again, Moneypenny might not know that.

Peg turned onto Cedar Canyons and pulled me out of my speculations. "Janet, where's the lake?"

"Tappen Road. A bit farther, on your left. The turn is hard to see, the sign nearly impossible. Slow down a little."

We turned onto the gravel road. Tom's van was parked just inside the property, on the driveway into Heron Acres, so I had Peg pull onto the berm and said, "Goldie, careful getting out. Hard to see the edge of the ditch for the weeds."

"Hey, how far are we going?" asked Peg. "These shoes aren't made for this. I dressed for an art show."

"Not far." I glanced at my own footwear and thought better of taking my only pair of decent pumps onto the beach. "Just let me see if I can spot them. They may be out on the island anyway."

There was no sign of George or Tom other than Tom's vehicle. I knew they'd be using Collin's bass boat, and it was nowhere to be seen either. They must have beached it on the other side of the island. I was more disappointed than I thought I'd be, although I realized that I had no idea what I would tell Tom if I did see him. *You're slipping, MacPhail,* I thought. I don't actually lie to Tom, at least not about anything important, but I didn't see any reason to let him in on every little thing, especially if doing so was likely to start a row, which any plan that took me near Rich Campbell was sure to do. And he'd likely have George Crane's support in this one.

"Okay, let's go," I said, turning back toward the car.

"Hey, look!" said Peg. "Someone's waving."

I looked across the water to the island. Sure enough, two men, one of them waving his arms like a windmill. I waved back, and suddenly wanted to get out of there quickly so I wouldn't have to dodge any questions. "Okay, ladies, let's go."

"Don't you want to say hi?" asked Peg. "I mean, isn't that why we came?" She was still waving at Tom. "We have plenty of time."

"I wasn't thinking," I said.

Goldie got it. "Right, let's go. We don't have a good cover story."

"Oh, gotcha." Peg looked toward the island. "He's yelling something."

"Can't hear him," I said, trying to get them moving.

"Wait," Peg said. "He's yelling 'wait'."

"Can't hear him, Peg. Let's go."

Forty-One

We hightailed it back to the car and drove to the Treasures on Earth entrance on Cedar Canyons. Two pillars built of rough-cut limestone stood like Colossi on either side of the driveway. They each supported an enormous wrought-iron gate, now swung open, away from the road. A sign just inside the entrance invited us to find our treasures here on Earth.

"Moneypenny seems to be the one finding the treasures. What do people have to pay to be in his crowd, anyway?"

"No idea how this works," I said. I thought of Giselle, and realized that I still hadn't called to apologize for breaking our coffee date on Sunday. "Rats."

"What?" asked Peg.

"Nothing. Never mind. I forgot to do something. Come to think of it, I doubt if they charge much to be part of this." Giselle wasn't rich. "Maybe they have membership levels or something."

"I could ask about joining," offered Goldie.

"They'll never buy that," I said, and they agreed.

We parked in the same lot that held the Beemers and Jaguars and Lincolns when they had things going on out here. Now there were only a couple of cars besides ours, both big and shiny new.

Goldie tapped my arm and said, "Isn't that your friend's car?"

"Could be." It was definitely the car Neil had been driving at Panera Bread, but part of me still hoped he wasn't involved in whatever was going on out there. "And stop calling him my friend."

We walked up a series of shallow steps to a massive double door. The wood had a warm golden glow, and the main panels were intricately carved with birds of all sorts.

"Wow." I'm not sure which of us said it. Goldie ran her fingertips up the long tail feathers of a peacock, and then stroked a cockatoo's crest. "Amazing. This is hand carved."

"Gorgeous," said Peg.

It was. If I had to guess, I'd say there were some thirty birds carved into the panels of each door, and I don't think any were repeated.

"So, then, birds are a theme?" asked Goldie. "I have to say, I can think of worse things to worship."

"Oh, we don't worship birds," said a deep voice behind us. We all jumped and turned. "Sorry, didn't mean to startle you lovely ladies."

Peg pressed her hand to her chest. "Didn't hear you coming, is all."

"Yes, so sorry. These new shoes of mine," he looked at his feet, which sported clunky looking black slip-on shoes with thick soles. Definitely not a fashion statement despite his pricey looking suit. "Very ugly, very comfy, and very quiet." He chuckled, then asked, "Going in?" and, stepping past us, held the door open. *At least the gatekeeper doesn't* look *like an ogre,* I thought.

The entrance hall was long and wide and well-lighted. The walls were covered with a lush jungle-leaf paper, and the gray marble floor gleamed. It also rang like a stone bell with every strike of our semi-dressy shoes. No wonder Mystery Man wore those silent soles.

When we were all in, our escort turned around and smiled at us. He took his time, making eye contact with each of us in turn and holding it briefly before moving on. Then he said, "Welcome, welcome." He bowed slightly, and said, "I'm Regis Moneypenny. How can I be of service?"

The man himself, I thought, and caught a look from Goldie. Moneypenny's tone was warm, but something about it made me want to back away from him. I forced myself to stay put, though, and held out my hand. "Janet MacPhail. Mrs. Willard invited me, well, us, my friends and I, to see the art exhibit." He was still holding onto my hand, and his smile didn't seem quite right. I pulled my hand from his grip and asked, "Is it open today?"

"Ah, Mrs. Willard." He nodded, and something soft passed through his eyes. "Indeed, it is open. Let me take you there."

As he turned away from us, I looked down the hall. Every fifteen feet or so there was a big pot, each one different, with an equally huge plant. Between each pair of palms and elephant ears and things I couldn't name stood a flight cage, maybe eight feet long and three deep, and from each cage I caught flashes of movement and color.

I stopped at the first cage. I don't know much about birds, but these I knew because I had photographed some at a bird show once and had fallen in love with their stunning plumage. Rainbow lorikeets. Blue and red and yellow and green and orange, all in one little bird. I had briefly entertained a fantasy of getting one, but when I read how messy the clean up is because of their fruit diet, I changed my mind.

"Shall we?" Moneypenny seemed determined to keep us moving, so I tore myself away, although part of me wanted to ask who appointed him to be our guide, head honcho or not. I kept loose track of which birds I recognized as we passed the cages. Cockatoo. A blue parrot of some sort. Several parakeets, or were they budgies? *What's the difference?* I made a mental note to find out. Next was a gray parrot of some sort. A flock of gorgeous little finches. Cockatiels.

"This is quite an assortment of birds," I said. "Why so many?" Our host had stopped at an open doorway and turned toward me.

"I have always loved birds." *Not exactly what I asked, but it was a start.* "But to answer your question, the birds are here for several reasons. They represent hope and freedom, and that's what we strive for here at Treasures on Earth. They are inherently beautiful, and as such eloquent reminders of the Creator who made us to appreciate the many treasures on Earth. And they are looking for homes."

"Freedom?" asked Goldie? "They're in cages!"

Moneypenny ignored her and continued walking.

"So you run a rescue program?"

"Of sorts, Miss MacPhail, of sorts." He stopped and turned toward me. He was smiling, but he stepped into my comfort zone and stood there, looking at my face. I gritted my teeth, determined not to back away. From the corner of my right eye I could see Peg raise her hand to her mouth, and it seemed as if Moneypenny were the only one still breathing. Then he broke the impasse by saying, "And now, I believe you ladies are here to see the art exhibit?" There was an edge to his voice and my muscles, already tensed, tightened even more, rather as they do when I hear a low warning growl from a dog I'm photographing.

We stepped through the door and into an enormous art exhibit. Paintings and sculptures and textiles, all depicting birds, were displayed around the perimeter, which I estimated to be about the size of two obedience rings, say forty by eighty feet. A series of free-standing display units, like cubicles without the desks, ran down the center of the room. They held more paintings.

"Holy crow," said Goldie.

Peg let out a low whistle.

Moneypenny swept his arm toward the display and said, "Enjoy." He bowed slightly and made for the far end of the room, where two women emerged from behind one of the freestanding displays.

"Ohmydog," I said.

"What?" Peg was right beside me. She looked toward the women and said, "Oh my . . . What are the odds?"

"Hundred percent in favor, I'd say." I turned toward the paintings we were supposedly there to see and whispered, "Come on."

Our erstwhile guide had reached the women and all three turned to look at us as he spoke to them. Mrs. Willard and Persephone Swann appeared to listen, then all three disappeared behind a display. We heard what seemed to be the click of a door closing, and we were alone.

Without taking her eyes off the painting in front of us, Peg said, "We knew they were both involved with Treasures on Earth, right? So it makes sense that they know each other."

Goldie had stepped up on my other side. "So that's Regal Moneypincher. He can't decide whether to be charming or weird, can he?"

I grinned and said, "Regis Mo . . ."

"Janet!" Goldie elbowed me and Peg snickered. "I know that!"

"So I wasn't the only one he made nervous?" I asked.

They both agreed that there was something unsettling about being in his presence. "And why did he try to stare you down like that?" asked Peg. "Still, I can see where he might be seen as, I don't know, not attractive, but . . ." She seemed to be searching for the right word.

"Fascinating?" I asked.

Peg nodded, and Goldie said, "Like a cobra."

The three of us moseyed along the walls as we spoke, taking in the artwork, which was consistently outstanding. I recognized only two or three names, but then I know only a handful of artists other than photographers. Unlike many exhibits, this one had not a single piece that made me wonder what it was doing there, and the pieces, as a whole and as individuals, were displayed with care. And every one of them depicted one or more birds.

We spent a good forty minutes admiring the artwork. I enjoyed that, but was disappointed that there was precious little chance to snoop around. The gallery had two main doors, the one we came in and another double door that led outdoors, but when Peg tried it, it was locked. A small alcove near the end of one long wall had a door as well, the one our host and the two women had used, but it, too, was locked tight.

We were almost back to the door we came in when Peg stepped close to me and said, "I think we're being watched."

"What?"

"Don't turn around suddenly or anything, but maybe in a minute you can walk back to the center display and sort of look around. Over each of the end doors and half-way down each side." She pointed and gestured in the general direction of the painting in front of us, as if commenting on the sweep of the white peacock's tail. "Pretty sure they're cameras, and that they move to follow us."

I played along with the charade, rubbing my chin and cocking my head as if studying the painting, and said, "Okay, I will do that." I stepped forward and leaned in, as if examining brush strokes, which actually *were* fascinating up close. "Amazing how many colors go into painting a white subject," I said. Then I looked around and made for one of the free-standing displays.

Peg was right, there was something mounted high on the wall and it looked like a camera, albeit a teensy one. I memorized its orientation, then checked it again after I had moved to another display unit. The camera had moved, I was sure of it.

It made sense to have cameras in a gallery displaying expensive artwork, but motion sensors? To track visitors? Or were they managed manually? If they were, that meant they didn't just keep a record they could review. It meant that someone was watching us right now. And that was creepy. It took all my self-control not to walk over to the camera and swing my purse at it, but I managed to pretend I hadn't noticed it.

Goldie joined me in front of a bronze of six California quail taking flight. It was a lovely piece, three feet or so in circumference, with the birds held, each at a different height, on supports made to look like tall blades of grass. Each quail seemed to launch itself on a slightly different trajectory, as if they were scattering to confuse a predator. Not a bad tactic, I thought.

"Gorgeous, isn't it? I think this is my favorite piece," said Goldie.

"It is. Look at the feathers on the birds."

She startled me by draping an arm over my shoulder and bending the two of us toward the sculpture. She whispered, "Don't react, but we're being filmed."

"I know. I saw them," I said. "They may be live feed."

We stood back up, and I said in a normal voice, "Well, ladies, I think we've seen everything. Shall we?"

The long hallway was empty of people and, other than a few squawks and whistles from the cages that lined it and the clack-clack-clack of our shoes on the marble, it was deathly still. I stopped in front of a cage that held a small green and blue parrot. At least I assumed it was a parrot. I don't really know what distinguishes a parrot from a lorikeet from a budgie. Whatever it was, the bird sidled to the edge of the cage and tilted his head to get a better look at us.

"Peg, give me your camera."

She reached into her pocket and slipped the camera to me. I flicked it on and held it against my body, hoping my aim was decent, and clicked off a few shots. On the last one, the flash went off and two seconds later a door opened down the hall. I lowered my hand and, as I turned toward the sound, I held the camera behind me where Peg could get it.

The man bearing down on us was backlit, so it was impossible to see his face, but I have a memory for movement. Dog, horse, human, I'm quick to notice carriage and style of motion, and I recognize the set of this man's shoulders and the way his arms hung.

"Aw, shit," I murmured.

"What's wrong?" asked Peg.

"It's just a photo. Big deal," said Goldie.

But the epithet rattled and echoed around my brain, and it took everything I had not to turn and run as fast as I could for the exit door. The man's face was clearly visible now, and the look on it was not friendly. It was too late to run to safety, so I followed the rules. When faced with a threatening animal, *do not run. Stand your ground. Make yourself as big as possible. Don't stare into his eyes, he'll take that as a challenge.*

I made my spine as straight as possible. Maybe they felt my energy. Okay, my fear. Whatever it was, I felt Goldie stand a little taller on my right. Peg did the same on my left. My elbows touched theirs. We were one unit, and I felt empowered by the time the man reached us and I found myself standing eighteen inches from the glowering mug of bird guy and possible killer Rich Campbell.

Forty-Two

"What an unpleasant man!" said Goldie once we were in the car and out the gates of Treasures on Earth.

"That's an understatement," I said, but I didn't share my suspicions about just how unpleasant Rich Campbell may have been to his former girlfriend, Liesl Burkhardt, and to my friend and student Anderson Billings. I focused instead on the failures of our mission. "We didn't accomplish much with that little adventure," I said. "Plus, Peg, I owe you a camera. But rats, I was hoping to take some photos of those birds back for George to identify."

Peg started to laugh. "You still can, my dear."

"What?"

She started rummaging around in her voluminous skirt and brought her hand out of the fabric with the camera in her grip. "Here you go."

Goldie let out a hoot in the backseat and tapped Peg on the shoulder. "Brilliant! Janet, you have brilliant friends!"

I flicked the camera on and brought up the most recent photos. When the little green and blue parrot popped onto the screen, I joined the laugh party. "So what was that you gave him?" Campbell had demanded the camera, growling that there was a sign outside the gallery that clearly stated the confiscation policy and no photos rule. "You can pick it up after we have a chance to remove all photos taken on Treasures property," he had said.

"That was my son's old camera. The one he dropped in the pool at the Y." The grin on Peg's face rivaled the one she wore when she drove me to the emergency room after Tiffany dear bit my behind. "Cheap little thing, wasn't worth trying to fix after its full immersion. Dead as a doorknob."

"You rock, girlfriend," I said, and thought *how appropriate, leaving Rich Campbell with a drowned camera.*

When the initial pleasure cooled a bit, Goldie said, "Janet, you'd better stay with Tom or me until this is all settled. That guy, what's his name again?"

"Rich Campbell."

"Right. He doesn't know us, but he knows

who you are. And he's not a nice man."

"Ah, the mistress of understatement," I said.

"What?"

"Never mind." She was right, I thought. He knew who I was and probably more than that. I wondered whether Goldie and Tom, and even Peg, might be in any danger. If Campbell had been to my house, he could easily have seen Goldie in her yard. She was out in the garden all the time.

"So?"

"She's right, you know," said Peg, sobering up. "He's not going to be happy when he finds out about the camera. He doesn't know me from boo, but . . ."

"But the women do," I said, "Mrs. Willard and Persephone Swann."

Peg gasped, but recovered and said, "All they know is that I work at the clinic. I mean, they don't know where I live or anything. I mean, why would they care?"

"They might care now, so just be careful." I added that Goldie could be in danger, too, but she waved me off so I dropped the direct approach and said, "Maybe I should stay at your house, Goldie, until this blows over. I'd feel safer." *And I'd feel better knowing you're not alone over there,* I thought.

Peg slowed the car so we could see down

Tappen Road, but Tom's car was gone. We drove back to the Kroger lot.

"Email me those photos as soon as you can, okay, Peg?" I asked.

"Here, just take it." She handed me the camera and a little black bag that she had tucked under the seat. "I think the download thingy is in there."

I chuckled. "I'll bring it back to the clinic tomorrow."

"No rush," Peg said. "I don't have any more top secret assignments scheduled for a few days."

Goldie and I got into my van and I sat with the door open to change my shoes. No sense scuffing the back of my one nice pair of shoes by driving in them.

"There's something under the wiper," said Goldie, pointing to the windshield in front of me.

I reached out and grabbed it, knowing what it was before I opened it. "Note from Tom."

"Uh oh. Busted!"

I read it and told her what it said, mostly. "They stopped here on their way back to Tom's office, saw the van when they came out of the grocery store. He went back into the store to find me and see if I wanted to join them there." I looked at Goldie. "I feel like I cheated on him or something."

"That's what happens when we sneak around and lie. But it had to be done."

"Thanks a lot."

"Just sayin'," she said. "So call him. Go find out what they found out. You'll find a way to get found out, and everything will be fine."

"What did you say?"

"You'll find a way to get caught," Goldie said.

I started to argue but stopped myself. She was, as she often is, right. "It's not as if I wasn't going to tell him eventually. Today, even."

"So, Janet, you know something about that nasty man, that Rich Campbell, don't you?" I glanced sideways and saw that Goldie was peering over the top of her glasses at me, which she only does when she knows I'm holding out. So I told her, then swore her to secrecy.

I parked in my own driveway but went straight to Goldie's to see to my boys. Jay bounced and wriggled as if we'd been gone for a month. Leo hopped onto the back of Goldie's big overstuffed reading chair and I bonked noses with him to say hello. We all went out to the backyard for a little R and R, and I called Tom. They were just leaving his office to go home and shower, so I said I'd meet them there. But I had to ask what they had found.

"We saw the bird. George is pretty blown away. Going to try to catch him. Or her. That's still in question."

I couldn't imagine how he'd catch a loose parrot, especially if it was wild-caught and not used to or fond of captivity.

"We'll only be home long enough to clean up and grab a bite to eat," Tom said. "We're going to the morgue for a look at the other bird."

"The morgue?"

"Yeah. If I can reach Jo for permission. That's where the bird is." They couldn't exactly stick it in the department fridge," Tom said. "If the cops are anything like people around here," meaning the university, "someone would eat it." Tom had installed a small refrigerator in his office because, he had told me, someone kept taking his lunches from the faculty lounge and he could never prove who it was, although he suspected one of the accounting profs.

I loaded Jay into the van, but Goldie wanted Leo to stay and keep her company, and since he was curled up on her reading chair I had to assume he agreed. She said she would take him home later. I was almost to the corner when I realized that I was still more "dressed" than was quite normal for me, so I backtracked, changed into jeans and a henley, and then hit the road. My thoughts ran around like a pack of terriers in a field of mice. I needed to go see Mom soon. I hadn't been there since . . . when? I couldn't remember, which meant either that it had been too long or that I was losing my mind. I needed to followup on some requests for portraits, too.

What I really wanted to do was find a way to get back into Treasures on Earth without raising suspicion. Or getting caught by Rich Campbell. I had no desire to sleep with the fishes, and having encountered the man up close, I was even more convinced that he was dangerous.

And I needed to know more about Regis Moneypenny. There must be information about the man somewhere. He had become a significant figure in Allen County, and I couldn't imagine how he would do so without someone knowing something about him. I made a mental note to call Giselle Swann after I saw Tom and George. If she was attending services, or meetings, or whatever they called them, at Treasures, she must have some information about the man and the group. Knowing Giselle, she'd be testy for a bit since I had forgotten our plans to meet on Sunday, but if I groveled enough I knew she'd come around. I also knew that if she thought for a moment that the people around her were abusing or exploiting animals, she'd be the loudest canary they ever heard.

FORTY-THREE

Tom and George were showered and changed when I got there. Jay was delighted to see his buddy Drake, and even more delighted to see his new buddy George, who for his part got down on the floor to give my dog a belly rub.

"Man after your own heart, eh, my dear?" asked Tom, right before he planted a big kiss on my lips.

"He won't find it," I said.

"Already taken?"

I shrugged and opened the refrigerator.

"Hang on," said George, getting up and washing his hands in the sink. "I'm just about to make my gourmet grilled cheese sandwiches. Hungry?"

What I took for the ingredients were laid out near the stove. I stepped closer. A block of Gruyère, another of white cheddar. *These are not cheap cheeses,* I thought, looking at the per-pound labels. A couple of home-grown tomatoes, no doubt from Goldie's garden. She'd sent several home with Tom. Whole-grain bread with sunflower seeds. Fresh spinach. My mouth started to water.

"I want two!" I said.

George grinned as he got to work and Tom filled me in on their morning at the lake. They had arrived before dawn and were on the island when the sun peeked over the treetops to the east. According to Tom, George did a mean parrot imitation, and it didn't take long before "our bird" flew in and landed on the old sycamore. That was exciting enough, but when he had enough light to see the bird clearly, George had confirmed its identity.

George stopped slicing cheese for a moment. He looked at me and said, "Honestly, I almost peed my pants. I've never seen one at all, anywhere, and here it is, flying around in northern Indiana." He choked slightly on the last word, then continued, "The Carmine Parrot is a gorgeous bird, and so rare and endangered, and these bastards . . ." He shook his head and went back to making the sandwiches.

"Carmine Parrot," I murmured. "What a lovely name."

Tom changed the subject. "You sure disappeared in Kroger this morning."

"Oh, yeah, that."

Tom rested his elbows on the table and his chin in his hands. "What did you do?" He sounded resigned to whatever might follow. I noticed that George was grinning as he layered cheese and tomatoes.

George stopped smiling when I got to our encounter with Rich Campbell and said, "Seriously, Janet, that guy is mental. You need to be really careful."

Tom just stared at me. I appreciated his ability to keep quiet even though he was worried, which was clear in his eyes. It must have been clear in his chemistry, too, because Drake came and laid his head in Tom's lap and gazed up at him, a perfect mirror of the look Tom had been giving me.

"Come on, guys, lighten up. I'm not going hand-to-hand with the guy." *Time to change the subject,* I thought. "Wonder why Jo hasn't called back."

"Oh, she did! Sorry. I meant to tell you," said Tom.

"She called you?" I asked.

"Said your line went straight to voice mail."

"What?" I pulled my phone out of my pocket. Dead. "Aww, crap. Again?"

George flipped a sandwich in the pan and said, "I used to do that all the time."

"I don't do it all the time." *I do, but I didn't need a scolding.* "Where's your charger, Tom?"

He handed me his phone and took mine. "I don't know that my charger will fit your phone but here, call her."

On the third ring, Jo said, "Did she show up yet?"

"Yes, she did," I said.

"Hey, I'm standing in your driveway. Where the heck are you?"

"Why are you standing in my driveway?" I asked.

"You at Tom's place?" She didn't wait for an answer. "Stay there! I'm on my way."

"What's go . . ."

"Just stay there, okay? I have something to show you." And she was gone.

"Those smell great, George," I said. He had two sandwiches done and on plates and was melting butter for the third. I turned to Tom and asked, "Do you know what's up with Jo?"

"Nope," he said, but he had a funny twitch going on at the corners of his mouth.

"How come you know everything about my friends before I do?"

He raised his hands in surrender and said, "I don't know anything."

"Let's eat!" said George.

Tom told the dogs to lie down by the wall. Jay slowly sank into a sphinx position but kept his eyes fixed at the correct angle to watch my sandwich, as if he had x-ray vision. Drake circled once and then dropped to the vinyl with a muscular *thunk* and let out a big sigh.

Without looking at the poor things, George grinned and said, "You never feed them, do you?"

We had just cleared the table and released the dogs when I heard a car door.

"Must be Jo," I said.

"Come on guys, let's go out back," said Tom, hustling the dogs out the sliding door into the back yard, a maneuver I found a bit odd. Jo loves dogs, and even if her partner, Hutch, was with her, he was coming around. Jay had taken Hutchinson on as his personal project, no doubt aware long before I was that the man was just afraid of dogs, and what we fear, we dislike. Jay was working on that.

Tom caught up with me at the front door, pulled it open, and let me go through first.

"Oh my God!" I blurted.

Jo Stevens stood in the yard with a gorgeous puppy of indeterminate breed.

"You got a puppy!" I had to fight the impulse to rush the pup and scoop him or her into my arms, knowing that from where the little guy stood, that would be terrifying. Instead I walked slowly toward Jo and the pup, sat on the grass a couple feet away, and let the pup come to me. Tom and George did the same, sinking to the ground next to me. The puppy, who appeared to be about twelve weeks old, launched himself into my lap and licked and nibbled my chin. Then he bounced from my lap to Tom's and tried to pull Tom's collar off.

"Okay, big guy, leave the shirt," said Tom, gently fending off the assault. "Nothing shy about this guy!"

The puppy had medium-long fur the color of corn stalks in autumn, but unlike a Golden Retriever, he had white stockings, a white chest, and a white stripe down his face. I held him out from me so I could look at him. His eyes still had a hint of deep puppy blue but were heading toward brown, and on closer inspection I saw that his coat was not a solid wheaty yellow as I thought at first, but mottled.

"Aussie-Golden cross?" I asked Jo.

"Wow, you're good. Yes, he is." She was grinning all over herself. "Daddy is an Aussie, mama a Golden. Accidental breeding — the Aussie boy actually opened the back door of the people's house to come visit."

"Interesting mix," said Tom. "He won't know whether to round the birds up or carry them."

"The door thing sounds familiar," I said. Jay had a habit of opening my back door and letting himself in.

Jo laughed. "Both parents, oddly enough, are champions. They live a few doors apart, train together. Neither of the owners was happy about this, but, you know, here they are. At least both parents had all their health clearances, so chances are these guys will be healthy, or have a fighting chance. And there were only two puppies."

I was trying to think who I knew with a champion Aussie in town and the only ones I could think of were bitches. "Who are the dogs' owners? I might know them."

"Maybe, but they're in Evansville."

So probably not. Evansville is the very far end of the state from Fort Wayne, and fits the old "you can't get there from here" joke because there is no major highway between the two cities, at least not until they finish the interstate extension. "We don't really see many people from Evansville at most shows up this way."

"Yeah, it's a long haul," said Jo. "We just

drove it, didn't we?" She stroked the puppy's head.

"Yes, the missing detective." I got the pup down on his back in the grass and calmed him with a belly rub. "What's his name?"

"Not sure. I want to live with him for a few days and let him tell me."

Tom winked at me and gestured with his head toward Jo. "Smart woman."

George came out and we made the introductions, then moved to the backyard and let the pup meet Jay and Drake. He licked their chins, then jumped on Jay's head. Jay was not amused, and gently but firmly pushed the little guy down and held him there for a moment. When he let go, the puppy gave Drake a try and although the black dog didn't look happy, he didn't object to the puppy rough stuff. "Better get used to it, old man," said Tom.

George threw a tennis ball, and Drake and the puppy ran after it. Jay looked at me as if to say, "I'm not getting into that mess." We all watched while George and Tom tossed the ball a few more times. Drake always got there first and picked up the ball, then let the little guy take it from his mouth and carry it. Finally the puppy's battery seemed to wind down and he flopped down next to Jay. He fought to keep his eyes open but was out cold in about two minutes.

We filled Jo in on all the things we had learned.

"I'd like to necropsy the dead bird," said George.

Jo looked thoughtful for a moment, then said, "I think we can arrange that. Today, if I can clear it?"

"Perfect," said George.

Jo looked at her watch and said, "Right. I'll get this guy," she nodded at the pup, "squared away and meet you there, make a few calls on my way."

Before she could stand up and wake the puppy, I said, "So, Jo, I thought you didn't want a dog yet? How are you going to manage a puppy?"

She smiled at me. "That's what I've been wanting to tell you." If you saw Jo in law-enforcement mode, you wouldn't think her capable of squealing, but excitement launched her voice about three octaves higher as she said, "I've been accepted into the SAR program!" Meaning Search and Rescue. Jo gave the sleeping puppy a loving look. "He's my partner. We're going to train together."

"Really?"

"I know, you're wondering about the breeding. They take a lot of mixed-breed dogs in this program. Often rescued or shelter dogs, if they have the drive. One of the instructors, you know, high-ranking SAR guy, heard about this litter and thought the cross would make for good workers. They passed the temperament and other tests with flying colors, so the owner donated him and his sister to the program. When I picked him up she said she felt guilty about not keeping her dog, you know, the mama, secure, and she thought this might turn a bad mistake to something good. And now he's mine."

The dogs got up when we did, but the puppy was groggy. Tom picked him up and carried him like a baby to Jo's car, rubbing his chest and cooing to him, and something in my own chest did a little dance. Tom slid the little guy into the crate in the backseat of Jo's car. The pup turned around in circles until he found the perfect spot, then flopped and went right back to sleep. Jo took off and we went back into the house long enough to grab what we needed, settle Jay and Drake, and lock up. Tom and George were off to have a closer look at the dead parrot. I had questions about living birds, although I didn't tell Tom how I planned to find a few answers.

Forty-Four

I glanced at my phone where it lay on the passenger seat. The screen was lit, the "new message" signal flashing. It was working again.

"Janet, I'm sorry I didn't call on Sunday." I had expected Giselle to be upset that I hadn't called her. One of us obviously misremembered the plan, but this worked for me. "I got really busy for a while, and, you know, I got my bird, you know, the one I told you I might get? I mean, she's not really mine, I'm a, you know, guardian. Just for a while." There was a pause, then, "So, Janet, can we meet, maybe, you know, maybe today? This afternoon? I sort of need to, you know, need to talk?" Pause. "To you?" Pause. "About something?" Giselle may have looked a lot better than she did four months earlier, but her self-confidence still had a long way to go.

I ran through my mental list of things I

really needed to do. Laundry was number one, unless I wanted to buy more undies. On the other hand, Giselle said she had her bird, the one placed in her "guardianship" by Treasures on Earth. I wouldn't mind getting a look at him or her. My phone hadn't been plugged in long enough during lunch to get more than a low charge, but I was pretty sure it had enough juice to get at least one photo of Giselle's parrot, assuming it was a parrot, for George to look at. My camera would be better, but if I pulled that out Giselle might have a nervous breakdown, so the phone would have to do.

I made the call.

"No, not there. I mean, I'm not at home," said Giselle. My first impulse was to try to talk my way into her house, but something in her voice stopped me and we agreed instead to meet at my house in half an hour. That gave me time to stop at Kroger for laundry soap. I spent a few minutes looking for the phone charger for the car, digging around under a pile of magazines, a towel, a rain poncho, and three sweatshirts on the back seat, then searched under all the seats. That turned up my missing stopwatch, half a dozen pens, and a bent paperback on organizing stuff. I tried to flatten it out, thinking maybe I should read it. There was no sign of the charger. *Don't forget to plug it in as soon as you get home,* I thought.

Kroger was busy. I grabbed the detergent and decided to hit the bakery as well. The carrot cake cupcakes called to me, but when I thought about how hard Giselle had worked to take off the weight and how I should be doing the same, I decided to pick up a bag of pita chips and some grilled red pepper hummus instead. I was just reaching for the hummus when a brain tingle made me look around. At first I didn't see anything, but at the end of the aisle a curved mirror mounted high on the wall caught my eye. The image was distorted and small at that distance, but I was sure someone was standing at the end of the row of freezers behind me. The figure was still at first, but as I watched, it seemed to lean in my direction. Someone peeking around the corner? Or just looking at products on display? I shifted my gaze from the mirror and was sure I saw something. Or someone. Hair? A face? It was such a fleeting image that I couldn't be sure, and when I looked back at the mirror, whatever it was had disappeared.

I dropped the hummus into my basket and scurried toward the end of the freezers. There was no one there. The image in the mirror was vague, and the memory of it even harder to hold. A blue shirt? Or gray? I walked as quickly as I could, given the crowd of shoppers, weaving between shopping carts as I crossed the back of the store. I looked down every aisle, and finally spotted someone in a blue shirt and baseball cap. Tall. Something familiar in the walk, but I couldn't place it. Whoever it was walked between the check out lanes and turned left toward the exit, then was gone.

I stood there for a moment, watching out the front window. My view was partially blocked by the displays spread across the front of the store, and I was partway down the aisle, but still I thought I might catch another glimpse. I was about to give up when I saw a blue shirt pushing a cart into the cart garage.

Rich Campbell. He always seemed to wear blue shirts. Or was it? A little shiver in my shoulders said yes, but my rational mind told me that was just silly. For one thing, would he be civil enough to put the cart away? That small courtesy was enough to make me think I really was overreacting. And even if it were Campbell, he had to eat, right? Had to buy groceries? *This far from Treasures?* a little voice asked me. And then another little voice told me not to be stupid, it wasn't him, and if it was, well, there were all sorts of reasons for him to be in town. *Get a grip, Janet.*

Giselle was sitting on my front porch when I pulled into my driveway. She had on a poncho, but not one of the old ratty-looking ones she used to wear. This one was a heathery blue blend, and looked good on her, if a bit out of season.

"Giselle! Am I late?" I glanced at my wrist but I'd forgotten to put my watch on when I dressed. Still, how could I be late? I hadn't dawdled that long in the store.

"No, I'm early? I just, you know, I didn't have anything else to do so . . ." She let the thought trickle off.

"Are you okay?" She didn't look okay, although sometimes it's hard to tell with Giselle.

"Oh, sure, you know, I'm fine?"

"Where's your car?" Giselle's hard-to-miss old Yugo was nowhere to be seen.

"Oh, I, umm, . . ." Giselle swayed from foot to foot and pushed a hand through her hair. She looked down the street toward the subdivision entrance. "Can we go inside?"

Leo met us at the door but ignored me to stand up with his paws on Giselle's thighs and meow at her poncho.

I grinned and said, "He's fine with dogs. You can put Precious down." I should have guessed the little guy was with her. Giselle goes few places without her Maltese, especially if she can tuck him under a piece of clothing. Hence the poncho in August. "Come on, let's sit in the kitchen. Let me drop a load in the washer, okay?"

Precious froze when Giselle set him down, and she said, "He's never been close to a kitty."

Leo extended his neck and sniffed experimentally at the little dog.

"I guess they're even," I said. "Leo's never been close to a dog that's smaller than he is."

Precious looked up at Giselle and Leo looked up at me, and then they both seemed to relax. By the time I got the laundry going and came back to the kitchen, the two of them were taking turns chasing each other to the living room and back.

"Aren't they cute?" Giselle put a hand over her mouth and giggled. "I didn't know Precious liked kitties."

"They are cute, yep," I said. "So Giselle, what's up?"

"Oh, you know, I wanted to talk to you?" I waited for her to continue. "It's just, you know, it's been a long time."

Ho boy. I was starting to lose patience, but knowing Giselle, I might as well settle in for the ride. Directness is not her middle name, but something was definitely on her mind, and it wasn't the months since we had our last heart-to-heart.

"How about some iced tea and hummus with pita chips?" I asked, getting to my feet and wondering whether I was becoming one of those have-a-cuppa old-lady sleuths. *Nah.*

"Tea would be nice. But hot, if it's not too much trouble. No food, please. And no sugar."

The interlude while I put the kettle on seemed to buck her up a bit, and when I sat down again she started a rapid-fire delivery.

"Janet, I'm so worried. There's something, I don't know, something wrong I think with the birds, you know, the bird I'm taking care of, you know, I'm a guardian now for the birds for Treasures, you know, for Mr. Moneypenny and them, and, I don't know what's, I mean . . ."

"Whoa, Giselle!" I reached across the table and laid my hand on hers. "Giselle, slow down."

She stared at me as if I'd slapped her and said, "Okay."

Silence. I waited. And waited. The kettle whistled. I filled the pot. Precious chased Leo into the kitchen, barked three times, then spun and took off with the cat right behind him. I sat back down and looked at Giselle, but didn't say anything.

Giselle finally spoke, and seemed a bit more relaxed. "Okay. I don't know what's going on, Janet, and I don't know who to talk to."

"So you called me."

"Yes. Well, I think you sort of called me." The corners of her mouth lifted and she looked at me out of the corner of her eye.

"Right."

"Okay, well, I think there's something bad going on." She paused. "You know, with the birds?"

Avian flu? "Is your bird sick, Giselle?"

"What?" Her eyes widened. "No! Oh, no, I don't mean that. I mean, you know, they're doing something wrong. Not the birds. I mean, you know, people there?"

"Like Moneypenny?"

Giselle's shoulders sagged and her voice shifted down half an octave. "I don't know."

I poured the tea and set a mug in front of Giselle. She wrapped her fingers around it and inhaled the steam.

"This smells really good. Sort of relaxing."

"Blackberry sage, my favorite brew." She was right about the fragrance, too. It always calms me down. "So why do you think something bad is going on?"

"Okay, I got my bird. You know, the one I'm taking care of. Mr. Campbell brought her to my house with the cage and food and all, you know?"

"Okay."

"He told me, you know, gave me a bunch of weird rules. Oh, look at them!" She pointed at Leo and Precious, who were both tanking up at the water bowl. It's big enough for a party of critters their size, since it's really Jay's bowl. "Maybe I should get a cat instead. The bird doesn't like Precious much."

I watched Leo and Precious lie down side by side on the cool vinyl. "I'd say they're having a good time. So, Giselle," I turned my attention back to her, "what kind of weird rules?"

"Don't take pictures of her. Isn't that weird? I mean, if they want to find her a home, why not let people know she needs one?"

"Does she?"

"What?"

"Does the bird need a home? What's her name, anyway, and what kind of bird is she?"

"Oh." Giselle seemed confused by at least one of those questions. "That's another thing. I asked what kind she is and he said 'parrot,' and I said, 'yes, but what kind of parrot,' and he acted like that was a dumb question and said, 'just a parrot.' " She shook her head and scowled. "That's like 'just a dog.' I mean even a mixed breed is a mix of something, right, not 'just a dog'?"

I sure wouldn't argue with her about that.

Giselle went on, "So I tried to figure out on the computer what kind of parrot she is but I don't know, you know, there are a lot of them that kind of look alike?"

"I know someone who would know. Would you let him have a look?"

Something like fear moved across Giselle's face, and her voice rose again. "No, I mean, I can't, he said not to let anyone see her, and, I don't know . . ."

"Moneypenny?"

"Mr. Campbell."

"Giselle, did he threaten you?"

"Not really." She stared into her tea.

"What's that mean?" I asked. "Did he or didn't he?"

"Really, not really. But, I don't know, I sort of felt like he'd do something if I didn't follow the rules."

"How about if you break just one little rule and take a picture of your bird? And then give it to me?" I asked. If she would do that, George could have a look and no doubt identify the bird.

Giselle reached into her poncho and produced an envelope. She handed it to me, a nervous twitch working on her eyebrow. Inside were three photos of a lovely blue parrot with yellow edges to her wings, like epaulettes, and a green band across her throat.

"Oh, she's gorgeous!" I spread the photos on the table in front of me.

"I know." Giselle's fingers were tapping quick time on her mug. "She's really pretty. But not too friendly. Really, I think she's kind of scared." I looked at Giselle. "I feel sad that she has to be in the cage but she's so scared, I'm afraid if I take her out I'll never catch her."

"Poor thing." I tapped a photo. "May I keep these for a few days?"

"No. I mean, they're for you. You can keep them."

"Giselle, you're doing the right thing, you know." At least I hoped she was. Mostly I hoped she wasn't putting herself in danger. If I was right about Rich Campbell, he wasn't a man to be crossed lightly. I couldn't see Giselle fighting back effectively if he attacked her, and although I was sure that Precious would defend her to the death, at his size, he couldn't really do much.

"Janet, do you think they're doing something with these birds? Something to hurt them?"

"I think they may be doing something illegal, yes." *How much should I say?* "Giselle, you can't talk to anyone else about any of this, you know. Not yet, okay?"

"I know."

"Really, Giselle. If they're up to what I think they're up to, there's a lot of money at stake, plus federal crimes. So hush hush, okay?"

"Okay."

I remembered that I hadn't seen Giselle's car out front so I asked her how she got to my place.

"I drove. I parked over at the embroidery shop."

I had to think a moment. "The embroidery shop in Georgetown Square?" That's a shopping center at least a mile from my house, and I couldn't think of a direct walking route. "Why?"

"In case . . ." She didn't finish the thought, but I did.

"You think you're being watched?" I flashed back to the figure at the grocery store, and suddenly was positive it had been Campbell.

Giselle shrugged.

"Let me drive you back."

"No, I'll walk. I mean, if he, you know, someone, is watching me, that would sort of blow my cover, wouldn't it?" She grinned at me.

"Your cover?" Somehow the idea of Giselle as a spy or secret informant struck me funny and before I knew it I was in a full-blown laugh attack and Giselle followed suit. Leo and Precious jumped into our respective laps to see if we'd lost our marbles, and somehow that just spurred us on.

When we finally came back down, I said, "Okay, at least let me drive you partway. I know a back way through the neighborhood that will land you a lot closer to the back of the shopping center." I glanced at my wrist, still bare, and asked, "How long have you supposedly been shopping for thread?"

Giselle looked at her watch. "An hour."

"Is that even possible?" I've never been good with a needle and hadn't been in a stitchery shop since I was about ten.

"Yeah, I'm in a class in their back room." She pulled a plastic bag with the shop's name and logo out from under her poncho. "See?"

"Giselle, how much stuff do you have

under there?"

"That's it. Well, you know, Precious's sling." At which she flipped the front of the poncho over one shoulder and lifted Precious into a contraption much like a baby carrier. "Okay, ready to go."

I drove her to a path I knew that led to the back door of the embroidery shop and left her with a caution to be watchful and not to talk to anyone about the situation at Treasures on Earth. "Not even your cousin Persephone, okay?"

Giselle blew a raspberry and said, "Oh, man, she's the *last* person I'd talk to. She's *seeing* Mr. Campbell, and I'm not sure which one is creepier."

Forty-Five

"Holy cow." George was studying one of Giselle's photos with Tom's magnifying glass. "Holy crap." He shifted to another photo, then the third. "Holy mackerel."

Tom and I looked at each other, and Tom said, "Holy ornithologist, Batman, tell us!"

George looked up and set the magnifying glass on the table. "I need to see this bird. I need to be sure."

"Giselle is pretty scared . . ."

"Janet, if this is what I think it is, it's one of the rarest parrots on earth. And it shouldn't be here."

"But you're not sure?" asked Tom.

"Pretty sure. I need to see the bird. For one thing, there's nothing here to show scale, so I don't know how big this animal is." He went back to examining the photos through the magnifying glass.

Tom looked at me. "He's sure."

George looked up, put the glass down, and

leaned back. He took a deep breath and looked at Tom, then me, then back at Tom. "Yeah, damn it."

It was two p.m., and I knew that George wanted to get out to the island soon, but his interest in Giselle's foster bird seemed urgent. "Do we have time?"

"The stuff I ordered to catch the island bird isn't here yet, so yeah, let's do it."

"I'll call Giselle." I flipped my phone open, then closed it and looked at Tom. "Give me your phone. Mine's dead again. It was just working a little while ago . . ."

"You need a new battery," said Tom. We traded phones and I went off to the bedroom.

Giselle's phone rang five or six times and I expected to get her recording when she squeaked, "Hello?"

"Giselle, it's Janet. I need . . ."

"Oh, hi, Mrs. White."

"No, it's me . . ."

She cut me off with, "Yes, I can babysit Saturday morning."

Silence for a moment, than I asked, "You can't talk?"

"Yes, that's perfect. Thanks for calling."

"Call me when you can."

"See you then."

She was gone, and a shiver started at my

shoulders and trickled down into my shoes. *What the heck?* I sat down on the bed and tried to think. Who could be there that would make her pretend I was someone else? Campbell? Moneypenny? Not likely, unless one of them came to check on the bird. Her cousin Persephone? That would be more likely, except that Giselle wasn't fond of the woman and claimed not to have had much contact with her in a long time.

"Did you get her?" asked Tom when I returned to the kitchen.

I told them about the call. "I'm a little worried about her. We should go anyway, make sure she's okay."

"Maybe not right now," said Tom. "She obviously didn't want someone to know she was talking to you."

"What if I go?" asked George. "Nobody knows me."

"What would you say?" It wasn't a bad idea, I thought, if he could come up with a reason to ring her doorbell.

"What if I'm, I don't know, looking for my lost dog or something?"

Tom and I looked at each other.

"We'll take the rental," said George, standing up. "No one knows that car, even if they've been watching the two of you."

"I don't like it," said Tom.

"Then you stay here and man the phone," I said, grabbing my purse from the back of my chair. George and I were out the door before Tom could protest further. He followed us to the car and said, "Call me when you know she's okay, will you?"

"We will," I said.

"Seriously. If I don't hear from you in an hour, I'm calling Jo." He looked at George and said, "You said yourself that Campbell is dangerous, so don't do anything stupid, okay? It's rare, but it's still a bird. Wait for help if you think you need it." He paused. "What if Campbell's there? He knows you."

"He won't know me. I had longer hair and a big bushy beard back then, and I weighed about eighty pounds more."

Tom looked doubtful. "Just be alert."

"Right!" said George, already backing out of the driveway. When we were out of Tom's subdivision he glanced at me and said, "Really nice guy, Tom."

"Yeah, I think so."

"Worries about you."

"Right." I started to get mad, and then it hit me funny and I began to laugh. "What is it with you men? I've lived alone for, jeez, two decades. I've photographed wild stallions and grizzlies. I've hiked most of the Appalachian Trail with my cousin. Girl cousin. And now I need a man to take care of me?"

"What is it with you women?" George sounded mildly amused. "A man shows concern for your safety and you think he's trying to stifle you?"

I didn't really think that about Tom, so I kept mum.

"What if Tom were snooping around that place, that Treasure House?"

"Treasures on Earth."

"Wouldn't you tell him to be careful?"

"Turn left at the corner."

He put his signal on and slowed down. "Wouldn't you worry?"

"That's different."

"My wife is a rock climber. I've never asked her to stop, but when she goes off somewhere with her climbing buddies, I don't eat and I don't sleep." He stopped for a light and looked at me. "I don't tell her to be careful anymore because she gets mad, like you."

"I'm not doing anything dangerous. I just want some answers." I thought of Anderson Billings and felt hot acid bubble into the back of my throat. My voice was thick in my own ears when I said, "Anderson was a friend, and I sent him out there."

We were both silent for a few minutes, but

for my turn directives. When we crossed the Columbia Street Bridge, George asked about the rivers, which come together there.

"The St. Marys and the St. Joseph merge here to form the Maumee."

"And if my sense of direction is working, the Maumee flows north?"

"It does a little while, then twists and turns its way east into Ohio for a while, then north again to Lake Erie." I gazed out the window at the muddy water. "I've always wanted to follow the river all the way to the end."

"So this is a regular river city, eh?" George paused for a moment, then said, "You didn't kill Anderson, Janet, and you didn't cause his death. But seriously, be really careful about Campbell. Rich was not a nice guy even before his world crashed around him, and if he's smuggling birds, he has a lot at stake." *Not to mention if he's been killing people,* I thought, but I kept my suspicions to myself.

We were on Giselle's street by then, so I had George park the rental car in the driveway of a vacant house with a for-sale sign. It was about four houses from Giselle's, and I gave him her address. We decided that he should pretend to be looking at the vacant house, go around back, and cut through some backyards until he was closer to Giselle's place. As George put it, "A little paranoia never hurts." He was starting to open his door when I had an idea.

"Wait a second." I grabbed a red sweatshirt from the back seat. "Take this. You can change in back of the house."

He smiled and said, "Sneaky," then stuffed the sweatshirt under his T-shirt. He grabbed a baseball cap from the back seat too, tucked his ponytail up under it, and got out. He strolled along the front of the house, backed into the lawn as if checking the roof, and worked his way around to the side, then disappeared.

I felt a little conspicuous sitting in the car until I remembered how dark the tinted windows were from outside. I doubted anyone could see me from the back or sides, at least not from any distance. A minute later a pony-tailed man in a red sweatshirt pushed a wheelbarrow from the vacant home's backyard into the yard next door. I shifted in my seat and watched, and soon a man of identical build in a green T-shirt and backward baseball cap strolled from the far end of the house next door to the sidewalk, where he turned toward Giselle's house and, half a minute later, knocked on her front door and disappeared inside. *Sneaky back atcha, Dr. Crane,* I thought.

I scanned the street and noticed a Cadillac SUV parked in the shade of a huge old sycamore across from Giselle's. Seemed an odd vehicle for this modest neighborhood. I'd only been in Giselle's house once, but I knew it was tiny. The whole neighborhood had been built in the shadow of one of Fort Wayne's General Electric plants, long closed now, to house factory workers. Like most of the houses in the neighborhood, Giselle's had a living room, kitchen, two tiny bedrooms, and a bathroom. The area was fairly safe, but was not exactly prime real estate. In fact, Giselle was the rare homeowner here. Her father had co-signed the contract, and she had moved in a few months earlier. She had told me that most of her neighbors rented and didn't stay very long.

George had left the keys in the ignition. I reached over and turned them so I could listen to the oldies station. You would think Creedence would distract me, but my thoughts just bounced around in time to "Bad Moon Rising," which seemed just too appropriate. I turned the key off and leaned into the corner where my seat met the side door, closed my eyes, took three slow deep breaths, tried to clear my head, and nearly had a coronary when someone knocked on the glass behind me.

Forty-Six

The knock on the window behind me sent my body straight up and my heart into overdrive. If I were any taller, I would have hit the ceiling of the car. I blurted something semi-coherent and turned around with my arm raised between me and the glass. A woman's face was smiling at me from about six inches away.

I tried to open the window, but the engine was off, so no power. Despite the temptation to slam the door open and knock the intruder down, I controlled myself and opened it slowly. She straightened up and minced backward on fuschia stilettos as I stepped out of the car. She started to say something, but her delivery got slower and slower in the two or three seconds it took me to clear the door and stand up.

Body language is something people don't think much about, but being around animals so much has taught me to pay attention to non-verbal cues, and I could see that the woman in front of me was now more frightened than I was. Some goofy image-centered part of my mind wished for a camera even in the midst of this opening parry. A camera and another photographer, since I was one of the subjects. My brain registered actions and reactions even as they happened and I realized that, on some fundamental level, the tables had turned. She may have prowled up behind me, but now I was the predator. The woman had stopped talking and was backing away from me, her eyes very wide and her mouth slightly open.

My shoulders relaxed and I almost laughed. That reaction probably came partly from my adrenaline leveling off, but I confess that whoever she was, the woman in the fuschia suit and matching heels suddenly looked very like a rabbit to me. Body language, no doubt. I was back in control and made myself turn away from her for a moment to close the car door. I figured it would make her feel less threatened.

"Oh, I . . ."

I turned back toward her and relaxed against the car. "Sorry, but you startled the snot out of me." Not the worst thing that's ever come out of my mouth, but the look on her face made me sorry I'd stooped to nasal discharge, linguistically speaking. *Gotta work a little more on your language, Janet.* "Did you need something?"

She tugged down on her jacket hems and then raised a hand full of long metallic-pink nails to pat at her short blonde hair. A "Price Reduced" sign had appeared on the for-sale sign behind her in the yard. A black Lexus was parked in the driveway next door, which wouldn't have meant much except for the magnetic sign on the door advertising the same Realtor as the one named on the for-sale sign.

"Patricia Gilhooley?" I tried to sound breathless at the prospect.

"Do I know you?" she asked, crossing her arms protectively across her chest.

"I've seen your photo, I think. Yes, I'm sure of it. *Fort Wayne Magazine,* right? There was an article about you." *And if you buy that, I'll sell you the old Wells Street bridge.*

Her fear gave way to flattery and she shifted into Realtor mode. "*Allen County Business Link.* You must have seen the interview with me in the April issue." I was nearly blinded by her oh-so-whitened smile.

"That must have been it," I said. It was a lucky guess. The second one, I suppose, although the first wasn't pure luck. Her name was on the sign in the yard. But she was, by all appearances, doing well with her business, so I figured her photo had to be floating around. I'd have put my money on her having paid advertising out there, but the interview was even better. Honestly, if I've ever seen that magazine, it would have been during a long stretch in a waiting room lacking in reading options.

"Are you here to see the house?" Patricia Gilhooley's glossy lips puckered. "I don't recall being notified of a showing today."

"We were driving by and saw the sign. Just, you know, having a preliminary look." I hoped George didn't walk into the middle of this. I could talk my way out, but he would be hard to explain, especially if he appeared from the neighbor's backyard.

"We?" She looked toward the house.

"Yes, George walked around back to see if the yard would work for our dogs."

"It's a rather small house." She sounded doubtful.

"Oh, it's for our son, while he's in school. He babysits our dogs sometimes, so they wouldn't be here all the time."

"I see. I'd better go see . . ." Gilhooley said, starting to totter toward the house.

"It's pretty muddy back there." I realized as soon as it was out of my mouth that it was about as ridiculous as I could get since we hadn't had any rain in ages, but decided to keep bluffing. "That's why I came back to the car." *Didn't want to get my oh-so-dainty beat-up running shoes damp.*

"Oh, dear. They were supposed to fix that sprinkler system yesterday. I'm afraid the timer is off." She fished a smart phone with a fuschia skin from her skirt pocket. I wondered vaguely whether she had skins to match all her outfits. "I hear it at all hours." She glanced at me, then back at her phone. "My dad lives next door. I've been helping him since his operation." Before she could check on the errant sprinkler guy, she smiled at something behind me and said, "Oh, this must be your husband?"

Oh crap, I thought. *Busted.* Bluffing had worked before, though, so I turned toward the approaching ornithologist and said, "George! This is Patricia Gilhooley, the Realtor for this lovely home."

George grinned and held out his hand. "George Crane. Cute little place."

"So, George, dear, what do you think of the yard? Big enough for our dogs when Tommy doggy sits?" I smiled at him.

"Might be a little small, honey." He took a conspiratorial tone with Ms. Gilhooley. "Hard to find a yard that suits three dogs."

"Oh, I know what you mean. I have two Yorkies." She was shifting back and forth on her feet and I wondered whether she might have overreached with the height of those heels. As if to confirm, she said, "Why don't we go inside, as long as you're here?" and turned toward the front door. "What kind of dogs do you have, George and . . . I don't think I got your name?"

"Janet."

"George and Janet Crane. Okay."

"Two Great Danes and a St. Bernard," said George, draping his arm across my shoulders. "They're just the sweetest little guys, aren't they, honey?" It was all I could do to keep a straight face, especially when Patricia turned back to us with a stricken expression. "And we're starting to get a handle on the barking, at least when we're home." George went on, "We do have to have an extra garbage can, though, if you get my drift."

That stopped the sales pitch cold.

"It sounds like you need a much bigger yard."

"I don't know. They would only be here a couple days a week. But you might be right. We'll talk about it." George took his arm back and said, "Well, shall we, my dear?"

Patricia Gilhooley looked relieved and, I

realized later, went down in history as the first Realtor who did not offer me her card. As soon as we were in the relative privacy of the car, George and I started to laugh and he said, "Now that's teamwork!"

"Ohmygod, George. I think you missed your calling."

"What, flimflam man?" He backed out of the driveway and drove back the way we had come, still avoiding Giselle's house. "You could be right, though. Two Academy Awards in one day. Purty good."

"So tell me!" I was dying to know what went down at Giselle's house.

But as I watched, George's smile vanished and he leaned forward slightly, staring out the windshield. I followed his line of sight and had just registered someone walking toward us on the sidewalk to the left when George reached over, pushed my head toward my knees, and said, "Duck!"

Forty-Seven

"What the heck was that all about?" I yelled, brushing George's hand away and sitting up. "Jeez, George, I think you sprained my neck!"

"Sorry." He was staring into the rearview mirror with occasional glances in the direction we were moving. "Campbell."

I tried to whirl around in my seat and nearly dislocated my right shoulder when the seat belt locked. "Shit!" I released the belt and turned to look out the back of the car. The person I'd seen walking toward us was still walking, but now his back was to us, and the glare on the back window made it impossible to tell much about him. I looked at George and said, "You sure?"

"No doubt."

"But you haven't seen him in years."

"It was him." George settled back into normal driving mode, his primary attention back on the road. "What's he doing there?

On foot, no less?"

"Good question." I rubbed my shoulder, knowing I was going to have a nice bruise from the strap. "No one can even see through these windows, you know."

"Buckle up."

"Yeah, yeah," I said, but I did it. I believe in seat belts. My brother, Bill, wouldn't be alive if he hadn't been wearing his a few years back.

"Well, Janet," and he broke into Music Man mode, singing, " 'Ya got trouble, my friend, right here, I say, trouble right here in River City.' "

"You saw the bird?"

He nodded.

"And?"

"Quite a bird."

"Is it what you thought? The rare one?"

"It is. And we need to get it out of there."

"Did you tell her?" Meaning Giselle, of course. "Tell me you didn't. She'd freak out."

"She wasn't alone, remember."

"Right! So who was it?"

"Her cousin. Penelope?"

"Persephone?"

"Right. Persephone."

I thought back to Giselle's comments about her cousin. "That's very odd. Did they seem, you know, friendly?"

"To each other, you mean?" asked George, glancing at me. "Don't forget I don't know where I'm going, by the way."

"Right. We're fine. Turn right at the light." I gestured ahead of us. "So, yes, to each other. I don't think Giselle likes Persephone much. I'm surprised she was there."

"I'd go with that," said George, slowing for the light, then turning onto State.

Then it hit me. "George! You didn't let Persephone in on why you were there, did you?"

"You mean to measure for the new carpet your friend won in the contest at our store?"

"What? Turn right at the next corner."

He grinned. "Had to come up with something quickly and it was all I could think of. Have you ever seen the bright green carpet in her living room?"

I had. He was right, it was all you could think about when you first walked in.

"How did you manage to see the bird?"

"The cage is right there in the living room. I told her it was the prettiest parakeet I'd ever seen. That's the house, right?"

As he parked in Tom's driveway, George told me that Giselle seemed very nervous around her cousin, but knowing Giselle, I wasn't entirely sure that meant anything.

George shut the ignition off and looked at me, a mix of anger and something like wonder lighting his eyes. "It was all I could do to walk out of that house without that parrot." He opened his door, then stopped and said, "We have to nail these people, and we have to get the birds into safe keeping." Then he smiled. "And we'll have to let Giselle know she didn't actually win a new carpet. I think she'll be disappointed."

Tom was at the kitchen table with a red pen in hand and two piles of student papers. Jay and Drake were wriggling and wagging at the sliding door, so I let them in. "Want me to clean the dog snot off the glass?" I asked Tom.

"Nah, I'll get it later when I water the pots. It'll keep." The master of understatement. In my experience, the slobbery snottery mess that dogs make of window glass will keep forever if you don't scrub it off.

We told him about our adventure. When we had finished, Tom waved toward the family room and said, "George, there's a package for you in there."

George reached into his pocket but came out empty handed. "You have a pocket knife? Couldn't bring mine on the plane."

Tom handed over his jackknife. George cut the box open and removed a hefty birdcage, a long coil of light-weight rope and another of even lighter nylon cord, and a small canvas pouch.

"What's all that?" I asked.

"Let's go catch ourselves a Carmine Parrot," said George. He set the cage on the floor near the door to the garage and laid the rope and bag on the table. "I need some bits of fruit and some nuts and bird seed, if you have any?"

Tom cross-stacked his papers and set the red pen on top, then went to the refrigerator and pulled out a couple of apples, some grapes, and a pear. "Will these work?"

"Perfect."

I got a plastic container from a cupboard and offered to get some birdseed from the garage, and Tom pulled a jar of mixed nuts from the cupboard.

"Got a colander?" asked George.

Salt, I thought as I pulled the door open, and heard George say, "Gotta rinse the salt off."

When I got back with the birdseed, Tom was lacing his hiking boots. "Coming with us?" he asked, looking at me.

"I need to make a call first." I wanted to check that Giselle was okay, and that Leo wasn't being any trouble to Goldie. It felt as if I'd been gone for days, not hours.

George stuffed the canvas bag, rope, fruit, nuts, and birdseed into the cage and moved to the door. "Maybe we should take two cars, actually. It could be a long wait."

"I'll catch up with you," I said. "You guys be careful out there, okay?"

George looked at me and started to laugh, which prompted Tom to give me a "what the heck?" look. I just shrugged, but realized that George was right. If I could tell Tom to be careful, I grudgingly admitted to myself that Tom could also tell me to be careful without getting an earful. I put my arms around Tom's neck and kissed him, then whispered, "Just be careful" in his ear. I turned away as soon as I let him go, and heard, "Love you, Janet," just before the door closed.

Jay and Drake stood staring at me, Jay's butt wriggling like mad and Drake's thick tail banging *wham wham wham* against a table leg. I chucked the black dog under the chin and said, "You're gonna break that table with that tail of yours, mister," and then asked, "Out?" They had just come in, but their body language was all about *ball game* so I decided to take a few minutes to let them have a run. Drake raced into the yard and came back with two tennis balls in his mouth, and Jay grabbed a floppy disk from a chair on the deck.

For the next five minutes I threw whatever the silly dogs brought me. Since the only mental effort necessary was to make sure I didn't set them on a collision course, I let my thoughts run to other matters. Of course, the lost parrot was on my mind. It couldn't survive out there for long. Food would be an immediate problem, and predators were a constant threat. That big red-tailed hawk I'd seen circling the lake, for one, and even the screech owl might be a problem, although the parrot might be big enough to discourage it. And then there were the human predators. Rich Campbell, Regis Moneypenny.

Campbell was mixed up in whatever was going on with the endangered birds. I felt sure of that, based on the man's history. And Moneypenny had to be up to his toupee in this. He owned the place and, from all reports, ran it. Who else? How many people would it take to shuttle birds illegally into the area, sell them to the highest bidders, and deliver them alive?

Giselle popped into my head and a felt an inexplicable fear run down my spine. "Come on guys, that's it." I told the dogs to leave the balls and floppy disks outside, and we went in.

Giselle's phone rang four times, and then her voice mail answered. I wasn't sure whether it was a machine that someone else might hear, so as I listened to the recording, I came up with a quick message. "Giselle, hi, it's Janet MacPhail. Hey, I just wanted to remind you that I'd like to borrow that new book you got on tracking. Maybe you could bring it to agility practice this week? If not, it's okay, no rush. Maybe you could let me know, though? Okay, that's all. Thanks. Oh, I don't think you have my number, so here it is." I knew even as I left it that I might be overdoing the "we don't know each other that well" bit, but I couldn't stop in the middle.

I felt a pressure on my foot and looked down. Jay was leaning against my leg with his head tilted back to gaze up at me, his paw firmly pressed into the top of my shoe. Who in their right mind could resist that? I set my phone on the table and got down on the floor so I could bury my face in Jay's silky fur. The next thing I knew, a big black muzzle had shoved itself in under my arm, so I wrapped that one around Drake, pulled them both close, and surrendered to the magic that is a dog's loving touch.

Forty-Eight

My mind was spinning faster than my radials as I drove north on Coldwater Road. After our group snuggle, I loaded Jay and Drake into the van and drove them to Bill and Norm's house for another visit to "the uncles." There was no way I would leave them alone at either of our houses with a crazy person out there. Norm was thrilled and greeted the dogs with a promise to "all bake dog cookies together while your mom is away." Bill had gone to the Clothing Bank drop box with another load of stuff. The clearing-out-to-move business was getting serious.

I missed Leo enough to call Goldie once more before I left their driveway, but I got her voice mail. Tom and George would already be at Heron Acres and I really wanted to watch the capture process, so I cruised about eight miles per hour over the limit once I cleared the stretch near Pine

Valley that was a notorious speed trap.

Who was that mysterious figure in Kroger's? The height seemed about right for Rich Campbell, and the blue shirt he always seemed to wear. Then again, if you counted the people wearing blue shirts in any given place, how many would there be? What about that feeling I'd had that I was being watched? Was I just plain paranoid, or had that been real? I hadn't gotten a clear look, and I had to admit that the baseball cap bothered me. Campbell had been bareheaded every other time I had seen him, hadn't he? I was sure he'd been capless when he scared me on the island, but I wasn't so certain about Anderson's photos, and I was annoyed with my own lack of attention to the details.

If they were smuggling birds and selling them for big bucks, I thought, they had to be bringing them in and shipping them out somehow. Peg had mentioned trucks coming in and out of Treasures on Earth in the wee hours. Could that be when they transported birds? The more I thought about it, the less sense that made. They weren't smuggling horses, after all. Even the biggest parrot easily fit into a smallish crate. Why draw attention with noisy trucks at odd hours when they could move the birds in automobiles? Or was the report of trucks exaggerated?

A bigger question was how many members of Treasures on Earth were involved in this. Conspiracy theories aside, I couldn't imagine most people going along with a federal crime. Certainly not people like Giselle. Mrs. Willard didn't seem a likely criminal, unless her cluelessness was all an act. Giselle's cousin Persephone wasn't very appealing, but that didn't make her a criminal. Then again, according to Giselle, Persephone was involved with Rich Campbell. Which reminded me, I'd have to try calling Giselle again later. I wanted to be sure she was okay, and find out why the long-lost cousin was at her house if they didn't get along.

One thought led to another, as they will, and I suddenly remembered Sylvia Eckhorn's odd comments at Dog Dayz. What had she said? "Be really careful"? That was it. She was talking about Rich Campbell. She had seen him behind Tom in the television footage of the training sessions, and she had brought it up, then dropped it. I would have to call her and find out what that was all about. Sylvia had a very level head, and I was sure she wouldn't throw out frivolous warnings. I added Sylvia to my growing list of phone calls to make.

The parking lot at Treasures on Earth was packed with the usual high-end vehicles when I drove by. *Don't any of these people have jobs?* I wondered, and then chuckled at myself. After all, if I was free to run all over creation whenever I wanted to, why shouldn't they? Maybe they also stayed up working in the wee hours as I did. Or used to, more often, before I met Tom. Not that I was getting more sleep now, but I had to admit that staying up late was more fun with him than without. I pulled myself back from a particularly fun memory and took my foot off the accelerator to make it easier to scan the lot and the front of the Treasury, as I'd come to think of Moneypenny's place.

What's the big attraction with this place? I wondered. That was something else I needed to ask Giselle, although knowing a little about her history of short-term affiliations with a variety of belief systems, she might not be the most lucid source of thoughtful analysis. But what would attract Neil Young to what appeared to be something of a cult? Or someone like Mrs. Willard, or any of the other people who parked their high-end cars in the lot several days a week?

By the time I passed the gate to the property I was barely rolling, but even so, there wasn't much to see, especially with the iron fence breaking up the view. I turned my attention back to the road and started to accelerate, figuring that a crowd at Moneypenny's place was probably a good thing when Tom and George were out on the island. Unless the whole bunch of them were in on whatever Moneypenny and Campbell were up to, it wasn't likely anyone could go skulking around right now, much less attack anyone close by. Besides, it was mid-afternoon.

My thoughts had just turned to Anderson Billings when something hit the back of my minivan *KAWHUMP!* Reflex took over and my foot moved toward the brake as I looked in the mirror. A second *THWACK* hit the back hatch just as I caught sight of the batter in my side mirror. Tall, blue shirt, baseball cap with the brim pulled down, face in shadow. "What th . . . ," I shouted through a surge of nausea. An hour later I wished I had had the intestinal fortitude to shift into reverse and back over bat and batter alike, but in the moment raw terror ruled and I hit the gas. My assailant turned away, arm raised as a shield against the stones my tires were spitting into the air, but I knew who it was. My heart felt like it might jump right out of my chest. I looked once more in the mirror. At that angle I could see only from the attacker's knees to shoulders. A baseball bat hung from one hand. The other hand came up, and although I couldn't see clearly, I knew the gesture. A fist pistol. Aimed at me.

Forty-Nine

Tom had taken the kayak with him and left it on the bank for me, which was a good thing because I didn't think I could have lifted it, shaking as I was. I had jumped out of my van and run toward the lake when I parked at Heron Acres, but by the time I reached the water, my knees had liquified and I let myself sink to the ground. My head throbbed, but the initial nausea had passed, and as I sat there I felt fear spin around me like a silken thread around a caterpillar. I closed my eyes, focused on breathing, forced my muscles to relax. When I opened my eyes and re-emerged, my fear was gone. All I felt was rage. Cold, dark rage.

Tom and George were out of sight on the island, but I could hear their wordless voices across the water, so I got up and headed their way. As I paddled, I took stock of myself. I felt better except that my cheeks seemed to be on fire, so I dipped my hand into the cool of the lake and wiped my face. It felt good, and the vague mucky fragrance of the water was comforting somehow. A small voice whispered to me as I started to paddle again. *Don't tell them.* I repeated the words out loud.

I had no idea how George would react, but I had a pretty good notion that Tom would be inclined to do something about the assault, and I had to think that would not be wise. What kind of person stands on a public road in broad daylight and hits a car with a baseball bat? Aside from the violence of the act, it was plain wacko.

What about the back of my van, I wondered. I hadn't even looked at it. All I wanted to do when I pulled into Heron Acres was get away. How much damage had he done? I should call Jo, I thought. I let the kayak drift toward the island and fished my cell phone from my pocket. The island itself got inconsistent reception for some reason, but maybe out here on the water . . . Four bars. I hit Jo's speed dial button and waited. Voice mail, as usual, so I left a short message. "Jo, call me. Today. Important. I'm at the island now, so probably bad reception, but leave a message or try in an hour, okay? This is an official call." That was lame, but I wanted her to know I wasn't just calling to ask about the puppy. “Rich Campbell just attacked me, well, not me, but my van with me in it, with a baseball bat, in front of Treasures on Earth.” My phone beeped at me and I spoke faster. “I’m okay, scared and furious, but okay. I’m on my way to the island.” More beeps. Battery must be going again. “Tom and George are there, trying to catch the . . .” Long beep. I looked at the phone. Dead. “Great. Just great.”

I pulled the kayak well out of the water and went looking for Tom and George. I found them at the base of the old sycamore. “See the bird?” I asked as I walked up.

“Yeah, he’s . . . ,” Tom started, turning to look at me. “What’s wrong?”

“What do you mean?” The smile I tried to plaster onto my face felt lopsided, and I wondered vaguely whether adrenaline rushes interfere with muscle control. George was looking at me now, too.

“Janet?”

“So, the bird?” I asked, looking away from them and up into the branches. “Oh, there he is.”

Tom kept staring at me, but George went back to work on the cage. He tied the end of the light nylon cord to the cage door and threaded it through the back wires, careful to leave the door ajar. “Okay,” he said, standing up and lifting the cage. "Let's do it."

We moved to within a few feet of the base of the tree's trunk. George set the cage on the ground and pulled the coil of nylon rope from the canvas bag he was carrying. He secured one end to a hanger on top of the cage, then pulled out a small pouch with a strap to which he fastened the other end of the rope. The pouch seemed to be heavy, so I asked, "What's in that?"

"Rocks."

"Rocks?" But as he looked up and started to swing the pouch like a lariat I got it.

"Won't that scare him?" Tom asked, eyeing the bird high up in the tree.

"Probably not, if I get it on the first toss. So cross your fingers." George glanced at us. "And you might want to stand back a little in case my aim is off."

I backed away and Tom moved to my side and took my hand while George swung the pouch in one, two full circles. As it whirled into the third swing, he heaved it upward and it sailed past a hefty branch about twenty feet up, came neatly down the other side, and plummeted to the ground, dragging the rope with it.

"You've done that before," said Tom. He squeezed my hand, and although I thought it was mostly a reflex in the presence of George's rope-pitching prowess, my eyes suddenly felt hot and wet. I sniffed for control, not just to keep from crying but to stop myself throwing my arms around him, all the time wondering why my emotions are sometimes so out of wack.

George grinned at us. "Once or twice."

I pulled my hand away and asked, "Okay, what now?"

In answer, George pulled the fruit, seeds, and nuts from his tote bag and scattered an assortment on the floor of the birdcage. He pushed the cage door open as far as it would go, then grabbed the rope by the weighted end, pulled it taut, and continued to pull gently, making sure to keep the light line attached to the cage door loose. It wouldn't do to pull the door closed before the parrot climbed in for the ride back down. The cage rose from the ground, swinging slightly and beginning a slow spin. George stopped pulling and steadied the cage. He waited to be sure it had lost its inclination to swing and spin, then resumed raising it slowly into the old sycamore.

"He's moving, George," said Tom, pointing beyond the cage toward our parrot quarry. The bird had his wings open and was leaning forward as if to get a closer look at the topsy-turvy sight of a cage flying toward him.

George looked toward the bird but kept his hand-over-hand rhythm steady on the rope. "I think we're good. He's just checking it out. He's probably pretty hungry, and he's been in captivity long enough to associate the cage with food."

I thought about my own routine of feeding my dog and cat in their crates, all the time at first, then sporadically to reinforce the idea that the crate is a good place. Probably worked for birds, too, I thought, even a wild-caught parrot if he's hungry enough.

"Okay, I think that will do it," said George. The cage was hanging just below the branch that held the rope. Two other branches grew at nearly right angles but lower than that one, so the cage was effectively "in" the tree. "Let's back off a bit. Now we wait." George pulled a tent peg from the canvas bag and secured the rope to it. He picked up the light line and found the end of it. Careful not to tug the cage door closed, he walked as far from the base of the tree as the line allowed and sat on a fallen tree trunk. We followed.

"Can we talk?" I whispered.

"Softly, sure."

"Think this will work?" asked Tom.

"Hope so. Other than darting him, which I don't want to do, I don't see any other way to catch him." George leaned forward and rested his forearms on his knees. "Might take a while, though. I'm sure he's spooked by the death of his friend or mate, and whatever landed them out here in the first place."

"Not to mention being captured, whenever that was. I mean, he probably wasn't bred in captivity, right?" I asked. It didn't seem likely with such a rare parrot.

"Oh, I'm sure he was poached from the wild. No telling how long ago or how old he was. Probably as a chick."

"You can buy parrots along the road in Mexico, Latin America, farther south," said Tom. "Habitat loss and poaching are the biggest dangers to birds and lots of other animals. And plants. It all goes together."

"Right," said George. "But the poaching problem isn't fueled by local demand. The poachers just want to feed themselves and their kids. The real problem is the buyers here in the U.S., and in Europe and other well-heeled markets."

"Like Moneypenny and his minions." My cheeks went red hot again as the rage I had managed to cool earlier in the kayak came back to the boil. The image of that bizarre pistol fist flashed behind my eyes. I like to think that I'm not a violent person, but as I thought of baby birds pulled from nests, and adult birds netted or killed, and of Anderson Billings and Liesl Burkhardt's untimely deaths, and of that pistol fist raised to threaten me, I had a sweet little daydream of smashing that threatening hand with that swinging baseball bat.

Fifty

I sat watching the parrot in the tree while the parrot appeared to watch the cage that hung fifteen feet beneath him, and Tom watched me. I fought the urge to look at him. He would see right through me, see the anger racing like blood under my skin, and I couldn't trust myself not to tell him what Rich Campbell had done. The last thing I wanted was to say anything that would prompt Tom to confront the guy. Someone would get hurt.

"What's got you all wound up?" said Tom.

"Nothing. Well, you know, this poaching and shipping birds and all. It's horrifying." I gestured toward the frightened, hungry bird in the sycamore. "I'm angry for that guy. And his dead mate."

Tom and George were both staring at me by that time, so I decided to try to shift conversation to something more uplifting. Maybe my cheeks would cool down before all the skin peeled off them.

"So, George, what made you become a bird guy?"

George chuckled. "Pretty sure I was hatched fully fledged as a bird guy. Can't remember a time I wasn't fascinated by birds." He shifted his position on the log and gestured toward our parrot. "Look."

The bird was sliding sideways along the branch, his head cocked as if to see the cage better.

"This is good, right?"

"Yep, but I wouldn't hold my breath. I doubt he'll go in this quickly." The bird stopped and George relaxed again, although he never took his eyes off the parrot. "I actually started college as pre-law. Went all the way through my undergrad years thinking I'd be a lawyer."

My behind, especially the bitten part, was unhappy about the rough bark we were sitting on, so I checked the ground for poison ivy, stinging nettles, and ants, found it clear, and sat down where I could lean back against the fallen trunk. Tom shifted so that he was straddling me. As he massaged my shoulders and neck, he said, "Ah, the lure of money, right? I started out in pre-med."

"Yep. Then I got an internship with a law firm. It was supposed to last the whole summer. I lasted four days and knew it wasn't for me. I spent the rest of the summer slinging burgers, and it took me an extra year to make up science deficiencies to get into a master's program in biology, but I've never looked back."

"I didn't know that," I said.

"How could you?" asked George.

"No, I didn't know you started in pre-med, Tom."

He shook my shoulders gently and said, "Janet, I confess, I've held a few things back. Have to retain some mysterious allure, don't I?"

That made me smile. Tom was one of the most open people I'd ever met. For me that was his allure. Part of it, anyway. I had enough of men with secrets a long time ago.

Conversation petered out after that and, other than the occasional comment from one of us, we sat in silence for the next hour. I may even have dozed off. When I snapped to, my first thought was for the parrot. He was hunkered down on his branch, possibly sleeping. Then I checked Tom's watch and figured we still had a few hours until sunset. It could be a long evening, and I needed a break.

"Will it bother him," I gestured toward our feathered friend, "if I get up and walk around a bit?"

"I doubt it," said George.

"Want company?" asked Tom.

I covered my hesitation with the clumsiness of getting up with a half-numb fanny. "Sure," I said, although I was anything but sure. Not that I didn't want to be with Tom. I just didn't want to slip and tell him about the assault on my van. Not until we got home, or at least away from here and Treasures on Earth. Even better, not until I'd spoken to Jo Stevens and the police had Mister Baseball Bat in custody. I decided I'd just have to try for a poker face.

We moved carefully until we were at some distance from the old sycamore, then walked more freely. Tom took my hand and I braced for more questions, but none came.

"I hope this works," I said.

"Yeah, me too. But George said on the way out here that it might take a couple of days."

"That bird has to be starving by now. I mean, what do parrots eat? There can't be much out here for him, right?" I thought about the birds I photograph in Indiana and what they eat. Some do eat fruit, but I didn't think there would be much available on the island. "Maybe some chokecherries," I said, thinking out loud.

"There isn't much, probably. He might not recognize some of it as food, either." Tom paused. "Must be eating something, though. I don't think he could go this long without eating."

I hadn't been paying attention to where we were headed, and realized that we had made our way to the shore closest to Treasures on Earth. As we strolled along the edge of the water, I couldn't help looking across to the fence that separated the two properties. Tom stopped and looked in the same direction and said, "That might be a way in."

"Obviously he came in that way."

"No, I mean a way into their place from here."

Mr. "Let the Police Handle It" wanted to sneak into Moneypenny's private property for a look around? I couldn't believe it.

"If my sense of geography is accurate, that," he pointed at the section of fence directly opposite us, "would lead into the back of the property. Seems likely that anything funny that's going on would be out back somewhere, doesn't it?" An edge of excitement colored Tom's voice now.

"Not a good idea," I said.

He looked at me, one eyebrow at attention. "What's this? Caution from the intrepid photographic investigator?"

"Stop it!" *You stop it, Janet,* I thought, realizing how dumb it was to be annoyed when he was right on target. "Just, you know, I think it would be dangerous."

"Probably."

"Really, Tom. I don't think they play fair over there. I think . . . I know they killed Anderson. Not they. Someone. Campbell." My voice broke, and I wasn't sure which emotion had the upper hand, fear, anger, or grief. "George said it, you know. Rich Campbell is dangerous."

"Glad you realize that."

"He probably killed his girlfriend, too. Liesl."

"What are you talking about?"

I had forgotten that Tom didn't know about Liesl's death. "She drowned."

"How do you know that?"

"Duh! Google, Tom. I looked her up. She drowned in a pond on Cape Cod, in cold weather. It makes no more sense than Anderson's death." The longer I spoke, the more solidly my thoughts congealed. "Don't you think that's a huge coincidence?"

Something moved in the underbrush beyond the fence on the mainland. I grabbed Tom's arm and pointed toward the swaying shrubs. I didn't speak and wasn't at all sure I could have if I'd tried. We were out of baseball bat range, but I wanted nothing more than to take off running and screaming to the other side of the island.

Then I noticed that Tom was smiling. He whispered, "Stand still."

The brush wriggled a bit more, and a doe and fawn stepped into the open, nibbling as they walked. The fawn still had faint spots on his back, but they were fading. As they stepped fully into the light, the doe froze for a moment, her head turned slightly to give her a better view. I felt the little tingle I always get when I know that an animal sees me, not in some abstract way, but as another individual creature who has impinged on a universe where they didn't know I existed. People, yes, but not *me.* I held my breath and listened to the pulse in my ears. The doe turned toward her fawn, arced her body around him, and they disappeared back into the brush.

"Wow."

"Too bad you didn't have your camera."

"No, sometimes it's better this way," I said. "They don't see me when I have the camera. She saw me." Tom never questioned what I meant. *One more thing I love about him,* I thought, as we walked back toward George and the feathered fugitive.

Fifty-One

George was right where we left him, but the parrot had moved about six inches closer to the cage. I knew that because he had been sitting just to the right of a clump of wilted leaves earlier, and now he was to the left. As we crossed the field of coneflowers and Queen Anne's lace, he unfolded his wings and flapped them two or three times, making Tom and me stop in our tracks. For a moment I thought our approach was about to spook him, but he relaxed and we rejoined George at the fallen tree.

"I'm thinking we might need to up the ante," said George. "I'm thinking tropical fruits that he might recognize."

I had been wanting to make a few calls anyway, so I offered to pick up the fruit at the same time. It turned out that George wanted to make some calls, too. We batted things around for a few minutes and finally decided that George and I would both go do what we needed to do and Tom would stay to watch the bird and, if the cage proved alluring enough, to spring the trap. We took the bass boat and left the kayak in case Tom needed to get off the island while we were gone. We left the remaining water with Tom, and I tossed him half a roll of fruit-flavored hard candies I had in my pocket.

We approached my van from the front, so George didn't see the damage. I wasn't sure how he would react, but I figured that if he saw it, he would probably tell Tom about it when we got back. It would be better if neither of them knew about Campbell and his bat until we were home for the night. I made sure to park facing the store as well when we got there.

The round trip took an hour and a half. I drove going in so that George could check for critical emails. We stopped at the grocery store at Coldwater and Dupont, where George grabbed a mango, a passion fruit, and some grapes.

"I have no idea whether these will be more appealing than the current spread," he said, "but it's worth a shot." I also checked the battery display, but they didn't have the right one for my phone.

8up the dogs. "I hate to leave them locked

up so long, and there's no reason they can't have a swim," I said. "They can stay in Tom's x-pen while we go back out to the island, or I can just stay with them."

"Don't have to convince me," said George, a big grin on his face.

We switched seats from Kroger's to Tom's house so that I could make a few calls. First, I tried my mom's number, but she said she didn't know a Janet and hung up on me. Twice. So I called Bill next. I told him we were coming to get the dogs and confirmed that he was going to see our mother that evening. He whined a little, but I heard Norm in the background say, "Oh, stop it. We're going to see your mother and that's all there is to it." *Thanks, Norm.* I hated arguing with Bill about Mom, and I knew he was having trouble dealing with her loss of mental function, but so was I. Not for the first time, I was glad he had Norm — both for emotional support and for a kick in the pants when he needed one.

Goldie was next on my list. Anyone watching my house would spot her sooner or later and realize she had been with me at Treasures on Earth, but I couldn't tell Goldie I was worried about her. I asked about Leo instead. Worrying about my animals, I've learned, is always acceptable. Everything was fine.

I thought about calling Sylvia Eckhorn to ask her what she had meant about being careful around Rich Campbell, but decided to wait until I had a little privacy. Besides, we had arrived at Bill and Norm's. When we pulled into the driveway, Bill was in the garage trying to drag some shelving units away from the wall. George offered to help him, and I went inside to find Norm and the dogs. Jay and Drake made a half-hearted run at me, then spun back around and gave their full attention to "uncle" Norm, who was loading a plastic container with homemade dog biscuits. "It smells like ginger snaps in here," I said, inhaling deeply.

"I know, isn't it yumscious?" asked Norm. He sealed the lid on the container, broke a biscuit in half, and told the dogs to sit "like gentlemen." They both sat, raised their right paws, and crossed them over their left legs. Norm gave them their cookies and grinned at me. "See, I *did too* read that trick training book I borrowed from you."

"You guys crack me up," I said, laughing. "All three of you."

"Did you catch that poor bird?" asked Norm, handing me the container of biscuits.

"Not yet, but George thinks it's a matter of time." I peeled the corner of the lid open, inhaled the gingery fragrance, and whined, "You never bake cookies for me."

Norm shrugged. "Have one of those. Just oatmeal, ginger, applesauce, and a smidge of honey."

"Really?" *Even I could make those, if I had the recipe,* I thought. Out loud I said, "I really hope we get him yet this afternoon."

"Oh, I know," said Norm. He looked like he might cry. "I can't stand to think of that little bird out there alone and scared and hungry. People are just terrible."

"Some are," I agreed. "And then I meet someone like you, and my faith is restored." I hugged him with my free arm. "I need to make a quick call."

Sylvia answered on the first ring.

"Sitting by the phone, huh?" I asked.

"As a matter of fact, I was just going to call you. I wanted to finish what I started last night." I heard a kiddy song start up and then grow softer, as if she had either turned down the volume or walked away. The giggles in the background suggested the latter. "So, yeah, listen . . . I don't want to go into a lot of detail, Janet. I mean, I can't really. Just be careful about that guy, you know, the one who was at the retriever training session."

"That's why I'm calling, Syl," I said.

"What are you talking about?"

"Look, don't repeat this, not even to Tom. I could lose my job." I heard a big sigh.

"Your job?" I asked. Sylvia is an emergency-room nurse. "What are you talking about?"

"Men who hurt their girlfriends and wives don't care who they hurt. So be careful. And that's all I'm going to say."

I decided not to probe any further. Sylvia obviously was uncomfortable about telling me, so I thanked her for the information and promised to watch myself. Rich Campbell's violent streak wasn't exactly news, but Sylvia didn't know that. Having someone else verify it didn't calm my fears, but did make me feel supported in an odd way.

"No, wait, it's not," said Sylvia just as I was about to close my phone.

"Not what?"

"Not all I have to say. This is hypothetical, okay?"

"Okay?" I was on full alert now.

"Sometimes violence is a two-way street. Sometimes we treat both partners in a domestic situation." I stopped breathing and thought, *Wow. Persephone?* Sylvia continued, "And even so, Janet, people like this will stand together when they're threatened." I remembered Jo and Hutch talking about how they hated responding to domestic situations because victims often turn on the cops that come to help them.

I promised again to be careful and closed my phone. The dogs bounced around me, ready for a ride, so I gathered up their leashes and the container of homemade biscuits and went back to the garage. I held my breath as I tried the back hatch, and breathed easier when it opened, despite the dents. Once they were squared away in the back of my van I more or less dragged George away from a debate with Bill and Norm over which bean goes better with rice, red or black, and we took off.

"How far out of the way is Tom's place?" asked George.

"It's not really. Do you need something?"

"I do." He didn't elaborate, so I didn't ask, and we pulled into the shady side of Tom's driveway about eight minutes later.

I popped the back of the van, opened the front windows, and slid open the side doors, then stepped around to the crate doors to turn on the little portable fans hanging there. A decent breeze was blowing so the fans were redundant, and it wasn't bad in the shade, so the dogs would be fine for a few minutes. I followed George to the front door and found the key between the one to my mom's, now Bill's, house and the mystery key that I'm afraid to take off my key ring in case it's for something important and I someday figure out what that is.

Just looking at the yellow and pink roses flanking Tom's front porch makes me smile, and the humid heat held their scent like a canopy over the door. Something about opening this door felt safe, like coming home. I turned the knob, pushed, and stepped over the threshold. George was right behind me, and the scene before me might not have fully registered until I heard him exhale as if he'd been punched. We both froze and stared and said "ohmygod."

Fifty-Two

George and I stood rooted to the floor of Tom's foyer looking into the living room where a tornado had apparently touched down. "Ohmygod," I said again, and then, "Do you smell gas?"

We looked at one another and scurried into the kitchen. The oven door was open, the pilot out, and the gas turned on. George pulled the front of his T-shirt up over his mouth and nose, and I folded my arm across my face, nose pressed into the inner curve of my elbow. We both reached for the knob, but I let George turn it off while I moved to the family room and opened the sliding door. When I turned back toward the room, I felt like crying. The wall of books across from where I stood had been torn apart. Books lay everywhere, pages torn out and ripped or crumpled. Tom's collection of Labrador Retriever figurines had been swept from their place of honor and lay in a heap, some of them broken.

The kitchen table had been tipped over and one of the chairs lay smashed against the end of the counter, where a strip of molding hung loose and broken. George started to reach for the edge of the table as if to right it, but I stopped him. "Don't touch anything," I said, pulling my phone from my pocket. "We should step outside. I'll call . . . Dammit!"

"What?"

"I just charged this!" I shook the stupid phone in his direction.

He handed me Tom's handset from the counter. "Wait until we're outside."

I didn't know Jo Stevens' number other than "number five on speed dial," so I dialed nine-one-one, reported the break-in, and asked them to notify Jo Stevens or Homer Hutchinson because it was probably related to a case.

"Tell them about the gas," said George. I looked a question at him and he said, "In case he monkeyed with more than the oven."

The dispatcher told me to wait out front, away from the house, until the police arrived, and said she was notifying the gas company as well.

"I'm glad the dogs weren't here," said

George.

I tried to say, "Me too," but my voice wouldn't work. I appreciated what George had said, though. Most people would have wished the opposite, thinking two biggish dogs would keep an intruder out. Truthfully, anyone nuts enough to go into a house in broad daylight and tear it up like that might be violent enough to hurt the dogs. Or worse. Then I thought of something. "George! Your laptop!"

He gestured toward the interior of the car. "Under the seat."

"What do you think he was after?" I asked.

"*If* it was Rich . . . ," said George.

I cut him off. "Of course it was him. Who else?"

"Houses do get robbed." He didn't sound convinced.

The handset rang as I was about to reply.

"Janet?" It was Jo Stevens.

I admitted that it was I.

"Where's your phone? I keep getting your voice mail." She sounded angry and relieved all at once. After I explained, and confirmed that we were not inside Tom's house, even though I had answered his phone, she said she was tied up but that two patrol cars were on their way and that her partner would be there as well.

"They're here," I said. Two cruisers with their lights spinning were half a block away, and behind them I saw a black Taurus that I figured was Hutch.

"And Drake?" asked Jo.

"He wasn't here," I said, and heard a sigh from the handset.

"I'm sending a car to your place."

"Okay." That sent a tremor through my skull. "Jo, have them check on Goldie. I'll call her now."

"Will do . . ."

"Janet, your friend, Anderson," she paused. "You were right. We don't have the full report, but preliminary shows it was no accident."

My face went cold and I leaned against the van to keep my balance. "He didn't drown?"

"He probably did. But someone cracked his skull first."

I forced myself to swallow the bile that shot into my throat.

"What's the code for your house? So my guys can get in." Jo's voice sounded like it was far away, but her words registered and I gave her the code to my new locks.

"I'll call you later."

"Jo, wait," I said, regaining my balance. "It had to be that creep Rich Campbell, you know, from Treasures on Earth. Moneypenny's henchman."

"Some of it, maybe. What time did you leave Tom's place?" That seemed like an odd question, but I told her we had an early lunch and left around noon. She said, "Wasn't him then."

"What?"

"He was picked up at a rest area in Delaware County a little while ago," she said.

So this was random? I wondered? Or if not random, at least not related to our amateur detecting? "Picked up?" I asked.

George mouthed questions at me. Who? What? I signaled him to wait, but he wasn't nearly as responsive to hand gestures as Jay is, so I turned away to hear what Jo had to say. A truck bearing the Northern Indiana Public Service Company logo pulled up behind the cruisers.

"I can't say much, but a wildlife dog indicated him in the rest area," said Jo, and I could hear the satisfaction in her voice.

Wildlife dog. That had to be Lennen, the Lab I met at my vet's office. He was the only wildlife detection dog I knew of in the area, and one of very few in the whole country.

A young man with NIPSCO emblazoned across the back of his jumpsuit got out of the truck, jogged across the lawn, and entered the house.

"Did he have a bird on him?" I asked.

"Let me talk to George," she said.

"Wha . . . ," I started to protest, then realized that George's status *vis-à-vis* wildlife smuggling might allow her to tell him what she couldn't tell me. I handed him the phone and waited. When he hung up he started to tell me, but I said, "Hang on. Let me give Goldie a heads up." She answered on the first ring, and was as cheerful as ever and didn't see any reason for a visit from the police, but she said she'd humor me.

When I had finished, George said, "The dog indicated on Rich's vehicle. That gave them cause to search it, and the dog indicated the back seat. The bench had been modified, hollowed out, and there were two birds inside. She said parrots. I'd have to see them . . ."

He cut it off as Hutchinson came out of the house and straight to us. The man was never long on social graces, so I was surprised when he nodded at me and said, "Janet. You okay? And the dogs?" He stopped for a nanosecond, then walked to the back of the van, where I heard him say, "Oh, Jay, glad to see you're safe and sound. How's my sweet boy?" I walked around to the back and found him sticking his thick fingers as far as he could through the bars of the crate. Drake squooshed the side of his head into the bars of his crate and Hutch gave the black dog's ear a scratch and said, "Yeah, yeah, you too, you too," in the semi-baby talk that some people use with animals. I made myself not laugh in case Hutchinson took it badly, but it would have been a "hope for the human species" laugh if it had come out.

"Listen, can we go?" asked George. "We've been gone a while and, well, our bird . . ."

Hutchinson pulled his hands away from the dogs and said, "Yeah, sure, don't see why not." He looked at the mobile handset in my hand. "That belong here?"

"Oh, right." I handed it over. "It won't do me any good at the lake, huh?" George gave Hutchinson his number since my phone was useless, and Hutch turned back toward the house. I stopped him. "Hutch, have you looked into Regis Moneypenny? I mean, he must be part of this."

"Can't say."

"Can't say because you don't know, or can't say because you're not allowed to?" I asked.

"Yep." Hutchinson's eyebrows had risen just about to his hairline and he was staring into my eyes.

"Okay. You have. And he is?"

Hutch just stared at me in reply.

"So, if you don't think Moneypenny is involved, just shake your head. I mean, should I be watching out for him at the lake?" I remembered my uneasiness on the island earlier, the feeling that someone was watching Tom and me on our walk. *A couple of deer,* my non-paranoid hemisphere reminded me. But something still bothered me about that section of fence where the brush thinned out. It felt like a conduit for evil.

"Won't be there," he said, starting to turn away again but still talking. "He's in Muncie posting Campbell's bail. I spoke to the jail down there on my way here and he had just arrived."

I did some quick calculations and figured it would be close, but Campbell could have made it to the rest area north of Muncie after he attacked my van. Perhaps I associated the open stretch of fence with Anderson's death. It seemed likely that Rich Campbell had come into Heron Acres that way. He could leave Treasures on Earth from the back of their property without being seen and, assuming he had a boat of some sort, he could cross the narrow stretch of lake without being seen from most of Heron Acres.

George interrupted my thoughts. "At least we'll have the place to ourselves. That should make it easier to catch ourselves a Carmine Parrot." I was too distracted to remember to keep George away from the back of the van, and when I closed the back hatch, he said, "Janet! What happened here?"

"Oh my! Someone must have backed into it." As soon as I said it, I knew how dumb it was. How could I not have seen the damage earlier? George gave me a look and seemed to be about to speak, but he didn't. We climbed into the van and headed back to the peace and quiet of Twisted Lake.

Fifty-Three

The sky was a clear, hot, August blue and the air was still as death in town, but when we stepped out of the van at Heron Acres, we entered a different world. A sweet breeze blew from the lake, the glare of urban concrete was miles behind us, and the air smelled of lake water and grass rather than petroleum fumes. Closing my eyes, I took a deep breath. That calmed me, but when I opened my eyes and looked across the field to the water, Anderson Billings came to mind. He died violently in this peaceful place, as creatures who live here do every day. Perhaps the Buddha was right. All is illusion.

Don't go all philosopher now, Janet, said a little voice, merging into a very real voice that was speaking to me.

"Janet, where do you want this pen?"

I shook off my complex feelings and helped George tote the x-pen to a nice spot in the shade, back twenty feet or so from the beach. Just beyond, a kayak lay on the grass. I walked over and took a look. "You go ahead and take the boat," I told George. "I'll let the boys play a bit, then take the kayak over."

"I thought you left your kayak on the island?" asked George.

"This one must belong to Collin, or one of his relatives. Mine is on the island. But they won't mind, I'm sure."

George started to move toward the boat but stopped and pulled his phone from his pocket and looked at it. He pushed a button, then said, "Aw, crap." He shook the phone and tried again, then started walking around. "Lost the signal."

"Something important?" I asked.

"Maybe? There's a text from the cop, what's his name? Hutch? Said 'need to talk, call me.' " George kept walking this way and that. "This happen a lot out here?"

"Yeah, it does, actually. Sometimes I can't get a signal at all, other times it's fine. Weird." I tossed him my keys. "Here, take my van and drive back to that little store on the corner where we turn. You can get a signal there."

"Listen, as long as I'm going . . . Are you hungry? I'll grab something for all of us. I meant to do that, but the mess at Tom's place distracted me."

I looked at my watch. It was after seven, a long time since lunch, and once George planted the thought, I realized I was famished. We walked back to the van and opened the back. Jay and Drake spilled out of their crates, barking with glee. Neither of them is a big mouth, but they were excited and feeding off one another, and apparently it was all too much to contain without making some noise. "Okay, okay, *shhhhhh.*"

I tapped on the passenger window to ask George to bring me a candy bar, too, and by the time I turned back around, Jay was racing around with a humongous stick in his mouth and Drake had scared up an abandoned tennis ball. To their credit, although they both love to swim, they had resisted temptation and stayed within about ten yards of me. "Okay, guys, lets go," I said. As soon as I pointed toward the lake, they were off, and by the time I got to the beach, they were both soaking wet and giving me the big-eyed "Throw it! Throw it!" look.

Which I did, for about ten minutes. Between tosses I looked toward the island, but there was nothing to see. The fallen log that had become our observation post was on the far side of the big old sycamore, and even if he were standing up, I didn't think I'd be able to spot Tom. I wondered if by chance the prodigal parrot had gone after the food in the cage. If not, it could be a very long evening. The mosquitoes and gnats were bad enough out there in daylight, I thought, and absolutely vicious at dusk. I wondered whether I had enough diluted skin softener left in my van for the three of us. Great stuff for fending off bugs. Then I remembered that George had taken the van.

I was not looking forward to telling Tom about his house, but at least Campbell was out of commission for the time being, and Moneypenny wasn't around. I pulled my cell phone out to see whether it might have come out of its coma so I could call Tom and tell him I was on my way back out, assuming he had any reception on the island. Sometimes I long for the days when we didn't expect to be able to reach people at all times. Expectations are so easily dashed.

The dogs seemed to be winding down, so I walked them back to the x-pen, filled their water bowl from the jug I'd brought, and locked them in. I draped my solar sheet over part of the pen, reflector side facing west to deflect the setting sun. Then I fastened their crate fans to the side of the pen and turned them on. With the breeze off the lake plus the fans, and the double shade of trees and solar sheet, they would be fine for a little while.

"Good boys," I said. "Take a nap." Drake set about tanking up from the water bowl but Jay was standing still, ears erect and gaze focused on the island. He let out a low *bfff.* "Hear Tom out there, Bubby? Is he talking to that silly bird?" Jay glanced at me and wagged his nub. "You'll see him in a little while. Lie down now. I'll be back." He sank slowly to the ground, his attention still on the island. He looked like a punk rocker with his wet hair sticking out in crazy directions. I started to walk away, but turned back when he let out a loud *yip.* "Quiet, Bubby, I'll be back in a little while."

I figured I'd paddle out there and see what was happening with our little lost bird. If Tom wanted a break, I could spell him. Either way, one of us could come back and stay with the dogs for a while, and if it got late I could take them home and come back. I heard Jay whine behind me, but he didn't bark any more, so I kept going.

The breeze had died, leaving the surface of the lake level except where the kayak cut a path and left its small wake. An engine of some sort was running in the far distance, but other than that, the murmur of water against paddle and hull, and a background buzz of insects, all was quiet. The sun was about halfway between zenith and horizon, so not so tough an opponent as it had been a couple of hours earlier, but the humidity made up for it. I was dripping by the time I reached the island and dragged the kayak out of the water, so I took a moment to wet my face and arms before turning toward the old sycamore.

Jay started to bark again. I turned to holler at him in time to see Drake stand up and join in. Nice duet, I thought, Jay's occasionally squeaky tenor and Drake's bellowing baritone. "Jay! Drake! Quiet!" I yelled, feeling like a bit of an idiot since I couldn't reinforce the command, or reward compliance, from that distance. I felt the breeze in my face and was surprised that my voice had carried across the lake, but apparently it had. Both dogs were quiet, though their postures said they were still watching. They'd settle down when I got out of sight, I thought.

I didn't want to trudge through the brush to cross the island — too many burrs and a lot more biting insects in the center — so I took the longer path along the shore. I had tramped around this place enough to know that there was a stretch of lower-growing vegetation a five-minute walk to the east, so that's where I was headed. I would cut inland to Tom's parrot-watching post from there.

It didn't take long until I was dripping again, and it wasn't lake water. *Hope Tom hasn't drunk all the water,* I thought, my mouth feeling sticky and dry in the evening heat. The island was usually cooler than the mainland, but now it seemed warmer. For a moment I considered stripping down to my undies and going for a swim, but what would be the point? I'd sweat up again as soon as I got back with the program. I kept walking.

I could hear dogs barking again, but wasn't sure they were mine. *Mine?* The thought surprised me, but I realized that I was indeed starting to think of Drake as my dog. Our dog. Not just *his* dog. I wondered whether Tom thought of Jay and Leo as *our* dog and cat. Maybe I'd ask him. *Maybe not.* From where I stood, I couldn't see the x-pen anymore. I was about to backtrack for a look, but they weren't barking, so I went on. I could always go back to stay with the dogs after I checked in with Tom. Besides, George would be back soon.

The island had a slight elevation gain from shore to sycamore, and I had reached the area where the taller leg-grabbing grasses and weeds gave way to low-growing varieties. I turned inland and looked in the direction of the fallen trunk where we had sat earlier that afternoon, and where we had left Tom watching the parrot. There was no sign of him, but if he was sitting on the ground, that made sense. I glanced at the sycamore. The birdcage still hung from the branch, empty as before. I scanned the branches above the one supporting the cage, but saw no parrot. Had he gotten scared, or bored, or hungry, and flown off? Then a movement caught my eye, and I shifted my focus to a scarlet figure hunched on the end of the branch from which the cage was suspended. He'd moved down. *Our luck is changing,* I thought, and smiled.

If I walked directly to where I expected Tom to be, I would have to pass almost under the cage, and I was afraid that would drive the parrot away. *I'll just have to deal with the burrs,* I thought, and took a detour away from the sycamore and through thicker, taller brush. Finally I reached the log.

No sign of Tom. I couldn't imagine why he would leave his post. If the parrot went for the food in the cage, Tom needed to pull the door shut. He wouldn't miss the chance,

I was sure. Not after sitting out here all afternoon. I looked around, but everything was quiet. I stepped up close to the tree trunk and took inventory. The canvas bag that George had used to carry his parrot-catching kit was there, as were a couple of empty water bottles. I sat down on the log to think. A deep-voiced dog started to bark. Drake? That seemed out of character, so maybe it wasn't him at all. Sound can be deceptive out in the country, especially over water.

When I swung my legs over the log and turned to face the other direction, I noticed a path through the brush. It was not a worn walking trail, but a line of broken vegetation, as if something had been dragged through the grass and flowers. The barking had stopped again, and everything else seemed to go still as well. All I could hear was a faint buzzing of insects. Heat, moisture, bugs, clear sky. All the parts were assembled for a peaceful, lazy summer evening, and yet something about it felt wrong.

Was that there earlier? I wondered, staring at the disrupted vegetation before me. I didn't think so. Had Tom walked through there? *Follow,* came a voice from somewhere inside me, and I felt a tiny tremor under my sternum. I didn't like the feeling at all, but I slowly slid off the log and stepped toward the brush. As I got closer, it became clear that vegetation had been crushed under a weight, as if someone had walked through here very recently. *Deer, maybe?* I stopped to orient myself, and realized that if I walked from where I stood straight through to the lake, I'd reach the water in about ten yards. It had to be the shortest path to the water. Maybe the doe and fawn had swum across from the other side.

Follow.

I took a couple of steps into the brush. The path zigged to the left for a few feet, then zagged to the right. And then, when I made the second turn, my heart jumped into my mouth. A baseball bat lay half hidden, as if someone had dropped it, and the path beyond widened, vegetation flattened to form a path about eighteen inches wide. And there was something else, something that wrapped a piano wire of fear around my throat and stifled the scream that tried to rise from my throat.

Fifty-Four

The bat was lightweight, and small. A child's bat, I thought, as I stepped over it and leaned to pick up the object that had stopped my breathing. It was a shoe, and not a child's. A man's shoe. Tom's. The lace was still tied. A green stain ran from the back of the heel down to the sole, where it feathered out and died, as if the back of the shoe had been dragged through the grass top first. I looked at the flattened vegetation leading down the shallow slope and considered the shoe again. *As if he were dragged and his shoe pulled off,* I thought.

The garrote that had tightened around my throat at the sight of that shoe slipped down to my heart. I started to follow the trail of crushed plants, then backtracked and picked up the bat. It was small, but better than nothing. I walked fast but didn't run. I knew I needed to hurry for Tom's sake, but I didn't want to give myself away by making a lot of noise, which was almost inevitable with all the dry sticks in this area.

After about a minute, the path turned forty-five degrees to the left, and it made another similar turn soon after that. The slope toward the water was a bit steeper here, and covered with scrub willow that blocked my view. I couldn't see more than a few feet ahead of me, although the drag path was still easy to follow as it wound through the trees. Finally I reached the break between willow and grass and had a clear view to the water.

The first thing that caught my eye was across the water on the mainland. The x-pen. As if on cue at my arrival, the panel nearest the water tipped over and the whole affair flipped on its face and went flat. As it did, the solar sheet whooshed into the air, and Drake shot out from between the prone panels and made for the lake like a furred cannonball.

My brain registered everything, and what must have been only a few seconds of elapsed time seemed like long minutes. My eyes tracked Drake's trajectory and landed on a glittering wake, its leading point aimed to my right. The light shifted, and I saw the swimmer. Jay. He must have jumped out of the x-pen. He was a strong swimmer and was coming fast, and even from this distance I could see that he was hell-bent on whatever he was after.

I tracked to the right. My heart skipped again and then went into overdrive. I dropped the bat and started to run.

A tall figure in a blue shirt and a baseball cap was dragging Tom, who was clearly unconscious, into the water. *But he's supposed to be in custody,* I thought. *Or getting bailed out. What is he doing here? And why did they let him go? Why? Why?*

Running has never been my strong suit. I run for exercise, but it's a jogging sort of run. Slow. I'm not a sprinter. As I angled down the slope toward the beach, my legs seemed to be wrapped in chains. It was like one of those dreams in which your feet are mired in goo, except that I was awake. My legs just couldn't move fast enough.

Tom was in the water, not moving, his assailant dragging him deeper and deeper. I could see that they were both soaking wet now, Tom floating still but seeming to ride lower in the water as his clothing took on weight. The blue shirt on his assailant was wet halfway up the torso, then to the shoulders, swimming, pulling Tom into deeper water. Letting him go.

"No!" I didn't know I had screamed until I

heard the sound of my own voice. I wasn't fast enough. I wasn't going to make it.

The figure in the blue shirt was waist deep now. Thigh deep. Knees. Coming out of the lake. I didn't care, couldn't look anywhere but at the figure floating on the dark water. Tom.

He moved. Rolled. I saw his face come out of the water, I was sure I did, but the next time I looked he was still again. Floating.

I registered movement in my peripheral vision. Both sides. Something moving toward Tom offshore. And something to my right, coming my way. I hit the water at a run, felt the soft ooze of the lake's floor give way beneath my shoes and slide my feet out from under me. Left alone, I could have righted myself, but something hit me from behind, across the small of my back. The muck beneath me threw my feet away, and I fell into the shallow water.

I pulled my knees under me, slipping against the gooey bottom but finding a purchase and pushing myself almost upright. I took a step, seeking water deep enough to hold me, deep enough to let me swim, but something caught my hair and the back of my shirt and pulled me onto my back. I tried to sit up, but hands shoved against my shoulders and forced me under the shallow water. My hair was glued across my eyes. I couldn't see, so I sent my hand straight up, coming close to a direct hit. I felt the heel of my hand strike bone and thought I heard a gasp.

My experience with animals sometimes comes through at odd times, and this was one of the oddest. As I fought, I flashed on the principle of zero resistance. If you try to push a dog's rear end down into a sit, he pushes back. But if you entice him to raise his head for a treat or a toy, his butt naturally goes down. I didn't intend to give my attacker a treat, but maybe I could use lack of resistance as a weapon. Don't the martial arts use the attacker's weight and momentum against him? I wasn't trained, but still, maybe I could make the principle work.

Hands grabbed my shoulders. I sucked in as much air as I could, knowing I was going under again. The hands shoved me down, and the force of the action knocked some of the air out of my lungs. My hair drifted away from my eyes and I looked up at my attacker and tried for another punch to the face, but my arms were too short to make contact. Thumbs dug under my collarbone and fingernails pressed into the tops of my shoulders. The pain almost knocked the rest of the air out of me, but I held on. I dug my heels into the slippery mud beneath me and pushed. My feet slipped away from me, but I got just enough traction to scoot my body a few inches, and that was enough to make blue shirt slip and fall toward me. I rolled with the pressure of the extra weight and got loose. Frantic, I splashed a couple of strokes and then stood up. The water was only halfway up my calves, and I was facing away from the island, toward Tom. He was floating on his back, but didn't seem to be doing anything else.

I started to move toward him, but instinct made me turn around. Through the entire encounter, I had Rich Campbell's face in my mind, but that was not the face that glared back at me now, and they were not Campbell's hands that held a huge piece of driftwood like a baseball bat and started to swing it at my head.

The water in front of me exploded and the figure in the blue shirt pinwheeled, hand releasing the stick, legs bowled out from under the body by seventy pounds of muscle, heart, and black fur. Drake. Tom always said that for a Lab, life is a contact sport, and I guess that applied to defensive maneuvers, too. Drake wheeled around and came back. I grabbed one of the blue-shirted wrists and told Drake, “Take it!” He closed his mouth over the wrist, and I said, “Hold it!” Then I turned to drag Tom out of the water.

I was too late.

Fifty-Five

"Janet! Tom!"

At least three voices were yelling our names. I looked down the beach, toward the source of the noise. George was running, flanked by detectives Jo Stevens and Homer Hutchinson. Persephone Swann, her blue shirt ripped and her baseball cap gone, sat very still in the shallow water, her arm held in Drake's soft but inescapable grip. He would hold on until Tom or I told him to let go, and every time Persephone tried to move, I could see Drake tighten his hold.

I sat on the beach with Tom's head in my lap. Jay was pressed against Tom's other side, his chin on Tom's chest and worry bright in his eyes. Tom smiled at me and said, "Thought at first that I'd died and gone to the arms of an angel, but I don't think I'd have such a blazing headache if that were the case."

"Don't even joke about it," I said, working harder than I wanted to admit not to dissolve into hysterics.

"Janet!" It was Hutchinson. He was standing in the water next to Persephone and Drake. He had one of Persephone's wrists in his handcuffs, and he said, "How do I get the other wrist away from the dog?"

"Drake, out!" I said.

He spat Persephone's wrist from his mouth and wheeled toward us all in one motion. In typical Labrador fashion, he slid into us, throwing sand into my hair, and started licking Tom's face and whining. Jay had jumped out of the way when he saw Drake coming, and now the two of them seemed ready to play wrestle-and-belly-rubs with Tom the way they did at home.

"Guys! Settle!" I said. It took two more commands to get them to listen, but they finally lay down, each being sure to keep at least one paw in contact with Tom.

George and Jo knelt beside us.

"Jeez, man, are you okay?" asked George.

"I will be, thanks to nurse Janet." Tom squeezed my hand and turned to me. "So let me get this straight. Jay, who is by rights not a water dog, dragged me out of the lake, and Drake, who is a water dog and not a protection dog, tackled Persephone and held her for the police?"

"That's about it," I said. I looked at Jo and asked, "She's Campbell's girlfriend, right? That's what Giselle told me."

"Was. I suspect the relationship is probably over." Jo had a funny little smile on her face.

"Why is that?" asked George.

"Campbell asked for a deal. He gave her up."

"What do you mean?" I asked, enjoying the warmth of Tom's hand in mine more than I ever had before.

"They've been pals for years, it seems. Met in the East. New Canaan, Connecticut." I remembered Giselle saying that Persephone had lived on the East Coast for years, in "New something. "He's a liar and a thief, but it seems Persephone is the killer."

"She killed Anderson?" I asked, and turned to glare at Persephone.

"So Campbell says. He claims to have evidence. And he says Anderson wasn't the first." Jo looked at Tom. "Might not have been the last, but thank God . . ." She stopped mid-sentence, but touched Tom's arm, then went on. "Anyway, seems Rich had an old girlfriend . . ."

"Liesl," said George.

"Right. Liesl Burkhardt. Apparently they'd

had a bad breakup, and he wanted to see her, tell her he was sorry, make amends." George snorted, and Jo looked at him with an eyebrow raised, then continued. "That's his story, anyway. So Persephone found out he had been to see Liesl, and went off the deep end. Or actually knocked Liesl off the deep end. Slipped her a Mickey and threw her into a lake on Cape Cod."

Tom wriggled himself into a sitting position.

"You sure you should be moving?" asked Jo. "We've called for an ambulance to take you out of here."

"Nah, it's just a bump." He reached up and rubbed the back of his head.

"With a baseball bat!" My voice cracked at the end.

"Cancel the ambulance," said Tom.

I nodded at Jo. "I'll drive him to the hospital and hit him again if he doesn't let them look him over. Just help me get him out of here." I changed the subject. "The smuggling? Was that why Moneypenny brought him here?"

"We're still looking into it, but I don't think Moneypenny knew about the smuggling or the endangered birds," said Jo. "I think he really wanted to run an educational aviary and a bird rescue, and hired the wrong guy." She paused. "Turns out he's had a few other odd schemes, maybe shady, maybe not. Real name is Willard."

"Floyd Willard," I said. It wasn't a question.

"Yeah," said Jo. "You knew that?"

"Not until now, but it explains where Mrs. Willard's money came from, and a few other things." Jo looked mystified. "Tell you later," I said.

Tom said, "Okay, George, if you get the boats, Nurse Janet will drag me along in a minute."

But George was pointing toward the sycamore and already walking that way.

"Perfect!" I said, and started to laugh. The parrot was in the cage. I couldn't see details at that distance, but his scarlet plumage was like a flashing light through the bars. As we watched, George pulled on the light line and the cage door closed.

George turned toward us, a huge grin on his face. He said, "I'll bring the bass boat right here. We'll get you and the parrot out first, then come back for the rest." He looked at Persephone and added, "I think she should sit here wet and miserable for a while." Persephone scowled, but said nothing. George walked off, and Jo joined Hutchinson where he stood watching Persephone.

Tom and I wrapped each other up in a hug to end all hugs, bolstered by a wet dog on each side. I don't know how long it lasted. Maybe a year. My doubts about how to proceed weren't all gone, but the fear that danced among them had drifted away across the surface of the lake. A veil of mauve and peach glowed on the horizon and dragged a fringe of color over the lake as the summer began to slip away. It promised to be a long, warm autumn.

ABOUT THE AUTHOR

Sheila Webster Boneham has been writing professionally for three decades, and writes in several genres. She has taught writing at universities in the U.S. and abroad, and occasionally teaches writing workshops. In the past fifteen years, Sheila has published seventeen nonfiction books, six of which have won major awards. A longtime participant in canine sports, therapy, and other activities, Sheila is also an avid amateur photographer and painter. When she isn't pursuing creative activities or playing with animals, Sheila can be found walking the beach or salt marsh near her home in North Carolina. You can reach her through her website at www.sheilaboneham.com.

The employees of Thorndike Press hope you have enjoyed this Large Print book. All our Thorndike, Wheeler, and Kennebec Large Print titles are designed for easy reading, and all our books are made to last. Other Thorndike Press Large Print books are available at your library, through selected bookstores, or directly from us.

For information about titles, please call:
(800) 223-1244

or visit our Web site at:
http://gale.cengage.com/thorndike

To share your comments, please write:

Publisher
Thorndike Press
10 Water St., Suite 310
Waterville, ME 04901